One
Rainy
Day

This book is a work of fiction dreamed up by the Author. Any names, characters, businesses, places, events and incidents are either the products of the author's imagination, or attributed to their original source material, or used in a fictitious manner. Any resemblance to actual persons, living or dead, or actual events is purely coincidental.

For Would You Rather

Both options are terrible

Choices must be made.

Chapter 1

Coffee and Kisses

Morning light streams through window

Uncomplicated

Naomi's fingers skated over the rough edges of the words carved into the wooden tabletop. With touch and sight, she read; with head and heart, she contemplated. As a rule, she did not approve of graffiti or defacement of property, however, it seemed the owners of the coffee shop did not. There were several other forms of graffiti about her table. A drawing of a Tyrannosaurus Rex trying to drink a martini, several "— was here," and written inside a heart with an arrow through it, someone named Erik loved Kevin. She again traced her finger over the poem. It was a form of time travel. A person from a past point in time had put that message there for her to find at this future point in time. And it was the last word of the message that held her attention.

Uncomplicated.

That was how Naomi liked her life—uncomplicated. And the poetic thought of waking each day to coffee and kisses sounded nice. She couldn't remember how long it had been since she had started a day with poetic coffee and kisses.

For longer than she cared to remember, her morning was a stale routine of pouring her own cup of coffee, an absent-minded kiss and a brusque "morning," from her husband as he fumbled for a coffee cup.

What happened to those easy and honest pleasures?

The little gestures?

Again, her fingers traced over the rough edges of the words. Lingering on uncomplicated. Her mind wondered if a future version of herself might have traveled back in time just to give this Naomi this poem. And if she had, for what reason?

Chapter 2

Hot Mud was the kitschy name of the coffee shop where Naomi sat waiting. It was like every other independent coffee shop. It was completely unique. The aesthetic was tasteful and simple—uncomplicated. The tables and chairs looked like they may have come from a furniture recovery business. One of those niche companies that bought old furniture from restaurants or churches or offices; then restored and sold it to business like Hot Mud. Naomi imagined several of the worn wooden tables and chairs could have come from her old school building.

However, unlike the school tables, her current table was small, but just big enough to be shared, in a comfortably private sort of way, with just one other person. Rectangular in shape, the once sharp right-angle corners now worn round. The once smooth top, now crisscrossed with creases and grooves, stains and graffiti. Naomi considered the table and thought she and it shared several similar attributes. The chair was a simple hard wood with a light natural stain and had well-worn ass-grooves stylized into the seat. Across from her its twin, empty, waited for its occupant. A thunder crack brought her attention back to focus on the world around her; to eight in the morning on a rainy Friday in May.

No matter how the morning or the rest of the day went, Naomi knew she would have a good day. She loved the rain. From a gentle mist to a thunderous deluge and all the types of rain in between, Naomi loved them all equally. Naomi wrapped her hands, her fingers interlacing, around the paper cup in a warming-like manner and sipped at her coffee while in the background the muffled sound of the rain found its way into her thoughts, soothing her nervousness.

Naomi thought about why she loved rainy days so much. There was something about the rain that spoke to her soul. She could not explain the exact reason. She considered the soul-soothing pleasure she felt from rain to be an ineffable enigma of life. Of course, there were lots of granular and quantifiable reasons why she loved gray rainy days. She felt emotional evocations, synaptically triggered memories resulting from the sound of the rain falling on the roof, or against a window. The smell of the rain, the wet air. The gray skies, the oversized water filled gray and puffy clouds—the full deal. Even the occasional crack of lightening and roll of thunder instantly made her want to just curl up in a blanket, sit in bed and experience the storm. She could do it for hours and did so on several occasions. Naomi inwardly blushed at the memory of how one time, the rain was perfect, the drops were small, almost tears they were so light, the wind was soft and the day not too cold, it was perfect. It was so perfect that she wanted to be part of the experience, an active participant, not just a spectator.

Naomi remembered the compulsion, the need to feel the rain on her body, her skin. In her memory she could see herself standing there in her living room in front of the sliding glass door that opened to the deck. Standing there as if hypnotized by the rain. It compelled her. It seduced her. It told her to take off her clothes, to step outside and stand naked in it, to let the rain caress her body with its touch. And she did. The rain soaking her hair; running down her face and dripping off her nose. She caught drops of rain in her mouth. She embraced the chill of the wind and water on her breasts and down her legs. The rain had become her lover.

Being the middle of the day, it did not matter. Her deck could be seen by several not close, but not so distant neighbors. It did not matter. To Naomi's soul the soft warm gentle rain on her body felt amazing. Naomi warmed and relaxed into the memory of that yesteryear morning.

And now there was today. Sitting, looking out the front window of the coffee shop. The rain falling. She sipped her steaming coffee. The air around her filled with the aroma of coffee and rain.

The clattering sound of life broke the hypnotic spell. The espresso machine hissing with a steamy release of pressure. A phone ringing. The chatter of conversation. And just like that Naomi was no longer a memory standing naked in rain, but was back in the present reality, clothed, and sitting at Hot Mud and waiting. She was there because had agreed to meet Colin. He was that someone from her past that unlike many of the other people from her life, he had never completely left. Naomi thought about that, people leaving. All the friends and acquaintances she had gathered and then parted from as she went through life. *Did they leave her, or did she leave them?*

Colin never truly left her life. It was more of a slow change of a situation, maybe something like water.

It was a liquid.

It was a solid.

It was a gas.

Yet it was always water, just a little different. The friendship she and Colin shared was like water.

Colin, from a geeky adolescent boy to the man he grew into, he had been there almost her entire life. They were friends in the truest sense of the word. Naomi sarcastically imagined that in some dictionary somewhere, next to the definition of the word *Friend* there would be a picture of her and Colin. The problem, the reason for her stupid, over-rationalized feelings was because over the past several months they had started to become something more than the standard definition of the word. Their friendship had changed forms.

Sometimes their conversations went to personal places— very personal. She told him about fights with her husband. The frustration of dealing with his family. Colin shared equally similar details of his personal life with her. Mainly how his wife was constantly annoyed about how much time he spent in his studio, especially when she constantly traveled for her job. They also shared other intimate details. Those physical things they enjoyed. Naomi did not, could not remember how those conversations even started. They probably started during one of their telephone happy hours. At one point they were talking about work, or the weather, or weekend plans the usual boring but also safe minutia, and the next thing she knew their conversation drifted into their favorite and least favorite sexual positions, which turned out to be the same, cowgirl and missionary, and opinions on oral sex, loved giving and receiving.

What bothered Naomi about it, about talking to Colin about those kinds of things, talking to a man other than her husband about what turned her on was supposed to feel wrong. But with Colin it didn't feel wrong. It did not feel tawdry or illicit. Instead, she felt the opposite. She felt unfettered and uninhibited. However, in those feelings Naomi also started to feel something troubling. That Colin had somehow become the other man in her life.

That was how Naomi had come to feel about Colin, *the other man* and it confused and frustrated her because there was not supposed to be another man. They could be friends. Naomi had multiple friends who were guys. However, her feelings for Colin were not those type of friend-guy feelings. Naomi and Colin had history, they had memories of growing up together, of sharing their lives both the good and bad, of drifting apart, and of reconnection.
Solid, liquid, and gas.

Those types of feelings had roots, and those roots were deep and strong. Naomi's current anxiety about meeting Colin was because of the strength of those shared feelings. Naomi wanted to, tried to, compartmentalize the mosaic of feelings she felt towards Colin, but it was as futile as trying to capture and hold moonlight in your hands. There was also the fact that besides pictures, they had not physically seen each other for close to twenty years.

Naomi could still remember the void in her life when Colin left West Lake, Minnesota for San Diego, California. He went there for boot camp then shipped off to live around the world, thousands of miles from where they had grown up. In her life, Naomi had traveled a little. She and her cousin went on a ten-day, girls' trip to the England and Ireland. But she never lived in those places. She had only been a visitor. Her actual everyday life had only moved a half hour away from where it had started. Point A was her parent's home in West Lake to point B, the town of Linder.

Their lives both grew and went in different directions but despite both time and distance their friendship endured. As with any friendship, there were periods of time when they drifted apart. The longest time had been a seemingly forever span of several years. Naomi had almost forgotten about Colin, almost.

She kept a picture of him from a high school graduation party. It wasn't just a picture of him. It was a group picture. She was in it. Another friend Nina and Nina's then boyfriend Frank—whatever happened to Nina? They all had plastic cups of beer and were holding them up in a toast of celebration. Naomi used it as a book mark and for occasional contemplation and rumination. They were all so young and naïve. They were also hopeful. Full of those dreams that only drunken eighteen-year-olds who just graduated high school can have. Those crazy dreams about how they were going to escape from that shitty little town and change the world—drunk teenager dreams. Now the picture was old and faded. All the corners, in varying degrees were bent and boxed. And during those quiet inward reflective times when Naomi drifted in memory with the picture, she understood how it felt. She too felt old, faded, and a little bent and boxed around the corners— just like the picture; just like those drunk teenage dreams.

As Naomi placed him between pages and moved him from book to book, she wondered about Colin. What he was up to? Where he was at? During those times, Naomi started to imagine his life. Since she didn't know what Colin's life was really like, she created one for him. Sometimes she created one for them. Then during those years when she hadn't heard from Colin and she had started to remember, wonder, and imagine about him more than usual, it happened. Rational Naomi knew better, but to superstitious Naomi, it seemed she had no more than thought hard enough about Colin when several days later her mom called. Among all the other family gossip her mom wanted to talk about, she told Naomi there was a letter addressed to her from someone named Colin Meyer living in California.

Naomi could not get over to her parents fast enough on her way home from work. She determined a speeding ticket was an acceptable consequence. Naomi felt like she was seven-years-old and it was Christmas morning, and once again, she had to wait for her parents before she could get her present.

When she arrived home, the excited Naomi wanted to rip the letter open and immediately read it. But dignified and in control Naomi stopped the action. She always tried to control those instant gratification impulses. Some moments in life were meant to be savored and enjoyed, and this was one of them. She took a breath. She changed out her work clothes, maybe a bit faster than usual, but still followed her usual after-work routine. Then after doing that, she went out to her porch and sat down with the letter. It was near sunset but enough light to still see and read the letter.

First all she could do was look at the envelope. She studied it. Committing it to memory. It was from Colin. His return address was Sonoma, California. Her maiden name on the envelope, her parents address. Naomi wondered about that detail, but she was certain she knew why, although she could not wait to read Colin's explanation.

She carefully opened the envelope, sliding her fingernail under the sealed fold and sliding it across like a letter opener. The letter was brief, only one page, but Naomi read and savored every word. In the letter Colin wrote he did not know her current address and hoped her parents still lived at the same house. He told her about his life and what he was doing. He gave her his current address and closed the letter by saying he hoped she would write him back. Naomi wrote her letter as she sat in bed that night.

Several days later a letter from Colin arrived to her home. Again, she immediately wrote him back. Even after several months, after the excitement of finally hearing from him again had worn off, they still kept writing with the same enthusiasm. He shared his life with her, and she with him. Just like those drunk teenagers in her picture. Once in a while there would be a photograph. Naomi, sipped her coffee and smiled at the memory of writing letters and taking film pictures. All those years ago when hand written letters and photographs were standard. Now it was all text messages, Instagram selfies, tweets, and Facetime—Life was instant, and it was live.

This was what Naomi was now experiencing. Life instant and live. At her table, sitting and waiting. Her fingers absently and anxiously picking at the edges of the cup. The time now five minutes after eight. Not that she was keeping track. Naomi's eyes moved from her watch to her wrist. Her wrist to her fingers. Her fingers to her nails that were busy picking apart the brown paper jacket around her coffee cup. Then, having reached the end of her appendage, her perception moved up to the plate glass door of the coffee shop and into gray and raining day what was waiting there. And superstitiously once again, just as she thought hard enough, a taxi was pulling up to the coffee shop.

It did not turn to park in one of the spots. It stopped behind several of the parked cars. Naomi found she was holding her breath as she saw movement in the car, a passenger in the back seat. The light on the top turned back on, the back-passenger door opened out into the rain and Naomi was, instant and live, seeing Colin getting out of the car.

Just like with the letter, it seemed all Naomi had to do was think about Colin hard enough and somehow, he would hear her. He unfortunately hesitated for a moment between exiting the taxi and looking at the coffee shop. Even for just that moment in the rain, the hesitation before action, was enough and Colin was soaked before he made it to the door. When he opened the door, for a short pleasant moment the warm smell inside the coffee shop was replaced with the cool outside smell of the rain. The people sitting closest to the door looked at him like he was an alien from a different planet.

Didn't he know it was raining?

Didn't he know he was supposed to have a rain coat or umbrella?

What kind of crazy person had just come into their warm and cozy place and interrupted their morning coffee?

And, come on dude, shut the door. It's raining out!

Colin stood there in the doorway and Naomi felt her heart begin to beat harder, faster. He did a quick visual survey of the room, spotting her sitting at the small wooden table next to the wall. A smile of happiness and relief lit his roguishly handsome face. For a brief moment Naomi felt an almost overwhelming and stupid urge to run and hide in the women's bathroom.

Their eyes locked and there was no running away. Even if she really wanted too. Although she was still toying with the idea of it. He kept smiling at her and Naomi felt a slow blush rise to her pale cheeks. She smiled back and began studying his face. His face, live and instant, not him captured in a picture, this face was animated and it had depth and character. Now so mature looking, the smooth softness of boyhood long gone, lost to a life of experience and age.

His hands moved to brush the water from his cream-colored linen shirt. Naomi did her best to keep the light short laugh from audibly escaping. Despite her attempt some escaped through her laughing smile and dancing blue eyes. Colin, by trying to brush the water from his shirt, only succeeded in making the fabric almost transparent. She could see his skin through the now semi-transparent shirt; his chest, his hair, his body. He shook his arms, still long and thin, but now with a muscular curve; now moving with a coordinated and graceful ease.

He no longer seemed to be the gangly and uncoordinated kid from so long ago. His hands, his firm, strong looking hands ran through his wet, dark brown salt and pepper hair. Brushing, pushing it back into place on his head. Naomi watched Colin walk through the coffee shop, something as simple as that and her tightly controlled and compartmentalized life started to come apart and feel messy.

She told herself to remain casual. This was just coffee. Coffee with an old friend from out of town. Despite her brain's best and rational efforts, her irrational body didn't listen. Her heart picked up its pace and she felt a nervous sweat starting.

What was wrong with her?

Naomi felt like she was a naïve teenage school girl. And if she was going to feel like a naïve teenage schoolgirl, Naomi wished she could at least have the boobs to go along with it.

Hell, Naomi thought, she would have even settled for her thirty-something boobs.

Naomi looked at his tan skin now covered in goose bumps. She watched as a shiver ran through him and his body did a little spasm from the chill. The cold rain, Naomi thought. He probably was not used to it after living in the warmth and dryness of California for all those years. Naomi wondered what it was like for him to be back in Minnesota in May.

Cold and rainy May.

He would not be used to this anymore, probably.

At least it's not snowing.

Naomi babbled the thoughts to herself.

It was no more than about ten feet between the door and the table and it seemed like forever for him to get to her. And in those ten feet of forever, on this one rainy day of forever, Naomi saw herself almost as clearly as she could see his chest through his wet shirt. She saw who they used to be. Where they had come from and how they arrived to the place they were now. Naomi saw all of it in that infinite ten feet.

Chapter 3

Ten Feet.

Naomi found herself back in seventh grade, when she first met Colin. They shared band class. He played drums and sat in the back. She played the flute and sat in the front. At first, he would walk next to her making some friendly small talk about what she thought of the music they were forced to play, or how stupid Missy Gilston kept challenging Naomi for first chair for the flute section. Naomi was obviously way better and never flat or off time like Missy. Naomi found she took an instant liking to the tall, sort of gangly but not bad looking guy walking to class with her. Him not liking Missy Gilston helped.

They started waiting in the hallway for each other. Not just to walk to band, but the other classes they had together or classrooms near enough not to be inconvenient. As their friendship grew so did their conversations. Evolving from banal school chit-chat to sharing their lives. Naomi smiled recalling Colin telling her once as they walked to a class that he wanted to marry her someday. Not, would you be my girlfriend, but jumping right to be my wife. Naomi warmed at that thought. It was original and it was so Colin. It was not the usual stupid comments guys would say when they were around her, trying to get her attention, to make her notice them.

Naomi had the good, misfortune of maturing earlier than some of the other girls. And not to be conceited, but also to be beautiful. Back then she had honey blonde hair, artic blue eyes, slim framed, and her developing breasts a head start on the other girls. She was beautiful. At least that's what all the guys told her, especially the older ones, so Naomi figured it must have been true; at least to a certain degree. Because at that tender young age, if a girl was ugly, or fat, or forbid the thought flat-chested, or in any other way not approved of by the ruling, trending popular boys at that time, those boys made sure those non-conforming girls knew they were outcasts. Body shamming was the new term they never had back then. But just because you lack the term doesn't mean it doesn't happen.

Of course, those same boys never noticed that she was significantly smarter than all of them combined. All they saw were the physical details. Naomi reflected on the idea that growing up in the nineteen eighties was a lot different, and entirely the same as it was in today's world. Boys and men were idiots then; boys and men were still idiots today.

But, because of all the attention the boys gave Naomi back then; the boys in her same grade and the older ones,

Naomi grew to know she was attractive, or at least was not one of the outcasts. As much as she did not want to care about that teenage school bullshit, instead wanting to focus on her classes, Naomi came to realize she had a place in that part of the school hierarchy, if she wanted it. She hated to admit it, but the youthful part of her did want it. However, despite the allure of being popular, there was something about Colin that made her not want to be part of that world.

Nine feet.

In the length of several months, they had gone from being two kids who had barely looked at each other, to inseparable friends. Back then he was such a goof. That was the best way to describe the young teenage Colin, a goof. Other than being tall and skinny, there was nothing significant, about Colin making him stand out against the plethora of other kids who were trying to find their place in the social position of school hierarchy.

He definitely was not one of the cool and in-crowd kids. That wouldn't come until years later. However, Naomi didn't care because she already knew Colin. She knew what was beneath the goof on the outside. Even though he quietly passed unnoticed by the majority of the other kids in the school, while she slowly found herself becoming one of the popular kids, Naomi still spent most of her time with Collin. He made her feel good. Everything was easy with him. It was uncomplicated. The so-called regular guys around her seemed capable of only saying stupid things about her developing boobs, or how her ass looked in her jeans and how the two of them should go out to the movies. The superficial and stupid shit only a boy who was starting to grow pubes would say.

Colin, despite being a stupid teenage boy, was still able to somehow not just talk at her but talk with her. He did not interrupt her life for the sake of self-aggrandizing posturing. He was not just taking something from her life. He offered details from his life in return. Once Naomi and Collin became comfortable around each other, Naomi discovered something special about Colin. Colin was not just able to sit still and be quiet, but he would actually listen. This was odd and completely out of place for a thirteen-year-old boy. There were times when they sat together at lunch without speaking. Not even how is your food. It was the best. It was enough just to be together.

At heart they were both teenagers and they both did love to talk about the microcosm of school. They talked about life. At thirteen-years-old he was wondering what she wanted to do in life as if she had already figured it out. He listened to her hopes and dreams. He never made fun of her when she told him she thought it would be fun to be either a horse trainer, or a nurse. Colin told her to do it if that was what she wanted to do. That she could do anything.

Naomi also found comfort in the fact that Colin could also make her laugh. He was good at it. No matter how depressed or sad she was feeling he could say something— no that was wrong. Colin knew her enough to say the right thing to cheer her up and make her laugh even if it was self-deprecating. He was funny but not usually gross or perverted, unless of course she initiated that type of humor. Naomi loved a good fart joke and could almost always win their burping contests. Most of their general conversations were Colin asking her about math class and did she get the assigned homework problems done and could he, please-please, copy it?

Naomi mentally admitted school-age Colin lacked the majority of school-related social skills, and basically had nothing going for him other than his goofy sense of humor. She never knew where he went for a haircut, but whichever parent took him there they should have stopped. It seemed every several months he came to school looking like he, Naomi paused, trying to remember an idea of his hair back then, but found it difficult. It had been a long time ago, and she was now distracted from her reminiscent thoughts as she admired the thick full waves of the wet, dark brown hair laced with white-gray in front of her.

Young Colin besides being unfortunately tall and skinny he was also lanky and uncoordinated. Colin seemed to be constantly at battle with his body. It was a weird unsure clumsiness, as if he was unsure of the exact location or length of an arm and hand or leg and foot. Naomi thought if people came with a user manual either Colin failed to get one, or more likely probablity, choose not to read it.

Instead, through some oftentimes, and unfortunately comical trial and error, he was trying to figure out the mechanics of how to make his arms and legs work together as they constantly grew, while at the same time battling all the new feelings that came with being a teenage boy. Naomi, was not sure what those boy feelings exactly were, although she suspected they were similar to those of a teenage girl; however, she had the added benefit of getting to learn about and experience cramps and periods.
Stupid boys!

But Colin was different than those other idiots and Naomi liked him and she definitely knew he liked her. What idiot boy tells a girl in seventh-grade he wants to marry her someday? For better or worse that was the first and last time he ever asked her that question.

Eight feet.

Their seventh-grade friendship seemed to fly by and soon the school year ended. They lived in different towns, she several miles outside West Lake and Colin ten miles south in Sunset. They didn't see each other over those summer vacations from school. Not until Colin got a car did that situation change. Until then Naomi never knew what happened to Colin, what adventures he had until that September when they reunited for school.

Naomi enjoyed summer with friends and family. The weekend trips to the lake for swimming, spending the majority of her weekdays over at a friend's house and riding horses or at her grandparent's farm playing in the barn hayloft with her cousins. But most of all Naomi enjoyed the idea of freedom during the summer. Despite abandoning her sense of responsibility and sinking into the freedom of summer, Naomi would find herself wondering what Colin was doing.

Was he having fun?

Was he thinking of her?

Naomi then wondered why they never exchanged phone numbers. It would have been so easy to have just picked up the phone and called each other. Of course, back in the '80s it was long-distance to make phone calls between Sunset and West Lake.

Naomi smiled at the thought of old rotary dial phones and long-distance phone calls to a town less than ten miles away. Now she could video call someone in Australia as part of her internet and phone service contract.

Since not accepting his marriage proposal, Naomi smiled at the silliness of it, she had to wait until fall to hear about his summer adventures. School would start again. The buses with kids from four different rural farm towns all coming to one central hub. It was the great State funded educational system; mandatory day care; social order establishment and hang-out with your friends, ditching class when you could; smoke until you got caught; cheat because you didn't want to study; and above all, prove yourself better by making others feel less about themselves.

All that shit packaged-up and delivered daily to a cinder block walled, cheap molded plastic chairs and pressed fiberboard tables and desks of the West Lake Public School system. It was the living definition of the oxymorn love-hate relationship. Every May it came to an end, and every September they had to start over.

Naomi could still mentally see how the new social order established itself. There would be those kids from the previous year that had been best friends but in the new school year, those former best friends became strangers. Sometimes that former friendship changed because of social clique's and soon former best friends became the worst enemies. Juxtaposed with those kids who hated each other the previous year, in the new year they became the best of friends.

Naomi's head hurt thinking about how that whole system worked back then. But all of that bullshit never happened to her and Colin. Within the span of several minutes, they found each other and they picked up where they left off. They went through each school year that way, saying hello and then saying good-bye, constantly repeating the cycle. The first change came when phone numbers were exchanged and over the summer, they would occasionally call each other and spend time talking. The second more drastic change came when they were old enough to drive and Colin got a car.

Seven feet.

As she watched Colin again shiver, Naomi's ruminations were interrupted. With each little spam of muscle, shaking of long and lean limbs, water slid and fell from his body. The butterflies in her stomach transformed into pterodactyls. And the barely contained nervous effervescence that had been corked inside her, was breaking free of its confines and exploding like a bottle of root beer in a paint shaker.

Naomi experienced a slight shiver of her own, not from cold, but fearful apprehension, and wondered if it was too late to run for the bathroom? Calmly and consciencely instructing her hand to stop picking at the edges of the thin brown cardboard protective sleave around her coffee cup, she placed it palm down on the wooden table top. She then told herself to stop thinking such nonsense. She was a grown woman and this was just coffee. And even that situation was a maybe.

She was in control.

She decided how the morning was to go.

Colin came another step closer and she saw the hairs on his arms. The subtle stubble of black and white whiskers on his chin and cheeks. She saw the happy twinkle in his brown eyes. And as she studied those little details about him, she failed to notice her hand once again picking at the edges of the protective sleave.

Naomi saw the memory of herself as clear as she saw the hair on his arms. It was several months earlier, during her lunch break. As usual she was sitting at her office desk munching on whatever microwave meal she had brought that day and glancing through the various news sites.

A Breaking News banner flashed across the CNN website. The musician Prince Rogers Nelson had been found dead at his Chanhassen, Minnesota home. Paisley Park. The initial details surrounding his death remained undetermined but it was alleged that drugs were somehow involved. The website insisted Naomi should stay there as they would provide more details as they became available. Naomi stared at the headline.

Prince was dead.

She liked Prince.

She liked his catchy lyrics and style—Darling Nikki was her favorite Prince song. Naomi, like all normal people, did not have just one favorite song, instead she listened to whatever fit her mood. Naomi usually found herself listening to non-mainstream music, songs with powerful lyrics and strong voices. Naomi's only exception was the Grateful Dead.

She would forever love The Dead.

Her love of The Dead did not come from memories of hanging out in the basement of a friend's house listening to albums and smoking cigarettes they had stolen from someone's parents. Or from going to their concerts, getting high and jamming with the crowd as the music and the audience became one. The crowd moved with the rhythms and the changes like the murmuration of starlings, feeling the music and the power of the crowd uniting. No, none of those were the reason. She would forever love The Dead because of her hippy-esk father.

Every time it snowed Naomi was six years old again. She was sitting at the kitchen table of the small farm house she grew up in. The warm smell of bread baking, the cracking for the fire in the woodstove. It was Saturday afternoon and her father was teaching her how to place chess. He insisted on listening to the Grateful Dead telling her she needed to be able to concentrate on two things at once.

"Besides," he would say, "music helps you learn, and there is no better music than The Dead."

Naomi's winter Saturdays were always the same and always special. Naomi knew her father, at first, was letting her win. However, he challenged her for each victory not just giving them away. She needed to learn how each piece moved on the board and how those movements allowed for strategies to be formed. He coached her on her mistakes, showed her how he could take her piece, how to setup moves. He kept teaching her and she kept learning.

Naomi met the constant challenge to become not just better at the game, but to earn both her victories and defeats honestly. Naomi's father quickly came to realize his cute-as-a-bug, rosy-cheeked, sunny-haired daughter was not just exceptionally bright, but equally determined to master any challenge set before her.

Several years later he found he had to rethink his strategic patterns as his precocious ten-year-old daughter, sang a duet with Jerry Garcia, not missing a word of *Uncle John's Band*, forced him to play blitz rules while she was making an initial gambit, leading to a bind or a castling and resulting in checkmate within ten moves.

Her father would laugh with love and frustration at his constant losses as she and Jerry sang their duet. Naomi knew she would forever be a Deadhead.

Naomi drifted forward to being at work, at her computer reading the story details about Prince and how he intersected with her life. As Naomi sifted through her memories one in particular came to mind, Prince's movie,

Purple Rain. She had seen it years ago, when it first came out. She thought about that day, going to the movie, which led her to think of Colin. Although she and Colin would email occasionally, they still had not quite become regular texting or emailing buddies. They were still friends, but there was a distance between them.

The distance was both literal, as he lived in California and she in Minnesota, but also figurative. They still shared some details about their lives, but they never tried to be as emotionally intimate as they had once been back in high school, it was something they both just let happen and now looking back, thinking about it, Naomi did not know why. Naomi's thoughts circled back to Colin and Purple Rain, the day the two of them went to see it. As she finished reading and thinking, following the lines of her memory that all seemed to lead to the same point. Acting on impulse, Naomi's cell phone was in her hand and she was texting Colin.

"Colin, heard the news? Prince died. Didn't we see his movie together years ago"?

Naomi was surprised to get a text back from him almost immediately.

"Naomi! Yes! At the old Har Mar movie theaters in Roseville. How are you doing"?

They spent the rest of the afternoon texting and catching-up. From that first casual text they started communicating almost daily. At first their conversations were text based, but it did not take long for texts like,

"My fingers are going numb, wanna actually speak to each other?"

to become phone calls. Slow work days and lunch breaks soon became an hour of talking. Naomi's tedious stop-and-go rush hour drive home listening to the NPR or the Current became an over-to-quick conversation with Colin. They could spend several hours talking, losing track of time as they shared their lives.

Colin was an artist, a painter. He did portraits and landscapes and some other art stuff. Naomi laughed at his vague description of "art stuff."

"What the hell is art stuff?" Naomi asked.

Colin explained art stuff as some large-scale contract art work for several of the local restaurants, like murals, and light setup, blending lines and form so the interior was appealing and would draw a person further into the room.

Further shared life details included marriage, from which Naomi experienced a pang of pain and jealousy. Sure, it was childish, but he had asked her first. Colin said he was married over twenty years to wonderful woman named Margo.

They met at an art exhibit and show she setup. He explained Margo did entertainment scheduling and event planning stuff. Their meet-cute was the suggestion that she had not only setup the art show, but set him up so he would have to meet her. Naomi found Colin's explanation and description of his wife's profession interesting as he told her.

"If a person wanted a banquet or party or some big conference of some shit, Margo would put it all together."

Because of the nature of her work, she traveled a lot, which Colin said was fine with him, since he spent most of his time alone in his studio painting.

Naomi thought about that, two people who were married, but didn't spend a lot of time together. In some ways she was envious of that situation. How many days did she just want to be left alone to her own devices? To have hours on end that were hers and hers alone. Even if she did nothing with her time but sit and watch the world go by. It would be her time to do with what she wanted. One the other hand, the thought of a relationship built on separation instead of togetherness made her sad. Sad because at the end of her day, it was always nice to know there was going to be someone there to share it with.

Colin told her about his nice house just outside of the actual town of Sonoma. It wasn't anything big or fancy, but it was cozy and it also had an old tool shed in the backyard he had converted and expanded into his studio, and that was where he spent most of his time.

While drinking coffee one quiet Saturday morning, Naomi, out of curiosity, started internet searching for Colin's artwork. She was amazed by the detail. His paintings were so beautiful. They were vivid in color and intimate in detail. They were a moment of life captured by a brush and kept alive in paint.

Naomi was caught by one painting in particular. It was of a woman standing on a dock, surrounded by trees, looking out over a river. The scene was alive, no detail too small to be missed—a dry leaf floating on the water, sunlight reflecting up off the water, even the idea of a breeze was imagined by several small locks of the woman's hair raised off her shoulders up to the left.

Naomi thought she could almost hear the sound of the wind through the trees, the light splash of a leaf landing on the water, the singing of the birds, and smell of the air. She found herself imagining she was the woman standing on that dock, how peaceful it would be. Reality checked her imagination into the boards, and knocked Naomi back to reality. She was amazed at how much money that original painting sold for. Soon she went from looking at his paintings, to how seeing the price tags. Naomi was shocked. No wonder Colin could afford to live in Sonoma!

Naomi's sticker shock faded, and she allowed herself to once again become emotionally and imaginatively absorbed into the world of Colin's paintings. She was again the model. She was in each painting. She was the woman standing on the dock. She was the woman standing in the rain waiting at a train station. She was even the naked woman partially covered by a blanket in front of a fireplace holding a cup with steam rising from it.

Naomi immersed herself in the idea of being those women. She also imagined Colin standing there behind the canvas, brush in hand, looking at every intimate line of her naked body as he painted her picture. She had never truly realized the extent of his talent.

Naomi had always known Colin could draw. Sometimes he let her see his drawings. Sometimes he did not. Naomi laughed to herself as she remembered the infamous tattoo incident. But all of those doodles were nothing like the artistry of paintings she now dreamed herself into.

Back then Colin never talked about his drawings. Other than the high school art teacher, Colin rarely showed his serious drawings to anyone, even to her. Naomi standing in the school lunchroom of her memory, seeing Colin eating lunch with friends. He would be listening and talking to the group, a sandwich in one hand, a pencil in the other.

That other hand seemed to move of its own volition and soon by that hand, Colin, would turn a paper napkin into masterpiece which he would then crumple up and throw away. Whenever she asked to look at what he was drawing he would reluctantly show her.

Although, there were times he flat-out refused no matter how hard she cajoled or tried to bribe him. She would even try to sneak-up behind him, to peek over his shoulder, to see what he was drawing. However, Colin always seemed to know she was there. He would call her out, not even turning around to make sure she was really there. He would just say,

"Nice try, but not this time."

Then he would crumple the drawing.

The only time Naomi was able to see Colin's full talent was in the art room display case. The art teacher Mr.

Murphy would pick his favorite pieces from various students and display the art for the whole school to see.

Naomi was amazed back then as she was now at what Colin could do with just a pencil. She would complement him. She would tell him how cool his drawings were. She would tell him he had talent. Colin told her it was just stupid shit. It was a waste of time. He needed to focus on real stuff.

He was supposed to concentrate on real classes so he could get a real job. He said it with an effacing edge to his voice, as if he were mimicking, and mocking, someone else speaking to him. Or for him.

Naomi remembered the day Colin told her he went to see the military recruiters when they came to school. She teased him, saying he had done it just to have a legitimate reason to cut math class. She remembered his stupid lopsided smile, a little laugh, telling her that was partially true, but he had also gone because he had decided to enlist, and had started the paperwork that day. That was spring of their senior year.

Naomi remembered being frightened and angry at him. She told him he was crazy. She could not mask her emotions when she asked, no she demanded to know, why he wanted to join the military? She told him he was not solider material. He was tall, skinny, and not very athletic. And besides, he was an artist, not a killer.

Naomi could still see his sardonic smile, the look of resignation and something else she did not understand at the time. That knowledge would reveal itself later in their life and friendship. He told her, he was not going to be a solider, *he was going to be a Marine*. Besides, there were other jobs in the military besides being a grunt with a rifle. Teenage Naomi tried again, a logical, non-emotional approach, not an offensive move to make him defensive. She asked Colin about needing his parents' permission or signatures. He could not just go off and sign contracts without them. Colin, still holding the same smile explained he in fact did not need his parents' permission. He had turned eighteen back in November. He could legally sign his own enlistment forms and once school was over, they were no longer his legal guardians.

"I will no longer be legally required to need them" he said.

End of May in nineteen eighty-six they graduated from West Lake High School. Five days later Colin was in San Diego, California for boot camp. Naomi remained in West Lake trying to figure out her life. Three months and almost a letter a day later, Colin graduated from boot camp. Colin sent her a graduation picture and she had to do a double take, almost not recognizing him. It was still Colin's face but he had fundamentally changed. He was wearing Dress Blues and looked so emotionally cold. Gone was his silly smile and the gentle softness of his face. That Colin had been replaced by an emotionless expression with hard edges.

In a letter he told her he was not going to return to Minnesota on post-boot camp leave. He was staying in California and going directly to his military training school. He was sorry he would not be able to see her but would send pictures. With that letter, Naomi felt her first great loss. Colin was gone.

After that Naomi started losing time to concern herself too much with Colin. She had moved in with her boyfriend, the older, break-up and make-up guy she had been dating most of her senior year. Six months later, Colin was stationed in Iwakuni, Japan as Naomi was getting married for the first time and still lived in the same town.

Even over distance and time they never lost contact with each other. They wrote letters to each other, sharing their lives. Naomi admitted she was a little jealous of Colin. He living over in Japan. All the interesting sites and experiences he was having. He would ask her about her life and how things were back in West Lake.

He told her he missed her very much. He had a picture of them together at graduation. He said he kept it taped to the side of his desk. It was the only memory of West Lake he wanted. Their worlds were definitely distant. The universe had pulled them in different directions and put them in different orbits around different distant stars. Yet even with all that distance between them, spread out across the universe, it didn't matter because they were always able to see each other's light and to feel each other's gravity.

Six Feet.

Prince, and his death, had been their watershed moment. Instead of staying small and easily contained within the course of their usual routine complacent lives, it became a swelling torrent and went over the flood barriers and swept them onto a new course. The daily texting grew to a constant conversation that would occasionally distract them from their actual jobs. Their first phone call was a little strange. Naomi found it curious to hear his voice after so long. It sounded so different and yet familiar. It was like the sudden remembrance of a forgotten memory.

Similar to the texts, the calls started out as casual, and then they grew into almost daily hour or more conversations. Colin once joked he felt like an eight-year-old girl. Naomi laughed and corrected him.

"No, they were more like thirteen-year-old girls."

Soon, at least once a week, around five o'clock Naomi's time, three o'clock Colin's, they would have what they called "Happy Hour." Which was still the preconceived idea of happy hour, except they did it across several time zones and over the phone.

Naomi would be home from work. Colin would be in his studio. They would share a drink and a conversation. The drink was ranged from water to the mutually appreciated a gin and tonic. They would then spend the next hour or so, before one of their spouses arrived home, talking about their day.

Naomi tried to control herself. She tried to keep her growing interest in Colin and his life safely pigeonholed and contained within its boundaries. She tried to rebuild the dams and the floodwalls, trying to redirect the flow of their relationship back into a safe and controlled situation. And the harder she tried the more tenuous her control became. Naomi felt like she was becoming an addict, addicted to that aspect of her life, addicted to Colin.

Their texts and calls had started simple enough and were all about reconnecting. They learned about each other's marriage—Colin on his first, Naomi on her second.

They exchanged stories of how they met their spouses, how long they had been married, and what about kids and why not. They talked about current interests, hobbies, movies, favorite foods, and even dabbled with some political and religious themed conversations.

Naomi, before she knew it, was once again familiar with Colin. They had moved past all the minutia-of-life bullshit and were once again true friends.

Thanks to the internet and her curiosity, Naomi decided to casually cyber-stalk Colin. He said he made a living as an artist, as a painter. She wondered if she had maybe seen some of his work somewhere. She finally convinced herself it was okay to be a cyber-stalker by telling herself it was okay because all the other kids were doing it.

A person could never go wrong with using that excuse. It was the universal panacea of excuses and justifications for any action.

But in her heart, she knew the reason for searching for Colin was to see a picture of him. It had been years since she had seen him and she wondered how he looked. Naomi knew if she asked Colin for a picture, he would send her one. But Naomi was not ready to ask that, not yet. Because if she asked him for a picture, he would ask her for one. And Naomi wondered if that was the actually the reason she did not ask? However, a little internet snooping was okay. Why was it okay? Because all the kids were doing it.

Naomi thought of all that as she typed Colin Meyer into Google.

"Google knows everything. Which is great and also terrifying" Naomi thought.

And in a matter of seconds, she had pictures of Colin. Some pictures from an art show, next to a painting. Some of the pictures were of somebody else taking a selfie with him. Naomi looked at those images and sighed, Colin had aged very well.

Naomi knew he had no current pictures of her and would occasionally ask for one. Naomi wanted to send a picture; however, she was self-conscience, not wanting to disappoint Colin. After the first request or two, he stopped asking her. Naomi figured he had taken her hint. Then came the day he blackmailed her. Naomi received a text from Colin. It was her high school graduation picture. Colin still had it and had dug it out from where ever he kept stupid stuff like that

"Rotten dirty hoarder!"

Naomi whispered to herself when she looked at the picture he had sent. It was Naomi from the 1986. She thought she looked like a reject from a hairband rock video, something from Poison, or Motely Crüe. Her hair big swept back and feathered. And her shirt! It had shoulder pads! She was even wearing pastels!

Naomi wanted to hate herself for looking like that. How could someone, anyone ever want to look like that? Then again, "all the kids were doing it."

After the close up of her graduation picture, Colin had sent a second picture. That picture was Colin standing in his studio. It was mostly a rustic white color although there were brush smears of various colors randomly across the walls. The shelves were filled with brushes and various tubes and jars. Along the wall were canvases and easels and what Naomi guess were paintings, although they were all covered with sheets. To her horror, what she did see was a canvas where he had painted,

"Your portrait here if you don't send me a picture. Yes, I will also post it on my website."

Naomi knew Colin was not serious. First, he would never do something like that to her. Second, the threat was followed with a laughing emoji face. However, there was a small paranoid part of her that decided she could not risk him being serious. Naomi checked her hair and outfit. It was a good hair day and the top she was wearing was super cute. Posing like she was checking her lipstick, her face turned slightly to the side, her lips pursed, looking right at the camera, Naomi sent Colin a picture. Naomi included the message,

"You win. Now destroy that old picture of me or face my wrath."

She included the devil smile face emoji.

After the first picture, Naomi found it easier to send more, not often, just enough. With the pictures, Naomi found they both seemed to need to include self-deprecating comments about themselves. Naomi's response was to tell Colin he was a stupid and how great he looked—Naomi was serious, age had been good to him.

Colin told Naomi she was even more beautiful now than she was when they were sixteen, in school, hanging out at her locker during their lunch period eating French fries. Naomi replied that she wished she had that metabolism again and those boobs.

They both laughed.

It was good.

Their happy hour conversations continued and once they even had phone date night. Margo was gone on a trip and Naomi's husband Brad was out with some of his friends doing guy bonding fantasy sports stuff. They spent several hours talking about everything and nothing and Naomi found herself relaxing when talking with Colin. She was becoming relaxed like she had been all those years ago, like they were, back in school and their cares were few and simple. Naomi liked that relaxed feeling, it let her breathe.

Somewhere in the process of getting to know each other again, as they relaxed and casual they started letting some of their more colorful personal habits and language come out. Naomi smiled as she remembered when she, not even thinking about it, burped when talking to Colin. She casually let out a carbonated diet soda induced thunderous belch.

Something she would only do if she were alone or with her husband. Naomi tried to apologize; Colin could not stop laughing.

Then there was the time Colin used the cunt when describing his sister-in-law. Colin then said fuck, because he could not believe he had just fucking said cunt while talking with Naomi. Now it was her time for uncontrollable laughter. She let him know it was okay, she actually liked the word cunt because it was so descriptive and not over used like the other good cuss words like shit, damn, and fuck.

They both laughed like titillated children using dirty, grown-up words for the first time. In the span of several sentences Naomi realized she and Colin were on new and more intimate area, a place she had never thought about going. Naomi determined she would not try to rationalize or deny those new feeling because she knew as irrational as it sounded, the heart wants what the heart wants.

Naomi knew they each had their lives and their happiness. They told each other they were content in the life they were living. Sure, there were bad times some squabbles and tense moments, but those were part of any long-term relationship. Naomi shared those moments with Colin and he shared his with her. It was a pressure release, a type of relationship therapy with a friend.

Then one afternoon, during a quick lunchtime text session, Colin sent her a link to a human-interest news story. It was about a family who lived out in the middle of bum-fuck nowhere Alaska. It was a picture biography about a husband, wife, and their teenage son. The parents were well-educated teachers and artists, and the family lived simply. They did some basic farming, a lot of hunting, and would trade with other families in the area around them for other supplies.

In that text, Colin told Naomi, he sometimes would think about getting away from it all, just like that family. Colin said there were times he just wanted to leave everything and everyone, starting over again somewhere else, maybe with someone else. Naomi responded to Colin, thanking him for the story. Then another text arrived from Colin. It was one line. It was a question. *Would she ever think of something like that?*

Naomi looked at Colin's message and thought about it. Naomi took several minutes to respond. The legal, educated, rational part of her mind went over the text as if it were a court document, some kind of sworn testimony that needed to be analyzed., She broke it down into parts and asked herself, how did this text differ from the others?

Sure, it could be a *what if,* or *what would it be like,* sort of question. It could have been one of those fantasies you think of when work is killing your soul or when sleep was elusive and you just spent several hours burning holes in the ceiling. But on cross-examination, Naomi found there could be implications, ulterior motives in that question.

She concluded based on knowing the personality of the defendant that in this case, a cigar was just a cigar, and she knew what her answer was. Naomi replied yes, she liked that sort of idea, getting away from it all. But, wanted a more post-apocalyptic world, maybe one with zombies.

Then came Colin's next text which made Naomi momentarily question if her original verdict was still correct? Colin asked if she wanted to run away with him? Just the two of them, up to Alaska, just go and no looking back. Naomi considered those words.

She thought about Colin and all the silly and stupid things they would say to each other. Naomi knew, at least she hoped she knew he was joking. However, there was a small part of her that sat in her light gray cube looking at her computer monitor and document covered desk. working as just another lawyer in the legal department of the multistoried building of the Midwest Bank and Insurance company. Naomi's thoughts shifted to the imagined possibility of a life that was more than the current "American Dream." Naomi replied with questions of her own.

"When do we leave?" and *"Will there be zombies?"*

Five Feet.

Naomi wanted to say it was against her better judgement that she and Colin were growing so close, but she also never truly tried to stop it. Naomi knew they had pushed some boundaries with some of their conversations and some of their pictures, and there was a part, a small part that kept reminding her, nagging at her. The small nagging part of Naomi questioned that if she would not tell her husband everything about her relationship with Colin, why was she doing it? But the greater part of Naomi enjoyed their intimacy.

It was unique and fresh without any small print or pressure attached to it. It was their secret other life and as long as they maintained the established rules, such as no nude photos and no phone sex—although Naomi would occasionally find herself enjoying an occasional private personal moment fantasizing about her and Colin. They were both comfortable with where they were and what they were doing. There was the original standing rule—Delete Everything!

There were just too many stories of people getting caught doing far worse, far more lewd and lascivious acts, because they kept the evidence on their phones or computers or both. Naomi wondered what the hell was wrong with those people? Were they stupid or did the just want to get caught? Naomi thought that same rhetorical question about most of the world.

Naomi happily continued her secret other life with Colin. They would talk about places they would like to visit. Naomi told Colin about wanting to go the Netherlands, to visit the museums and parks. Colin told her about a hotel in Finland with special cabins people could rent, the bedrooms were shaped like igloos, with high walls and glass ceilings and during the winter months, you could lie in bed and watch the Northern Lights. The places they found to visit always changed, but their response never did—*"When do we leave"?*

Four Feet.

Naomi was content in where she and Colin were as friends. Finding places to imagine they would run off to together, passive and not so passive flirting. They had their frequent happy hours and occasional date nights. They were both happy just spending time together and enjoying each other's company. Then Colin had to go and change everything.

That was the day of the email.

It was the early afternoon for Naomi when her phone dinged at her. She had an email. Naomi absently looked at the phone while working on a contract that was needed before the end of the day. She tried to ignore her phone. She tried to ignore the unknown message. She tried to ignore the fact that because of features on her phone she had set a special text and ringtone letting her know it was Colin. And because she knew it was from Colin, Naomi instantly started to feel giddy and excited wondering what Colin might say.

This time Naomi told herself she had work to do. Yes, she had to finish that contract. Naomi kept telling herself those same things over and over again as her eyes kept darting between the screen of her computer and the phone sitting by her coffee cup. After several hours and a lifetime later, she finished the contract. She saved it. She attached it to an email. She positioned the mouse arrow over the send button and left-clicked.

"*Now*", Naomi thought, "*now I can see what Colin wanted to say.*"

Colin only sent emails when he knew it was not safe to text or when he had something important to say. Naomi opened the file and read.

Naomi,

I just received a call from, and for lack of a better term, my agent, I have been invited to be part of a gallery show in Minneapolis on May 11th. I guess I'm coming to town. I arrive late on Thursday night, have the show Friday evening, then fly back home on Saturday morning. Margo will not be with me, as she has other commitments that weekend. I'm telling you this because I would like to see you and spend some time with you on Friday. If you want, are able to, we could meet someplace Friday morning for coffee or something before you work? Or maybe lunch? Or maybe a drink after work? Or all three? It would be nice to talk to you, actually speak to you, to see you laugh. Let me know if any of those options can work. If not, then I offer this; you and your husband come to the show. I will make sure your drinks are free and at least we will still get to see each other. Of course, you will have to keep your hands to yourself.

Love,

Colin.

Naomi's brain monetarily vapor-locked. Colin was coming to town. Not Santa Claus, but Colin. He had some work there. He would be by himself, his wife had other business of her own. He asked her if they could meet. Maybe before-work coffee? Maybe lunch? Maybe afterwork drinks? Colin even gave her the option of coming to his show with her husband, just so they could see each other.

Naomi's hesitation was not because she did not want to see Colin, but there were logistics and timing, responsibilities and other bullshit excuses Naomi could not think of at the moment but knew they existed. Her life suddenly came to a hard, quick stop and all her life's meticulously organized bins and files of thoughts and feelings suddenly and uncontrollably came crashing down around her.

Naomi knew she needed some time to think. This was not a quick response situation. She needed to clean up and organize the mental chaos that just crashed into her organized life. Naomi also knew all the excuses she had just come up with, and the many more waiting to be creatively constructed, were nothing more than the fear of having to see Colin, or more aptly stated, to have Colin see her

There were a lot of what-if questions. The biggest one being, could two friends who hadn't seen each other in literally decades still really just pick up and be the kind of friends they once were? Of course, this wasn't a sudden reestablishment of their friendship. That had already happened. This was now facing the reality of all the *just silly talk* during all their conversations. This wasn't suddenly going from zero to sixty, because they had already gone well over the speed limit of their rekindled friendship. Naomi knew all those contemplations and questions could wait. She could save them for the drive home, that was her contemplating time. Naomi also didn't want Colin thinking she didn't get his email so she sent him a quick text,

"Got your email need some time to think."

Several seconds later he responded, "No worries. I understand."

Naomi considred Colin's email on her drive home. It was a nice day and the traffic wasn't bad, so Naomi let her mind drift in thought, besides, her car knew its way home.

"Meet Colin for coffee." It sounded nice. That might be a nice way to start the day.

"Meet Colin for lunch." Also, an option but problematic since eating and talking didn't go well together.

"Meet Colin for an afterwork drink." That option, like the morning coffee, also had some appeal. But, unlike coffee, the afterwork drink had the danger of becoming several afterwork drinks and then having to drive.

All the options were good and all the options were also bad. The bad part was, besides the awkwardness of actually seeing each other after so long, they would be rushed for time. A quick "Hello, and, how are you?" wasn't what either of them would want, despite what Colin said in email.

And there was still that strange feeling about actually seeing him. Naomi couldn't shake it. She didn't know why she should feel strange about being in the same proximity, the same room, the same table, across from, looking at him, seeing each movement of his face as he talked or smiled.

Colin wouldn't be the picture, the digital image that no matter how many pixels and colors and depth enhances techniques which made up that image, but would never capture the true soul of a living person. Colin would be the living person there with her. Each line on his face moving as he moved. Those lines under no control of Colin, of their own volitions would form creases and furrows or curves and dimples, the sum of his unconscious expressions live right there in front of her. No way to hang up or be disconnected. Naomi should have wanted that, but she felt nervous, an apprehension of adequacy,

"What if they had both changed too much"?

Naomi knew she was being stupid, but she also thought she was being realistic. They had both changed. They both had lives. They both had grown so far from where they had started, and everyone knows, you can't go home again. And isn't that what they were trying to do, if even a little bit? Trying to make their lives like they were back in high school, before he left.

It wasn't until lately in their discussions, their happy-hour gossip and confession time when war-stories and drinking tips were exchanged with honest abandon. That was when Naomi figured it out.

Life is the act of living.

In their discussions, and from living through it, Naomi came to understand one of the reasons for the sense of personal distance back when they were kids. Naomi was having the typical personal family crisis shit. Rhetorically Naomi wondered why family crisis shit was never just stuff, it was always shit.

Naomi told Colin about the situation with her brother and his wife, and how lucky Colin was to be all the way out on the West Coast, to not have to deal with family. Usually,

Colin responded right away. But this time he didn't. He didn't and Naomi started to wonder what happened? Maybe he had to answer another phone call? If he had to go do something and just hung-up. Or maybe the connection failed? All of these were arguments for actually sitting down and having a face-to-face conversation. It may have been only seconds, only two or three breaths, but it seemed longer.

Naomi's intuition told her something was wrong. Either way she would just have to wait. Then finally on the intake of her forth breath Colin's voice was back, but it was different. It was no heavy, it carried a weight, and it seemed he was going to now share that weight with her. Naomi listened as Colin with a cold, dispatched voice medicinally explained he didn't interact with or visit his family. Their shit was not their own.

He hadn't been back home since he left. He never came back home for a specific reason. There had been some domestic abuse in his home growing up. That was all he said. He never gave specific details. She could never remember him coming to school with obvious bruises of any kind. But she knew there were many forms of abuse and not all of them left bruises or scars.

Because he didn't go into any further details, she didn't ask. She didn't know what to say. What could she say? So, she responded the only way she knew how, the way a friend would.

"I'm always here to listen if you want to talk," Naomi said.

"Thank you. And for what it's worth. Thank you for being my friend. I really do love you," Collin responded.

Naomi understood that was the reason he left Minnesota after graduation. Why he could never, would never let himself become emotionally invested back then. He wanted to get away from that life.

Naomi reasoned that was why he never came back home on leave or after he was discharged. It made her sad. There was the warm wet meandering down her cheek. They were such good friends and she never realized. Naomi mentally went over his missive. Colin asking her that if they wanted to, they could meet for coffee or they could meet for lunch or they could meet for after-work drinks.

He even invited her and her husband to come to his art show. That was how much he wanted to see her. And Naomi, once again had to admit, secretly to herself, she wanted to see Colin bad enough that she was considering doing just that, going to art show with Brad. Knowing it would be awkward, she would still do it. Afterall she and Colin were just friends. Very good *just* friends. But still just friends.

Naomi often wondered about that as well. The two of them had spent so much of their time together in high school. They hung-out together constantly, even to the point where it caused break-ups with the other people they were dating. But they never once went on a real date. They stayed *just* friends. Naomi once again felt the need for a mental confession. She hated the need for mental confessions.

"Forgive me Naomi, for I—Naomi—have sinned."

Since it was only her mental confessional contained inside the church of body and soul, and no one else could ever and would never hear her confessions she never lied, usually. And if she as the poor sinner seeking wise counsel and some gentle consoling, did try to lie, well she, as the confessor, knew immediately and would admonish herself for lying to herself. Although the penance she gave herself was never severe, Naomi found this mental processing helped.

It also made her think she needed some professional help or maybe some anti-psychotic medications. Her inner priest became her inner doctor who, as needed, diagnosed her as certainly being a little off-balance, but still quite normal, and she prescribed one to two gin and tonic to be taken orally as needed as treatment. Naomi liked her doctor.

But there had been times, a few in the past and more recently, when she had been thinking about Colin in more than just a friend sort of way. Even while sitting with her husband watching a movie, Naomi would wonder what it might have been like, if she had—she and Collin had—acted on their impulses all those years ago. And the movie on the television became one in her head. It was her and Colin on the couch. It was her and Colin in bed together. It was the two of them married to each other for all those years instead of the two of them married to other people.

Three Feet.

Naomi waited until the next day to respond. She had thought of all the different approaches and moves to the problem, to the day. Naomi knew the problem wasn't that she didn't want to meet, to see Colin. The problem was it had been so long.

They had been apart separated by time and distance and life. Now their friendship, although still a strong and wonderful friendship, it consisted of the two of them being nothing more to each other than words and voices, not flesh and blood.

And Naomi knew that was the crux of the problem. She was willing to admit she loved Colin, but the Colin that she loved was the Colin from her memory. The Colin she kept in a special shoe box in her closet. The Colin who could be neatly laid out on the floor in a collection of pictures and letters. Naomi could talk to, and look at pictures of, an updated version of that Colin on the phone—his sound and his words and his images became part of the collection. But the physical Colin, the Colin of flesh and bone and blood, Naomi hadn't known that Colin for over twenty years. That Colin was a stranger to her.

"Can we just get coffee? I know a great little place not far from my office."

It was about twenty minutes later when Colin responded. He said, yes, he was looking forward to it. As long as the coffee was the good stuff, not the shit Bonnie buys when she does the shopping.

Two Feet.

He was right there in front of her. Naomi could see each individual hair on his head and face. She could smell the rain on him. Each drop of rain catching, collecting, mingling together to once again drop from the gray and black whiskers on his chin. The details, and lines of his body through his rain soaked, semi-transparent shirt.

He stopped in front of her, looking down with eyes filled with a brilliant fire fueled from a bottomless inner happiness that was trying to escape. He smiled the stupid lopsided smile, and the room was filled with a barely contained happiness. The people around all seemed to be brighter. The coffee hotter, the sweet rolls sweeter. Naomi being the focus of such pure unabashed emotion felt herself become swept up by it.

The pterodactyl sized butterflies in her stomach were gone. The nervous earth moving shaking of her hands had ceased. Then in her heart, in the ineffable, intangible ether of the soul, that place within her, that place where she kept love hidden; against her will, against her determination, against her self-control, she felt something she hadn't felt in a very long time.

One.

Chapter 4

Colin wasn't just wet, he was soaked. He had forgotten how unpredictable and crappy the weather was in Minnesota, especially in May. He hadn't packed a rain coat. He did not think to bring an umbrella—or even thought to borrow one from the hotel.

He should have known the weather was going to be bad because the weather in Sonoma wasn't much better. There had been a lot of rain over the winter. That made the water-starved southern part of California happy. It made the grape growers in the northern half a little cranky. At the moment, Colin wasn't sure where he should direct his loathing.

If it was not directed at the rain, was it being in Minnesota? Or was his current emotional state brought about by the memories of someplace he once called home? Colin contemplated, reflected on his rhetorical questions as if he were in a therapy session.

During the ten minutes for the taxi to drive him from the hotel to the coffee shop address Naomi had given him Colin determined he didn't care about the answer to his inner questions. What he cared about, what he could believe in, was the taxi had just turned into a small mostly empty strip mall where he was going to again meet Naomi after years apart.

Colin looked around the brick and glass structures. Due to the early hour all the shops were closed except for a corner gas station and a small coffee shop two doors and four display windows away from the gas station. Both places were busy with people dressed for work. They were either trying to fill cars with fuel or bodies with caffeine while trying to stay dry but succeeding at only one.

Colin wiped at the breath-fogged window with his hand, and looked toward his destination—so many years away now so close. The coffee shop busy with people going in and out, trying to get a morning coffee without getting wet. Not getting wet, seemed to be the major objective of the morning. The taxi stopped behind the row of cars parked against the sidewalk in front of the coffee shop. Colin looked at the meter and handed the driver a twenty-dollar bill, and a keep the change. Colin took a deep breath. Reaching for the black plastic door handle, he opened the door.

Colin, in the moment it took him to open and close the car door, determined that the world had decided it wasn't already raining hard enough. For no sooner had his foot splashed down into the small lake forming in the parking lot, at the signal of a loud crack of thunder, the heavens' added another million gallons of water to the ocean already coming down.

Colin further determined, as he waded the fifteen feet from the taxi to the sidewalk, he could have skipped a shower that morning. In fact, he could have worn dirty clothes because he was soaked to his skin. Colin emerged from the parking lot lake up onto the draining shore of the sidewalk. He then moved to the relative shelter and safety of the overhead awing of the coffee shop and tried to determine what he had enjoyed more.

Was it the wading through the parking lot and stepping into the water so deep that his shoes became soaked?

Or was it the unexpected drop-off next to the curb, where the water was at least two to three inches higher and the raging swell which carried plastic bottles and cigarette butts down the storm drain flowed over the top of his shoes and soaked his pants?

Or finally, was it the waterfall pouring off the awing in front of the coffee shop with all the force and capacity of Niagara Falls?

Colin found he had only one response that would be both elegant, eloquent, concise and completely sum up his exact feelings at that moment.

"Fuckin-A"!

Colin stood for a moment under the semi-safety of the coffee shop window awing. The rain pounding down making the awning sounding like a tribal drum at the height of some celebration. Colin knew there was no use getting mad about it.

What good would it do?

He was wet.

He was soaked.

He was standing in front of the coffee shop trying to look through the windows hazed over on the inside with warm condensation, where at some table Naomi was sitting and waiting while he stood outside being splattered with cold rain.

Colin took a breath, shook his arms trying get rid of the worst of the water and opened the door to the coffee shop. The small brass bell over the door made a jingling ringing sound and alerted everyone in the place of his entrance.

So much for making a quiet entrance thought Colin.

Which was exactly what he had wanted to do. Just slip into the small shop and find Naomi without making a scene. Which, again, was how Colin preferred to go through life, quiet and without making a scene. He always thought publicity and big social events were just so people could feed their egos.

Even on a small scale, like the locals, those regulars who always had to go to the same place, arriving at the same time, to do the same thing over and over again. They did it because they found a certain level of self-satisfaction in knowing all the other people at that place were doing the same thing and were waiting for everyone to show up. Colin hated pretentiousness. He hated having to make public appearances. All those petty ego-feeding actions were nothing more than a dick-measuring contest.

He really, truly, honestly, and again back to really, hated having to answer the question of,

"So, what do you do for a living?"

Especially when he was at an art show. The way the person asking the question would put such emphasis on the "O" in so. The stupid fucker new what Colin did, but they asked him anyway. They always thought it was funny.

Fuckers.

Colin would often in his imagination come up with many colorful and often time offensive remarks, but rarely if ever used them, especially if Margo was with him. She wouldn't tolerate his self-deprecation and effacing to avoid talking about, and of course the all-important, marketing himself to people and aggrandizing his art work. Margo would take the initiative, lazily put one of her freshly manicured hands on his arm with the force of a bear trap. The other arm casually around his waist, like a steel band cinching him to her. She leaning her perfect groomed hair against his shoulder so he was sure to hear her whispered comments. She smiled her practiced easy-going with just right shade of red lipstick, oh he's just being silly and shy smile, and deliver her unctuous, mellifluous one sentence oration,

"He's an artist, a painter."

Colin would start looking for a rock to crawl under and hide from everyone who now wanted to talk art with him. And why should he give two-shits about how someone didn't understand Picasso or thought Van Gough looked like a child's finger painting, but they loved to watch the reruns of The Joy of Painting with Bob Ross.

Colin found one of the many perks of being a painter was, like a being writer, no one generally knew who he was. Even with social media he maintained a semi-private existence. Besides, Colin didn't do any social media, he had his friend Nancy do it all for him, it was just easier. The multitude of social media platforms were changing too fast for him to keep up. Then again, he had never cared in the first place.

Plus, there were the code words that unless you knew what you were doing and saying, an innocent posting about grandma's secret coffee cake recipe became an anti-sematic comment that somehow also supported child-molesters. No, Colin felt no need to share the intimate details of his life with so-called friends and followers.

When Nancy updated his website and social media accounts the pictures were him next to a painting. That was if he had decided to be in the picture. Usually, he declined. He wasn't for sale, the painting was. He let Nancy fill in the text. She was good with words and computers and people.

Besides, Colin enjoyed the removed sense of autonomy painting gave him. As a constant reminder to himself of that idea, Colin, using an airbrush, had painted a mantra in graffiti-style on the inside of the door of the small bathroom in his studio. While taking a personal moment, his polite euphemism for taking a shit. He would reflect on this mantra, to look at, to read and contemplate the full implication of its meaning while dropping a duce. It was part of a quote from the artist Banksy, *"they forget invisibility is a superpower."*

Colin liked that idea. He liked that mantra. He also liked his private bathroom. After that first piece of graffiti, and after contemplating his mantra several times, he did some further bathroom redecorating.

On a rainy afternoon and while suffering from some painters' block and, also being, admittedly, slightly drunk and bored, Colin once again let his inner street-punk-graffiti-artist out. Something he hadn't done since high school. Colin broke out of his painter's block by loading up several air brushes with a collection of garish colors, put on his respirator and goggles, cranked Queens of the Stone Age on his stereo and graffitied his studio bathroom.

When he was finished the bathroom looked like the side of a railroad car, a bridge underpass, the wall next to a basketball court—it was a pure uninhibited expression of his feelings and talent. Although, he did think about covering up, or at least painting some clothing on the naked woman leaning forward against a car, bending over, leering at him as he would stand at the toilet.

While standing there a person would look right at her spread legs and ass. The contour of her back turned as the viewers gaze progressed from her ass to her head. Her face was turned and looking at him, or whatever man went in to stand at the toilet and pee. She had long jet-black hair. Her skin the color or lightly tanned leather. Her face was defined by oversized, dark black eyes with exaggerated lashes, bright red lips set in a defiant pout—part slut, part challenge. Her over-sized breasts and nipples hanging like firm pendulums of ripe flesh waiting to be tasted, but only if a person could meet her challenge. She was leaning over part of a car hood, the rest of the car missing into the background of color. Obviously, he must have painted this bathroom puta much further into, or at the bottom, of the bottle of wine. Or was it the start of a second bottle?

Colin also added a special personal touch. It was a homage to all the graffitied bathrooms of the world. Written in black felt tip marker, just above the toilet tank, he wrote "Bob Dylan's Dream" and drew an arrow running down to the handle.

Colin didn't just like this bathroom, he loved it. Fortunately, no one, including and especially Margo, ever used his studio bathroom. Not because it wasn't clean, he in fact cleaned it religiously every Sunday morning. No one used it because he didn't allow people to stay that long in his studio. So, Colin left his bathroom puta as he had painted her. She would be there on the wall to look at, and to challenge him, every time he went in there.

The little ringing of the bell above the door making its tiny metallic clanging sound did not echo with an exited buzz causing all the people in the room to run toward him wanting to take selfies. It didn't boom with fate and Colin did not have to worry that it tolled for him. The only action that little metallic ringing sound did was tell the workers behind the counter another morning customer had just come into their shop.

It told those poor over-worked and under-paid baristas another customer was about to join the already long queue of patrons who were desiring a morning cup of coffee. The several people sitting about the coffee shop took no interest in him, other than to passingly acknowledge someone had come in.

Although some patrons near the door did glare at him. Colin realized that was because he was keeping the door from closing. Cold air and some rain were coming in the shop. Colin's introvert-fueled paranoia went safely back into its designated mental psychosis hole. His autonomy was safe. He was just another nobody. He was no one to give a second thought about and wonder if they recognized him from somewhere. All of that was true, but for one person sitting at a small wooden table over by the wall with fingers absently picking at her coffee cup. Colin stepped into the shop and the door shut with another innocuous jingling of the bell. He was about to casually shake off the rain, like something a dog would do. Then Colin saw Naomi.

She was sitting by herself at a table by the wall. Colin tried to start walking to her but for the moment he couldn't. His brain wouldn't release the body, to let the legs lift, to put one foot in front of the other. The brain was too preoccupied with once again noting her every detail, absorbing and filing away every nuance no matter how subtle; the way the light fell on her, the highlights, the shadows, the rise and fall, every angle of her was committed to, and compared to every memory of her— Colin was seeing one of his paintings come to life. Naomi was wearing a pair of low-heeled strappy sandals, cropped blue jeans, a black spaghetti strap shirt with a matching light black cotton jacket. Her blonde hair, still long and golden, but now with some silver, spilled out across her jacketed shoulders like a golden waterfall. Her hands delicate, regal looking, trimmed nails with classic French manicure, her toe nails painted a dark purple. Her right hand, possibly in reflex, went to her hair and pushed it back when she looked up and saw him come in the coffee shop, the left still holding the coffee cup.

Did he just see her hand shaking?

Naomi's blue eyes, Colin could see them from where he stood— those eyes along with her perfect smile lit up the room. Naomi was forever etched in Colin's heart and once again his heart rhetorically asked for the gazillionth time, *why didn't I try harder? Why did I let her slip away?*

Colin knew he couldn't just stand there like some idiot. He was supposed to start moving towards Naomi. He was supposed to walk over and say hello. But his brain was still busy. It was mesmerized. It was memorizing. Naomi was radiant as she simply and patiently sat there at the plain wooden table, her hands holding and picking at the brown paper insulated jacket on the white paper cup with a black plastic lid affixed to the top. Naomi's left hand trying to keep steady, wrapping itself around the cup, the nervous fingers opening and closing, holding and letting go.

Colin suddenly forgot that he was wet. He didn't care about being cold. He no longer was concerned with the water soaking through his thin linen shirt and blue jeans.

Oblivious to the concept that the body was cold and already soaking wet from the rain, Colin's hands started to sweat. Absent mindedly he rubbed his hands on his shirt to try to wipe the sweat off, to dry them. He didn't want to touch Naomi's hand, or hug her with his nasty sweaty one. That would just be gross. His hands pushing, wiping against his chilled wet shirt woke him up. Colin realized the problem with wiping his sweaty hands on his soaked shirt didn't really help. The only thing the action actually did was make his shirt look like he was going to a wet T-shirt contest. Colin wanted to die!

He wanted to die because there was Naomi sitting at the table. She looked so amazing! She was still so gorgeous! While one part of Colin's brain was still absorbing every detail of Naomi, another part woke up and memories long misplaced, crumpled and stuffed into dusty old file cabinets and desk drawers suddenly started to be found, started unfolding and opening up.

How could she have ever liked him?

Colin took a breath. He was better than this, he knew that, and those were just memories. Memories of someone else, someone he used to be. And yes, Colin knew he was still, sort of, that person, but he had become something more. He had evolved and grown. He had done and seen so much. But looking at Naomi sitting there he couldn't help but once again experience those feelings of helplessness because of her. Naomi had always had that effect on him.

Colin knew that even if he was the coolest guy around, the king of the mountain that with just her quiet easy smile and flash of those sparkling ice blue eyes, she could level any mountain he stood upon. He would fall and become nothing more than a stammering putz. It wasn't because he had put and still held Naomi on some ivory tower. The situation the simple and complex conundrum of a boy liking a girl.

Colin knew he was so much more now, more than what he had been back when they were just kids, but he still carried some of those albatross feathers. Besides, Naomi didn't care about any of that juvenile shit. He learned from all the long conversations, both text and talking. Colin came to remember not only how amazing Naomi had been back then, but also how amazing she remained.

Just as he had, Naomi had also grown, evolved, become more than the others around her. Naomi had become her own person and never let anyone ever hold her back from her goals. She gave Colin strength to face some of his past shit. He told her about it. She never judged. She hardly ever talked. Naomi just listened. And in the cathartic silence of their conversations, Colin realized, he was the one still carrying those feathers. He could brush them off anytime he wanted and let them go, to be carried off by the wind. What good were they doing him? Of course, it wasn't as easy as saying, *hallelujah, I'm fixed,* but with time and an honest friendship and conversation, some of those feathers did blow away.

Colin started to get control of the deluge of memories pouring into his consciousness from seeing Naomi. He had to pause a moment to once again pick himself up, because without evening trying, just sitting there on the other side of the room, Naomi had once again knocked him off his mountain and turned him into a stammering putz. Colin smiled at his jovial self-deprecating comments and felt his confidence and strength returning. He didn't know why he was getting all flustered. Besides, their time was limited, she had still had to go to work. The brain had to start giving orders.

"Quit standing here you idiot. Get moving!"

Colin ran his hand through his wet hair, trying to push it back into place.

"I should have got it cut."

He also took that moment of hand combing to pull at his hair, hard, trying to get his brain to start working again. Colin took a breath to physically and mentally steady himself, He figured he had better, because he had to walk about ten feet to Naomi's table and he didn't want to trip over his own feet because he forgot how to walk. Because, right at that moment, as Colin looked at Naomi, deep in his heart he felt like that nerdy, dorky kid back in seventh grade who had just met the most wonderful girl in the world and became confused by all those feelings he was feeling.

Ten Feet.

Colin didn't want to remember the last time he had seen Naomi. He knew it had been a long time. He tried not to think about it. Because to do so would be to admit that they were both getting up there in years and middle age was now a fully vulgar and profane term. It had been around high school graduation, those last days of school, and the graduation parties where they bumped into each other.

In those last days Naomi's boyfriend was always with her so Colin was never able to talk honestly with Naomi. He was never able to tell her all those things, those feelings that were always on the tip of his tongue, always on the edge of his heart. All those words that could have changed his life, their lives, fixing all the wrongs; at least that was what he had thought and dreamed.

Colin recalled it was about a week after graduation when he left for boot camp. When he had left Sunset. Period. Done. The End. And outside of occasional pictures, he never again saw Naomi in person, until today.

Colin looked at Naomi sitting at the table with her cup of coffee. Naomi looked like she did in all her pictures, from the old film photographs they exchanged through the mail, to the digital ones, the selfies taken on their phones and instantly shared via text. Now she was sitting there at the old wooden table, her fingers holding, playing with a cup of coffee, now she was three dimensional instead of two. Colin found Naomi just as beautiful as the day he actually built up the courage to start talking to her. He couldn't believe she would let him hang out, walk with her to class. He did everything he could to make her like him. He was such a schmuck back then. Colin smirked to himself,

"And how has that changed"?

The simple innocence of those days. He missed that. He missed the idea that the world could be as simple as a boy walking with a girl. Even if that thirteen-year-old boy was naive about the world and decided he already found the girl of his dreams. A dream he was allowed to walk with through the hallways going to and from class. Those moments were the best part of his day.

Colin thought about those days, walking through those old gray and beige brick and tile hallways. The sounds and voices of the other kids were mere footprint background echoes because Colin heard only he and Naomi walking together. Colin moved through those thoughts, thinking back, *didn't he once ask Naomi to marry him?* What thirteen-year-old kid does something like that? He almost deserved the beatings he was given just for saying something so stupid.

Even though he had physically left her life, emotionally they were never apart. It wasn't like they had ever stopped being friends. Colin didn't know if such an act was actually possible. Colin knew, sort of, about Naomi's life and she knew, sort of, about his. He may have left, but they still walked together, sharing their lives, writing letters to each other all the time.

However, Colin knew he held back, almost, always circumspect in what he wrote, what he said. Even when they were literally almost on opposite sides of the world, Naomi could still make him feel nervous, and silly, and scared out of his heart and soul that if he said the wrong thing, she would never want to talk to him again. The almost part, Colin knew was in part due to several lonely, drunken, and homesick nights in the barracks.

Feeling sad and alone so far away from home, he spent too much time looking at pictures and dreaming about the actions, the word he should have said, what he should have done when he had the chance. Then he would start to scrawl a letter filled with fevered ideas of an unrequited love, and in that intoxicated state, the drunk impassioned and empowered Colin knew the sober, rational and cowardly Colin would never write, much less send such a letter.

Drunk Colin wouldn't stand for that shit. Drunk Colin would stagger his way to the mailbox and deposit the letter and let hungover Colin deal with the ramifications. The next day when he woke up, he would remember what he did and immediately write a letter of apology and forgiveness. Then several days later a letter from Naomi would arrive. He could hear her laughter in the words she wrote. Telling him to relax and not drink so much, and to not worry about it, she understood.

Those were the days when he would check his mail as soon as he arrived back at his barracks, or later on after leaving the military, his mail box. He loved to arrive home and find a letter from Naomi, it made a bad day better, it made a good day great. Colin never knew why the two of them seemed to drop off and drift away at times. It wasn't like he wasn't thinking about Naomi. It was just somehow, she became a background figure, not the focal point of the picture.

Then one evening in the not too far distant past, after meandering his way home after having enjoyed a night out at the Blue Moon Bar and Grill, and maybe just possibly having had a little too much to drink, he found himself once again looking at old pictures and thinking of Naomi. And in his alcohol fueled drive down memory lane, Colin figured he would write Naomi a letter.

It had been six or seven years and he didn't know where she was living. So, Colin put her name on the envelope and sent the letter to the only address he had, her parent's house. Several days later, once again there was a letter from her waiting for him in his mailbox. As the world evolved and technology improved, soon he and Naomi slowly went from paper, or what would come to be called "snail-mail" to the digital e-mail. Now there was no waiting for the end of the day, or for the mailman, whom in fact for Colin's street was a woman, but the term mailman was just sort-of ingrained into his personal lexicon.

One day as she was delivering the mail, Colin was sitting in his yard, under the oak tree, and randomly sketching the neighborhood. As the female letter carrier approached his mailbox with sincere politesse Colin said, "Hello Mailman."

The vocal tone of her response let Colin she did not appreciate being called a mailman.

"Hi, my name is Jenny. I already know you're Colin. It's nice to meet you."

She smiled as she introduced herself, and Colin found himself politely apologizing to Jenny. Although Jenny still delivered Colin's mail, she no longer delivered letters from Naomi. That task had, at first, gone to as large tower computer system with a buzzing cooling fan. Then several years later the tower lost its job to a smaller, quieter laptop. Now it was his silent and more technologically powerful than his first computer, smart-phone. Although, technology had evolved and improved, no computer processor could open a text or email from Naomi fast enough.

Nine Feet

Then there was the day Prince died. Colin was in his painting studio. His studio in its past life, an old backyard workshop slash tool shed that he had converted and remodeled. It was shaded by a large, old, valley oak tree, which for Colin, was the true selling point of the home. Sure, the house was nice and he saw the potential in the tool shed, his mind sketching out what it would become. But the tree was magnificent.

It was living history and Colin could hear it talk to him; in the creaking of limbs as they moved in the wind; by the smell of the moss growing on its trunk; by the multitude of acorns which always seemed to be arrhythmically falling like a ball in a pachinko machine from some high branch to the ground below. Colin barely looked inside the house. He had seen enough. He had found his home.

But that morning as Colin had just started sketching out a new painting, he received Naomi's text. He stopped what he was doing to respond. Either by fortune or fate he wasn't in the middle of a painting. It was bad to stop mid-stroke, doing so changed the lines, the brushing. Colin honestly wouldn't have cared; he was still surprised that people thought so well of his work and would pay for it.

Of course, Colin wasn't going to complain or tell them otherwise, painting paid his way in life. Unknown to either of them, with the death of Prince and the subsequent text from Naomi, the universe had changed the weight of a distant star. By doing so the orbits that he and Naomi had been on were subtly changed, and now they were once again moving towards each other. Colin wiped off his hands and picked up his phone to read Naomi's text. Besides the *Hello and how are you* she asked if he had heard the news about Prince?

Colin looked at the words in puzzlement, something happened to Prince? Colin had been in his studio since sun up, he liked the first corpuscular rays of the sun filtering through the sky. He was currently sketching the large valley oak, his ancient friend, Colin liked the way the sun came through the leaves, causing subtle changes in their viridity. The leaves casting shadows across the acorn covered ground. Colin found his life was less stressful if he ignored the news in all forms. It wasn't that he didn't care about current events, he just didn't need to constantly inundated with multiple updates of the same story.

Colin maintained two newspaper subscriptions. The local Sonoma and Santa Rosa paper the Press Democrat and the New York Times. The Democrat being the local paper with all the local events and the New York times because Colin enjoyed knowing what was going on outside of California, and of course, the crossword puzzle.

The newspapers arrived daily and when he was done, they ended up on floor under a painting until being recycled. Colin also rarely listened to the radio. He thought why listen to commercials? Besides, when he worked, he liked a certain music, a continuous flow. Colin couldn't explain it. There was something about certain songs that could help to steady his mind. Close off one part of the thinking process and engage another.

To that end he listened to a wide eclectic range of music. From Aerosmith, Bach, the Cowboy Junkies to Townes VanZant, White Zombie, and Frank Zappa. Much to his wife's displeasure, Colin also listened to Tom Waits. Margo could tolerate most of the music playing in Colins studio, but she hated Waits. Margo said she couldn't stand Tom Wait's singing or discordant rhythms.

Prince?

Colin did like some of Prince's stuff, there were great metaphors in his songs. Obviously "Little Red Corvette" was not about a car, not with lyrics like, "she had a pocket full of horses, Trojan and some of them used." However, Prince was not part of his usual working music. Colin read

Naomi's text. Prince had died. He was found in his home. Naomi then asked if he remembered seeing Prince's movie, "Purple Rain" all those years ago? Colin did remember and he replied immediately.

After that first text, they started texting more often, several times a day, almost constantly to the point of distraction or addiction. Then facing a dead line on a project, but also wanting to text with Naomi, Colin sent the message,

"My fingers are going numb. Wanna actually talk?"

Naomi responded by calling him. It was strange hearing her voice, so many memories once again came falling out, echoes of the past. The next thing Colin knew it was an hour later, his project was done, and he felt good inside, lighter somehow. After the phone call they shared some recent pictures of each other, selfies and pictures from their lives and the people and animals in them.

Colin felt a pang of jealousy when he saw a picture of Naomi with her husband. Colin didn't know why? He and his wife Margo had been together for many years. Colin tried to ignore those other feelings trying to crawl back up from the abyss. It didn't take long and soon he and Naomi couldn't go a day without texting. Even on the weekends.

The weekends were supposed to be separate from the week. The weekends were supposed to be the time when they would spend it with their spouses, not digitally with each other. But somehow, one of them would find an excuse to text the other. Why not? They were just friends. Right?

Even though they did their best to hide the bulk of their texts and phone calls from their spouses, those who were supposed to be their significant others. All it took for their friendship to be renewed was for Prince to die. Apparently, for something good to happen something bad had to also happen. Colin always believed the universe demanded a balance and would settle for nothing less.

Eight Feet.

As he took another step, Colin thought about he and Naomi back in school. Colin thought of how much he hated the last day of school. The usual tense excitement of the last week, especially the last class of the day, the teacher trying to maintain a sense of control, the students a sense of restraint—all of them just waiting for the bell to ring so they could be rid of the other.

But for Colin the last bell of the day meant saying good bye to those few friends that lived in distant and separate towns, or at least not in his town. Colin didn't have many friends to begin with, and he didn't look forward to losing a large portion of them for several months. But, worst of all, it meant saying good-bye to Naomi for the summer.

They would spend the last day talking about their summer plans; what they would do, what they hoped to do. Colin thought about how those plans changed as they grew older. Going from excited kid stuff to more mature activities, they were growing up and looking back now he could see and reflect on the process of that subtle maturity.

Personally, Colin hated summer vacation. To be constantly at home, to have no escape, no release, no chance to be a kid. Back then, Colin's family lived in

Sunset on twenty acres of land which soon became a small hobby farm. Which was a standard paradigm for most of the people in the small country township of Sunset. The proper town of Sunset was a ten-minute drive. And sure, there were other local kids that lived along the same road, some were walking distance which back then was about a quarter-mile away, some further which usually meant riding the bike to get there.

The problem was those kids weren't really his friends. A better term for them would have been associates-of-convenience. Someone close to the same age as yourself, someone you could go play with, a group to get together to play a game of baseball or football in one of the fields. The problem was Colin was neither very coordinated nor did not have the physical attributes to be athletic. Because of that he was always the last person no one wanted on their team, or the last kid to be asked if they wanted to go do something like ride bikes or build a fort.

Inversely he the first kid if someone needed to be laughed at or made fun of. After several public humiliations both verbal and physical, Colin by choice, found himself alone. Those alone places included anyplace, from his room and house, which had only limited privacy due to constant invasion by siblings, to the big, wide, outside world.

A sunny spot in a field watching cows or horses as they lazily meandered about eating the long summer grass. Or sitting on the bank of some creek, cool water running over his bare feet, watching the water bubble over some rocks. Another favorite place was an old fallen tree out in the woods. It was back deep in the woods and Colin found it by accident while following a deer trail. He could sit in and listen to nature while watching birds and squirrels and the occasional deer.

And in those alone places Colin always brought his nonjudgmental friends, tablet and pencil. The three of them finding their place in one part of the world, while distancing themselves from the other.

The only change to his usual routine was when his mom loaded up the car, and forced he and his brothers and sister to go to their grandparent's place for a weekend. Colin remembered his father never came along, usually. Even thinking about it now, Colin was happy his father didn't join them. Colin knew, at least for several days, there would be a little less tension and fear in his life; however, because his brothers and sister were along there would never be complete escape. But at least there was a little less tension, and sometimes that was the best he could hope for.

Besides, Colin would always think to himself, *if nothing else there would always be something new to draw when he found the time to get away, to hide from everyone.*

Back in the present-day coffee shop, Colin shivered from the cold rain and shook the water from his arms as he shook the memories back into their usual safely guarded and locked holes. He had survived those summers of stone, just as he survived everything from back then. A person, no matter what age, could come to cope with pretty much anything, if they set their mind to it.

Colin knew his coping mechanism was autumn and the coming school year. A glimmering distant light that with every passing day grew brighter. As long as he held onto that light, he remained steady. It helped him cope and live with his life, to survive the stones of summer. September when school started, Colin knew Naomi would be there.

For Colin, the first day and week of school was the complete opposite from the final week and last day of school Then he started to feel depressed about leaving, packing up his locker. Now he was excited and would go through all his supplies for the start of the coming school year. As soon as he got off the bus and entered the school building, he would start looking for her.

It was usually Naomi finding him—it wasn't hard to find someone who was always a head taller than everyone else. They would find their lockers, get their class schedules and compare their coming days. Colin always hoped they would be together, in all of them, but that never happened. Unlike the majority of the other people in his life, Colin found it easy to like Naomi, she made it easy.

The two of them were friends, that was how it worked. It couldn't be explained or rationalized. It didn't need to be. Back when they were just kids their friendship was uncomplicated and almost free from explanation and rationalization.

The first week of school would be spent on catching up about the past summer. Naomi would tell him about all the stuff she had done, from a family trip to some fun place, to just going over to her cousin's house to ride horses. Colin would tell Naomi about some of his more socially acceptable activities, things families are supposed to do, intentionally leaving out and personally trying to forget the more lurid parts.

That was how they spent their first week of school, just talking and reviewing the summer and catching up. Colin would never admit to Naomi he was jealous of the other friends in her life, the time she spent with them. As they matured, as they would grow closer over the year and then have to leave, those feelings would become more intense. Colin did his best to push those feelings down, hide them, let them fester with the rest of the shit he wouldn't deal with. Of course, now Colin could look back and understand the reason; puberty was a beautifully horrible thing.

Seven Feet.

As the school years came and went Colin came to the socially grim realization that he was, in several ways, behind the other kids, especially the popular kids. First and foremost, Colin never developed the hand-eye coordination or any amount of muscle to go with the height which might have made him remotely athletic. And socially, because of his days of solitude and creative introversion, he was awkward and shy. The only talent Colin did have was a talent to not just draw but to use his skills to capture the world he immersed himself in. But that wasn't going to help him be accepted, or at least not be completely neglected.

It seemed so easy, he could look at something and draw it. As far back as Colin could remember he had a knack for art, for drawing. Although there were times when he thought being able to dribble a basketball, catch a football, or hit a baseball might have been better talents, at least in the neighborhood and on the playground. But there were those few times during the early days of art classes in kindergarten and the first couple years of school when the other kids would like to watch him draw, amazed that he could stay inside the lines and make such good faces.

Crayons were okay, colored pencils were better. And as he grew older and the art classes advanced, he discovered paints. Paint! Actual paint was the best. Paint could be blended, new shades discovered, hidden in between two other colors. Several of his teachers realized his talent and would encourage him and suggest books for him to study on the subject, and for once Colin wanted to study and read.

It took him a few awkward years, but he finally came to understand, and eventually accept, he was doomed to be a tall skinny uncoordinated kid who could draw. In those early years after the novelty of being the kid who could stay-inside-the-lines wore off in favor of the kids who were smarter and athletic, Colin started to fade from the social light. Then the teasing about being a sissy artist started and Colin began to hide his talent from everyone, only drawing when he felt safe. Then came the day he met Naomi and his world started to not seem so futile, so alone, so colorless.

Together through the years they went and finally they made it to high school. Colin was sure he had done something bad in a past life, something really bad to deserve the fate of being doomed to be a tall dorky artist and all-around social pariah. Despite his social status, Naomi was still there and they were still friends. Naomi on the other hand, had apparently done something good in a past life. Something really good.

She developed into one of the hottest girls in school. Her hair was honey blonde, her eyes a vibrant ice blue, her skin smooth and fair. And yes, Colin being a guy, he had to admit, Naomi developed some nice boobs. Even though Naomi didn't seek out any of the attention, she would confess to him how irritating it sometimes was, she became one of those girls in school who could strike any guy stupid. And those teenage boys were always around her, flirting with her, asking her out, doing all those things Colin wished he would have had the courage to do, but for so many reasons he just couldn't. Because there were guys around Naomi, that meant other girls were always around her.

Soon Naomi inadvertently found her way into one of the upper social cliques, where kids like Colin's kind were not welcome. He tried to join in, but being a devastated wreck of teenage existence, he was usually driven away by the disgusted looks and comments made by everyone else. But Naomi always had time and a special smile, just from him. He could breathe. Each day, because of that smile, he could continue to breathe.

With each smile, each breath, Colin refused to give up. He had a certain inner tenacity that drove him to want to succeed at something that was important to him, and his friendship with Naomi was very important to him. So, he kept working at the problem, looking at it, studying it like he would a painting, trying to find the lines, the layers and the meaning behind what the artist was trying to give the world.

Colin wasn't about to let the teenage social structure, a bunch of idiots who only came to school to hang-out and talk about parties they had gone to the previous weekend and who was having a party the coming weekend; Colin wouldn't let those types drive him away from Naomi. So, he persevered and studied, and looked at each brush stroke of their world he finally found the right color pattern. Or at least one of the shades used for climbing the teenage hierarchy ladder.

It was so simple.

It was one dimensional.

It stick-figure simple.

Colin rebelled.

The summer before his junior year he stopped cutting his hair. He started going to rock concerts. In fact, he and Naomi, along with a large group of other kids, all went to a

Judas Priest show. It was great. He was in, a member of her crowd and all it took was alcohol, drugs, and rock-n-roll. When junior year started Colin socially excelled, while his grades declined. In fact, Colin thought if he was any good at math, he could have drawn a flow-chart or graph that showed how the social aspect of his life increased in value, while the educational aspect decreased at an equal rate.

However, if becoming a slacker-burnout was the price for social acceptance, Colin was more than willing to pay his debt, his dues. He determined he would have done pretty much anything, whatever it took to be next to Naomi.

Colin, even with all his teenage rebellion drama, never gave up his art. It was as important to him as Naomi. Colin remembered how Naomi would often try to sneak up behind him to see what he was drawing. Sometimes he let her, sometimes he would just sit with and draw as they talked.

But there were times, when he was alone working on a drawing, he would feel her coming up behind him. He knew she was there. He could just feel it. There was a subtle warm feeling that grew in him whenever she was around. It was like a Naomi-radar. Some of those times he would quick crumple up his drawings. Colin was embarrassed by them. He didn't want Naomi to see some of the sketches he was doing.

But despite his reluctance to share all his drawings, soon his new cadre of friends started to take notice. It wasn't as if Colin would try and completely hide his talent, they had at different times throughout all the years of school all been in art classes together. However, now Colin was different. He wasn't just some art nerd. He was now one of them. In fact, now some of those same kids who used to taunt and bully him, in his new social clique, Colin and they were best friends and they thought Colin's drawings were cool. They told him he should become a tattoo artist They told him he would be awesome at it. They would all come to him for tattoos and he would be rich. So, to continue to fit in Colin did just that, he became a sort-of tattoo artist.

Using multicolored ink pens and felt tip markers, Colin would draw on the arms and hands of his new friends and giving them semi-permanent tattoos. The usual requests were for logos of various rock bands like Led Zeppelin, Van Halen, or AC/DC. One kid, *what was his name? Yes, Scott Leonard!* Scott was one of the more interesting dirt-bag stoners with whom Colin had become friends. First quarter of his senior year Colin sat next to Scott in a study hall. Colin found his friendship with Scott odd. Two years earlier Scott made it a routine habit to terrorize kids in school, including Colin. Now they were literally beer drinking buddies.

About a month into his senior year in school, Colin started his tattoo business again. One day in study hall Scott had Colin ink him with the pinnacle social landmark of a tattoo. Scott wanted a full-frontal naked woman on his forearm. Colin was pretty sure it would get them both in trouble, but if he didn't do it Scott might have thought him a pussy and Colin didn't want to lose his tenuous social status.

It took Colin all study hall to draw and color Scott's tattoo. And in the end Colin was both amazed and a bit embarrassed—the woman looked almost like a Hustler centerfold—almost as good as his current bathroom puta. All the guys thought it was awesome. All the girls thought it was disgusting.

The teachers and school Principal didn't think it was funny. Both Colin and Scott were given after-school detention for a week. Colin became a legend in school because of that incident. Senior year of high school had started out both good and bad. It all depended on a person's point of view. Colin spent more time with Naomi, and made some new friends. Granted some of those people ended up in jail, but back then they were still friends. Hey, losers didn't get to be choosers.

Six Feet.

Senior year was supposed to have gone well. Colin had a car. He had friends. He looked like; well, apparently, there were two sets of opinions. Colin could remember his father and mother continually telling him the family dog looked better. His father, during his semi-friendly/semi-threatening drunken states would call Colin "Collie" or "Lassie." Which of course his brothers and sisters found hilarious, so they started doing it.

Comparatively, several of his friends told Colin that with his long hair, skinny height, and when wearing an old leather jacket and sunglasses, he looked like Joey Ramone. Colin liked the dog, but decided Joey Ramone was more his style. As the school year came and graduation was getting closer, everyone started to prepare to move on with their lives, and Colin realized so had Naomi. Since the summer she had started dating an older, already graduated guy. He was a *bad boy*. Naomi had a thing for the bad boys. Colin knew that was one of the reasons for his transformation.

Naomi and her boyfriend were make-up and break-up, and Colin was content with the role of, *always be there for her*, friend. And that role worked out well. He hated it of course. But life was becoming unbearable, especially with graduation looming, an unknown specter of the future waiting for him. During lunch, he and Naomi would eat French fries at her locker and talk about the future, what they would do after graduation. Colin told her that according to his parents he was supposed to have a future plan. He was told he needed a job waiting for him. The specter of future was joined by the constant menacing threat of *or else*.

It was around mid-way through the school year when the military recruiters started making their regular visits to the school. Colin usually went just to cut a class, but now something was different, Colin started listening to what the recruiter was saying. A guaranteed job for four years, and depending on your aptitude test scores, there were a wide variety of military occupations to choose from. All of that appealed to Colin, but what really sold him was the military offered the chance to leave Minnesota. After several minutes of discussion about service commitments, and job options, Colin joined the Marine Corps.

Colin told Naomi later that week after it was too late to change anything, after the ink had dried. Naomi freaked out. Colin couldn't blame her. Colin could still hear the echoes of her frustration and outrage, *"What business did he have in the Marine Corps?"* Colin on both a physical and intellectual level, certainly didn't look like Marine material. Naomi asked about Colin needing his parents' permission. Colin sort-of lied to her, one of the few times he did; telling her he didn't need their permission, he was already eighteen. What Colin didn't tell Naomi was that he hadn't told his parents yet. He was going to wait until it was absolutely too late to stop it from happening.

At the end of May in nineteen eighty-six they graduated from West Lake High School. Five days later Colin left for boot camp in San Diego, California while Naomi was back in Minnesota starting her life there. Three months later Colin graduated from boot camp.

Unlike everyone else in his platoon, he opted not to take leave and go home. Instead, Colin went right to his military technical correspondence school. Naomi was working in a call-center taking orders for custom automotive parts and had moved in with her boyfriend. By December of that year private first-class Colin Meyer was stationed in Iwakuni, Japan, working as a writer and artist for the Far East edition of Stars and Stripes newspaper. Naomi Johnson had a winter wedding.

Despite literally being half-way around the physical world from each other, with their personal worlds in very different orbits, they were never so distant a letter couldn't find them. Sadly, handwritten letters now seemed funny to Colin.

Sitting down with paper and pen and hand-writing words on a piece of paper. Then folding up that piece of paper, putting it in an envelope, writing the address of the recipient in the middle of the envelope; not forgetting your return address in case the person no longer lives where you are sending the letter. Then adding a stamp in the upper right corner, opposite of the return address, and putting it in a blue metal box and knowing, not hoping or wishing, but absolutely knowing somehow that piece of paper would several days later find its way to the recipient. To Colin it was almost as magical as the internet and email.

Out of all the people he grew up with, partying with, doing stupid things with; all of those great friends who said they would write and stay in touch, Naomi was the only one to stay true to those words. Colin sent Naomi his new address after he left Japan and was stationed at Camp Pendleton in Southern California. He told her how he was so happy to be back in the United States. Not because he disliked Japan, but because he felt closer to her.

Naomi wrote about her life. How she was constantly fighting with her husband because he refused to stop living like some high school burnout and be an adult with a wife and responsibilities. How she thought something might change; how once again he had gaslighted her. After Colin's four-year service contract was up and he was honorably discharged, Colin wrote to tell Naomi he decided to stay in California. How he and some Marine Corps buddies decided to move up north to the Sonoma and Napa area. That he was using his GI education benefits to earn a degree in fine arts from the Sonoma Valley Community College. He was also working part-time as a free-lance artist and as a stock-boy at a grocery store.

Naomi wrote to tell Colin how she was also starting college classes. Nothing fun or frivolous as art–her chance to give him shit; she was going to earn a law degree. She also told him about her divorce.

Five Feet.

After that first text about Prince, the two of them just kept texting. Colin never fathomed why he and Naomi hadn't reconnected sooner? Of course, Colin knew why, but he still pondered the question. He wasn't sure if Naomi wanted to be bothered by him. She still intimidated him. After all those years, even right now, as he saw her sitting there. She was the one person in all the world who could walk up to him, reach into his chest, rip his heart out, drop it on the floor and crush it like a spent cigarette and all he would be able to do was look at her and say, *Thank You.* Outside the rain was still falling, now beginning to lighten, the deluge slowed.

The rain made him think of all those texts he sent Naomi. About places he thought it would be fun to run off to. Those were some of the fantasies he thought of when going for a morning run or bike ride. When sitting and painting, his mind would imagine those places and as it did, his hand would start to draw and paint them. Those special places where the imagined Colin and Naomi would run off to together. The solitude of nature giving freedom to the soul. Colin began to express those feelings in paint. Fred, Colin's agent and art rep, loved the new pieces. He told Colin those paintings were selling very well, and several smaller galleries wanted to put together a show of the new work. Margo didn't understand or like them. She liked his golden beaches and oceans, or the vineyards and people.

Four Feet.

Then Colin received the phone call that started to change everything in his life. It was morning. He was sitting and drinking a cup of coffee. He was absently contemplating the blank canvas in front of him. Colin wondered if Stephen King ever felt like that, just sitting and staring at his keyboard and screen and wondering how to start? Colin's phone rang as he had just started forming the idea of painting Stephen King sitting at his desk, staring wide-eyed and terrified as an evil clown in a spray of blood and gore, burst forth from his skull.

Colin looked at his own screen and became agitated at the intrusion. It was Fred. Colin wasn't sure what Fred wanted. At that moment Colin also wasn't sure if he wanted to talk to Fred. Fred didn't talk to someone as much as he talked at them. And talk wasn't even accurate. Fred told. He made direct statements, not conversation.

Colin took another sip of coffee. The phone rang again. Colin decided he had better answer. Fred wasn't likely to stop calling. In fact, if he was nearby, he might even drive over and intrude himself into Colin's studio. Besides, the image of Stephen King who was now entangled in a giant spiderweb as the evil clown gruesomely burst from his skull could wait. Maybe a new piece of graffiti?

Colin remembered the excitement in Fred's voice, the thrill of telling Colin how several galleries had contacted him about Colin's paintings and how those galleries wanted to include Colin in some up-coming exhibits. Fred, of course, accepted on Colin's behalf and booked several shows in different cities where Colin's work sold best.

Fred kept speaking at Colin and Colin kept absently nodding his head in silent agreement and sipped coffee— mmmm, fresh coffee in the morning was so good! Also, there should definitely be a spider in that painting.

Fred started naming dates and locations. Colin didn't need to try write down or even remember the names and dates, Fred would send an itinerary as soon as he stopped talking. Colin stopped nodding in agreement and pretending to listen after Fred said one of the shows was to be in Minneapolis, Minnesota.

Colin's ears heard the sounds, but the brain decided it was no longer going to translate those sounds into language. Fred's voice registered as only background static. The infinite length of a breath, mechanically, without thought or reason, repeated several times, and then once again Colin was hearing Fred tell him congratulations, and for Colin to get his ass in gear and generate some more paintings. The numbness clung to Colin as he hung up the phone.

The numbness followed Collin as he walked out the door of his studio, across the yard, the sound of acorns a they crunched underfoot. Colin stood under his oak tree and shared his numbness with his ancient friend.

They stood there in the growing morning sunlight. Colin's hand feeling the bark covered trunk. The layers of each section of bark. Pieces of armor grown from, within pushed outward, put in place to protect what was inside, to keep the heart safe and hidden. Yet it would be so simple to pick each layer off. To dig in and get to the living tissue. It had been years, decades since he had been anywhere near Minnesota. Now he was going there.

Of course, Colin knew he didn't have to go. He didn't have to do anything he didn't want to do. Until his signature was on the contract, not Fred's; only then was Colin legally obligated.

He ran his hand over the bark over the raised hard surface. Into the deep damp grooves feeling the small moss and lichen that cohabitated with the tree.

He looked up and watched the flash of the leaves as they started to turn and move in the light morning breeze. The crepuscular rays of sunlight, the god-light filtering through the thin clouds, through the branches, slowly rising casting shadows across, then down upon the tree.

He watched the birds moving about, dropping down to grab an insect or worm for breakfast, a squirrel grabbing one of the many acorns that no matter the season, they were always hanging from the tree, waiting to fall.

He stood there watching the world go on as it had, does, and always would whether he was there to observe it or not. Colin found his mind wandering to a story someone once told him. He couldn't remember the exact details and was confident he had modified and changed the story from how it was originally told to him, but he didn't care, as long as the essence of the story stayed true.

The story, as Colin thought about it, was of two monks walking along a road. They came upon a river they had to cross. The river was neither to deep or wide that they couldn't safely wade across, however, there was also an old woman wanting to cross, but she was too frail to make it. One of the monks without thought or question picked up the old woman and carried her across the river. After several miles the other monk full of question and anxiety finally asked his fellow monk, "How could you break your vow to never touch a woman by carrying that woman across the river"? The other monk turned and replied, "I only carried her across a river. You have been carrying her for miles."

Colin knew in his heart he had been carrying his old woman for far too many miles. Big fucking deal. He had a show in Minnesota. Big fucking deal. Life didn't come with a Disneyland-fairytale happily ever after guarantee. Isn't that what Naomi would say to him? Those times they would talk and he would complain about some drama about life—she would cut through all the bullshit, tell him to put on his big-girl panties and suck it up. Naomi knew how to give tough love. Colin looked at the sun and leaves, the filters and layers of sunlight and shadow, that was what life was, it was layers of light, shadow, depth, and movement. Life was a living canvas.

Without realizing he had moved, Colin found himself sitting in front of his old paint splattered laptop. He turned the computer on, and sipped at his now room temperature coffee. As Colin waited, he tried to keep his brain focused on what he wanted to say. He opened his email and started typing the letter to Naomi.

Colin tried to maintain control, but between the head and the hands was the heart, and the heart completely, without holding back, offered itself to Naomi. Colin told Naomi about the show, how he would be in town for only one full day, arriving late on Thursday, the show on Friday night, and leaving Saturday morning. Colin told Naomi he wanted to see her. That it would be nice to look at her as they talked, and not talk over each other because of a several second delay.

It didn't matter if they met for ten minutes for a quick cup of coffee before she went to work. Or maybe he could meet her for lunch, or an afterwork drink. Another idea, and although he wasn't a fan of it, he decided it was a better than not seeing Naomi at all, Colin told her if none of those times could work, then she and her husband should come to the art show. Colin threw in the enticement of free drinks.

It was simple and honest and from the heart. Colin did not care if Naomi said yes to a five-minute coffee or a shared evening with her and her husband. Colin decided to stop carrying his old woman because he wanted to see his friend again.

Colin picked up his cup of stale room temperature coffee and walked over to his easel next to the window. As his ears listened for the ding of an email, his imagination moved the hand across the sketch pad in front of him; a face with a delicate down-turned eyes, a lock of loose hair falling down across a sharp petite nose, caught next to pursed buttercup lips while delicate feminine fingers picked at the collar of a generic paper coffee cup.

Later that day his phone chimed. It was a text from Naomi. She had gotten his email. She needed to think about it. She would let him know. He couldn't sleep that night. His restlessness irritated Margo to the point that she asked him to go to the guest room and not sleep.

The sun was warming the sky and Colin, with a restless brain running amok with too many questions and only moments of fitful sleep finally abandoned the bed. Dressing quickly, he walked out into the sunrise to his studio. He knew it wouldn't matter to Margo. Over the years she had become used to his erratic behaviors and habits, besides, she had banished him to the guest bedroom. If Colin wanted to wake up at six in the morning and go to his studio to paint, she wouldn't say anything because that was just how Colin worked. That morning he didn't paint as much as he waited.

The first layer of paint was setting. Colin's gaze floated across the canvas seeing where the shadows were to begin, when his phone dinged. "Morning coffee would be great."

Three Feet.

Colin read her answer and was happy and also sad. He was sad because in his stupid heart he imagined Naomi saying something really stupid like, "no, not just coffee. I want to spend the day with you.", and many other stupid imagined scenarios and comments. Colin knew in reality even a quick morning coffee with Naomi was still going to be the best cup of coffee ever. So, he responded with a line, a quote from one their mutually favorite movies.

As long as it wasn't the shit Bonnie buys.

Naomi was so close now Colin could inhale the light citrus aroma of her perfume. She was right there in front of him, no more than three feet away. Colin found himself caught in her eyes, caught in the memories of their shared and intertwined life. She was looking at him with an expression he couldn't read anymore.

Years.

Years?

Decades had passed.

Years ago, he would have known her thoughts from a subtle flexing of her hand or blink of her eye, purse of her lips. But it had been decades and all those little things between the two of them were now between her and someone else. Now Colin couldn't be sure what she was thinking or feeling. If he didn't know better, he thought she was either going to cry or laugh. Her blue eyes were still the color of glacial ice. Back in school he had dreamt about melting that ice. Now there was a subtle hardness to that ice brought on by age and experience and pressure. Those same forces that could transform raw carbon to diamonds had had a similar effect on Naomi. But what the hell did he know? Maybe that was just life and what it did to people. For all Colin knew he carried the same hardness in his brown eyes.

Aside from all the years and the bullshit and time physically apart, all around her she radiated a subtle, calm warmth that he could still read. She was still as beautiful. She looked like she had in school, in the pictures he had of her then, of the recent ones she had sent him.

Colin looked at Naomi and he didn't know what was supposed to happen. They were just looking at each other as he continued to walk towards her. He was nervous. He was scared. His body shaking, goosebumps on his arms, not just from the cold but from seeing Naomi. Colin was trying to keep himself under control. He tried to be cool. He tried to be calm. Colin tried to not be the stupid, dorky boy he had been thirty some odd years ago. He failed on all fronts.

Two feet.

Colin's heart was trying decide if it wanted to stop, or to beat faster than he thought either safe or possible. His brain had become a tied bag of feral and rabid weasels fighting each other as they tried to escape.

He told himself this was just Naomi. This was no big deal. How was this any different than all those conversations they had had on the phone? How was it different than texting? What did it matter? This was just Naomi and they were just friends. Right? This, right here right now in the coffee shop getting a friendly cup of coffee and a good conversation.

One.

Chapter 5

Colin was standing in front of Naomi's table. He was standing in front of Naomi. There was a subtle fragrance about her which was just strong enough to find its way over the smells of the coffee and the rain. The legs of the chair made a wooden dragging sound as Naomi pushed back from the table and stood up to greet him. Her eyes were shining, her red lips parted with a radiant smile, her body and arms opened to greet him, a mirror of his own, and they came together in an embrace. Their arms wrapped around each other with an unexpected ferocity and veracity. More than a friendly, light holding and a pat on the back, greeting hug between two friends. It also wasn't a heavy, holding, exploring, clutching passionate lovers embrace. They held each other as if all that had been missing or forgotten or misplaced between them could now be resolved in that one simple physical act.

Colin felt Naomi's head fit nicely into the crook of his arm and shoulder. He felt her arms tighten around his waist, not squeezing or desperate, but a subtle idea of, *yes, he really is here. This is real.* Colin responded in a similar manner, making sure Naomi really was in his arms and he in hers. He wanted to make sure this wasn't just one of those super-realistic dreams. The one in which he thought he was with Milla Jovovich and the two of them were spending the day driving a convertible Aston Martin along the Pacific Coast highway. They were laughing and singing along with the ABBA songs blasting out of the speakers. The late afternoon sun warming them. The sound and smell of the ocean in the air as they navigated the curves of the road.

Then waking up from the dream and requiring several moments to realize he was in fact in bed in his home with his wife Margo. He was not driving along the Pacific Coast highway with Milla Jovovich and sadly, he did not in fact own an Aston Martin.

There in the coffee shop holding Naomi, the fragrant smell of her hair, her body presedagainst his, the sound of the low murmur of unnoticing and uncaring background conversations, this was a dream come to life.

After reassuring each other they were in fact actually there, they were actually real, the embrace ended, but they did not move away from the other. They did not move out of each other's intimate personal space. Instead, their hands remained resting on the others hips. A physical contact was still required. Their eyes holding the other as much as their embrace. An infinite moment passed before they thought about doing anything else besides just holding and looking at each other. Colin's started to speak before he remembered to open his mouth. What was supposed to simply be *"Naomi!"* Instead sounded like *Naughmmphi!*

Colin's attempt at loquacious elegance broke the emotional stillness and they both started laughing a low quite smirking laugh.

"Colin, you're still a goof." She said.

Naomi smiled her barb at him.

"You're the goof. Goof." He replied.

Colin smiled his childish retort back to her.

They hugged again. Simple, friendly, the kind of hug when two friends meet, a renewed connection. Both still smiling and lightly laughing, they released the hug and stepped apart. For a moment, they once again stood looking at each other, unsure of what they were supposed to do. It felt like an awkward kiss at the end of a first date—do I or don't I?

Naomi took the initiative and made the first move.

"Let's not stand here like two idiots. Sit."

"Okay. Oh, before I do, more coffee?"

Colin gestured at her cup.

Naomi held her cup and gave it a volumetric appraisal, swirling the liquid inside it and feeling the weight of the cup.

"No. I'm good. I've barely touched this one, it was too hot to drink fast. Go get one."

Colin was still standing there, rain slowly dripping from his wet shirt and arms; water from his rain soak hair running down his face. He was soaked. Coffee would be good. It would be warm. Colin also hoped it would help to settle his nerves.

"Be right back."

Naomi watched Colin go to the counter to order his coffee. She smiled at the puddle of water where he had been standing. He was soaked. And by hugging him so hard and long, the front of her shirt had strategically placed water stains. She didn't care, although the water and the chill also affected her in a different way, and she quickly wrapped her light coat over her shoulders and across her front.

It wasn't that she was embarrassed, maybe. She was just a little chilled and wanted to be warm, and not all inappropriately pointy. She looked at Colin again as she sat and swirled her coffee cup in her hand. He looked good. Naomi wasn't prepared for that. The pictures of him, those were not him. Those were digital two-dimensional images. They weren't the firm body. The strong arms. The hint of cologne and smell of rain. The bristle of the unshaven face.

The feeling of his body pressed against hers in an embrace, an embrace she returned. The years of missing him. So long without touching that person who had been one of her closest friends.

Their last embrace had been a drunken goodbye in a field party several nights after graduation. He was leaving the next day for boot camp and all of their friends thought it would be great to give Colin a proper send off. So much should have been said that night, so much she wanted to tell him. Instead, all she could do while her boyfriend watched—staring at her and Colin— was to give him a quick friend hug goodbye. Their only words were bland goodbyes and take care and write when you can. But, in the campfire illuminated darkness, their eyes found each other. In a brief glimpse their hearts shared feelings never said, never shared, never dared. So many years ago. Now she was watching Colin add some milk to his coffee.

Even if she hadn't been watching Colin, Naomi would have heard him returning to the table. He had a slight squish and sloshing sound as he walked. She smiled. It was funny. Not that she thought a rain-soaked Colin was funny. Well maybe a little funny.

Colin pulled out the chair opposite of her and sat down. His face was alive and beaming and Naomi knew it was because he was there with her. Naomi knew he didn't care about the water. The slight shiver to his skin. The slow drips of water falling from his hair and clothes. All he cared about was being there with her. Naomi knew this was how he felt, because she felt the same way

"How are you? How was the flight?"

Colin smiled at the small talk.

"I'm good. I'm wet. But otherwise, I guess I'm okay."

Naomi smiled as Colin absently wiped at the water running down the side of his face. She wasn't sure if he even cared. He just kept talking to her.

"The flight was good. I landed last night around ten. Got a taxi to the hotel, and by the time I got into my room I thought I was tired, but instead found myself wide awake. I don't think I fell asleep until about one in the morning."

Naomi frowned a little bit. She almost told Colin she didn't sleep well either and around one in the morning she got out of bed to stand quietly in her kitchen and look out the window at the night world. She didn't tell him, because these were just warm-up questions and an admission like that now in the conversation, would move them to a more serious place. And Naomi wasn't sure if she was ready for that place, or if they had time.

"I guess I was excited about meeting you today. It has been so long. And I guess there has been all that silly stuff between us, the pictures, texts, and phone calls. I guess I was excited to actually see you again. To actually be here with you"

Colin smiled.

Naomi smiled.

They were at an awkward conversation moment. Naomi knew they could either continue with small talk until she would have to politely excuse herself to go. Or they could talk as friends. When they would share their lives, the good and bad days. They would say things they probably shouldn't, the stupid, emotional, from the heart stuff. Shit Naomi would not have said if it had not been for the safety of the phone and the both the physical and emotional distance it provided.

They both smiled and awkwardly looked at their coffee cups.

"How are you doing? What has the big-time lawyer been up too?"

Naomi sighed. She didn't want to think about her work. She hated work almost as much as she hated talking about work. But, she had only herself to blame. She started their phatic conversation. Colin responded for her.

"Oh, you've had that much fun. Sorry, I didn't mean to ask."

Collin's comment made Naomi realized she had failed to hide her feelings about work. She never had been good at poker, at least not with people who knew her.

"No, it's okay. It's work. Unlike some people" Naomi smiled and gestured at Colin with her coffee cup, "most people have to get up and drive to their place of work. Once there they have to get situated in their cube, one of many in a small office where they have to put up with other people who work in the place, doing variations of the same work. One big happy family. Those kinds of people, possibly people like me,"

Naomi gave Colin a wink and smile as she continued to tease and poke him with the answer to his question.

"Some people don't get to sit alone, spending their day out in their studio painting. Or go to some house and paint naked women. Yes, I have looked you up on Google."

Naomi smiled. Colin smiled back at her. She wasn't sure if he was smiling because he was sitting there with her, if it was her making fun of him, or both? Either way, Naomi knew he didn't care.

"It must be nice to be a rich, famous artist who can just do what they want, whenever they want."

Colin's smile faded a bit to more of a passive, tolerant and self-effacing grin.

"Oh, I don't know about that. I have my off days. And, I also have commitments and deadlines to agents and galleries and commissions. And I'm not all that rich and famous. I just can't go around writing my name on a piece of paper, tossing it at the waiters in the restaurant while shouting I'm Picasso! Or, if I had one, let my pet ocelot named Babou piss on an expensive rug and then not only refuse to apologize or pay for the damage, but tell the owner the rug was now worth more money."

Naomi smiled at the memory of the Saturday Night Live skit with Jon Lovitz playing Picasso. However, she had no idea about the reference for the second comment about the ocelot.

"Says the rich and famous painter who is trying to make the lowly hard-working people of the world feel better about themselves."

They both laughed. Colin started to relax. He became anxious as soon as he walked in and saw Naomi. Even after all the years, she still had ability, the power to reduce to an idiot prepubescent boy. But she also had the ability to make him feel like he could lift the world. Right now, she made him feel relaxed and happy. Even if it were only for a couple of minutes before she went to work, Colin decided to live in those moments.

Colin's imagination had tried to see the morning coffee become something conceived by romance writers. The two of them would see each other and after the initial hug, lips would have met, and then blah-blah, yack-yack. Colin momentarily contemplated the defective gene that all men seemed to share. The one that made all men believe the most innocent of situations could instantly turn into a porn movie.

Their laughter subsided. They sat at their table. Their coffee cups in front of them. The movement of the people around them. The sound of the espresso maker behind the counter building pressure, the hiss of the steam unit frothing milk. The mechanical crushing sound of the bean grinder. The low chatter of the people and the conversations around them. The occasional dinging and binging sounds of various electronic devise signaling calls and texts and emails. The sound of the rain coming down and the occasional sound of thunder in the distance. The music from the overhead speakers quietly filling in the spaces between.

Naomi and Collin sat in their own intimate silence. It was a moment they would try to do over the phone, but never able to achieve because eventually one of the them would ask if the other was still there. Now, there together, the silence, the quiet comfort of being with someone and not having to speak, but just being able to be with them and know they are with you, and both understanding the world no longer mattered. They were comfortable. They were uncomplicated. Days later, Naomi would remember that moment. Before everything became complicated.

Colin let his hand drift across the table to where Naomi's hands were still absently moving around the paper coffee cup. His hand, if of its own volition, found Naomi's and covered it. Her hand was small and soft, and there was a slight tremble to it as he touched it. Then it relaxed again, moving from the side of the coffee cup to the table, to turn and hold Colin's hand; continuing the hug they shared earlier.

There was a smile between them. A small comfortable smile that accompanied the silence. Naomi didn't know when she had felt this quiet with another person. It had been years, if ever. The ability to just be still. She sipped her coffee. It was now a good drinking temperature. Being there with Colin she was happy she had said morning coffee. Afternoon drinks would have been good, but after two gin and tonics, and Colin looking so good, Naomi was sure she would have probably said things to him that she shouldn't have said.

"What's the smile for?"

Once again Naomi thought she had kept the smile and thought to herself, apparently either she didn't have a very good poker face, or Colin could read her mind. And at the moment, Naomi didn't care which one it was.

"Oh, to be honest, I was just thinking how nice it is to be here with you. To be in this quiet moment we don't get when we talk on the phone."

Colin smiled at her. He understood. Naomi liked his crooked smile. She wasn't sure where it came from, she couldn't remember his boyhood smile; but this smile with his scruffy, uneven beard, it was a very nice smile.

"I like it too. This is nice. Even if it is only for a little while. Thanks for meeting me."

Colin smiled. His hand squeezed her hand.

"When do you have to go? How much time do we have? I don't want you to be late for work."

Naomi smiled at Colin. Sitting there with him was easy. It was their childhood again. It was just the two of them with the universe moving around them, and they didn't care. Naomi looked at her watch.

"We have time, don't worry. Drink some coffee and wake-up. Relax. It's us and this is no different than talking on the phone. Except now you have to sit here in wet clothes."

They were both smiling, Colin raised his coffee cup up towards Naomi's in a gesture of a toast. She responded by raising hers and they touched their cups together.

"And what are we drinking to sir?"

Colin smiled, his lopsided smile with just a hint of his teeth showing under his black and gray scruff.

"To us and to finally being able to share the intimate silence we have both been wanting. To where the universe has brought us."

Naomi responded with a quiet smile, and a sip of her coffee.

Colin brought the paper cup against his lips to drink. The lid came loose. Instead of pouring a small sip of hot coffee into his waiting mouth, there was a large dump of hot coffee down the front of his shirt and onto the crotch of his pants.

Colin was able to control his response, barely. He didn't jump up and shout, "Mother Fucker Is That Hot!" like he wanted. He, instead, made a slightly more dignified muffled sound. He did not to slam the cup on the table which would have made more of a mess. He did not push his chair back sending it against another table to clatter loudly and obnoxiously to the floor. He did not jump up and brush the hot coffee off of his rain soak clothes.

Instead, Colin managed to slide the chair back without further incident. He managed to set the cup down without spilling to much of it onto the table. He tried to brush the hot coffee from his already wet clothes, but it was too late. He was now rain and coffee soaked. As for the coffee being hot, he was still chilled from the rain, and after the unexpected initial shock, it really wasn't that bad. In fact, the hot coffee warmed him up. Now he was just embarrassed. In a matter of seconds, he was that dorky, clumsy kid again, and Naomi was still the prettiest girl ever.

Naomi laughed. She couldn't help it. She tried to contain it. She didn't want to laugh. It was just so funny. The poor guy. Poor Colin. He didn't do anything to deserve it, but here he was soaked, and burnt, and cold, and so funny looking Naomi couldn't help but laugh.

"I hope you're laughing with me and not at me. Although I know you're not."

"I can't help it. I'm sorry. You. You just can't get a break today, can you?"

Colin tried using the several meager paper napkins to wipe and soak up the worst of the spill but it was useless. He was a mess. He had to laugh as well. It was funny. It was life.

"No, apparently, I can't. Well, I was wet anyway. At least now I'm warm"

"Okay. Maybe today is your lucky day and even you can catch a break."

Naomi was still laughing. She knew they couldn't stay sitting in the coffee shop, not with Colin a hot wet mess. It wasn't fair to him. But it was funny. He didn't do it intentionally, at least she hoped he hadn't, but he could still make her laugh.

He was still Colin. He was still the guy who had always done his best to be there for her. To be the friend she had always needed when she needed one. Despite time. Despite distance. Despite relationships. They were still the friends they had always been. They were the friends that would always be. Friends forever and then some.

"I'm parked right in front. Apparently your hotel isn't too far away? Let's get you there and out of those wet clothes."

Naomi saw the expression on Colin's face, the smile was not quite as lopsided. She knew she was smiling as well, and for all the wrong reasons.

"Shut up goof. I'm going to take you to your hotel. You can change. And maybe we will have time to drink a cup of shitty hotel coffee before I have to go."

Naomi thought about that, the having to go part. It made her feel sad. She was just getting comfortable. The nervous tension had disappeared. The two of them had found that moment of relaxed silence that comes when two people are truly comfortable with each other. No need to fill the air with useless phatic words. Speaking so much. But saying nothing. Then Colin had to go and spill his coffee. Naomi started to chuckle to herself, again.

"Yes, I know. But you knew I was going to say something like that."

Yeah, I did. That's why I called you a goof"

They both laughed and stood. Colin picked the lid of his coffee coup from his lap and tried to put it on the cup. The lip of the cup had been crushed at some point and the lid wouldn't stay on. That explained why he was now wearing more coffee than was in his cup. He tried to drink the remainder in the cup and only succeeded in burning his mouth.

Naomi could only smile and shake her head at him. He was still somehow, still that clumsy guy. She wasn't sure how, considering all he had achieved, how he looked now, but he still had that funny clumsiness about him. It seemed the universe gave as much as it took.

"Are you sure you want me in your car?"

"I think we will be fine. I had a priest bless it before I came here today."

They both laughed an easy casual laugh that only two friends know. Colin walked to the trash, cautiously took a last sip from his cursed coffee cup, and then threw it away. He didn't know what fate or hell awaited it, but he wished it all the misery it had recently poured upon him. He felt so stupid as he walked over to meet Naomi waiting at the door. How could the morning have gone that bad! Soaked by rain. Spilling coffee on himself. The morning was slipping by so fast. He would change clothes and maybe, maybe, they would have time for another quick conversation as she had one foot out the door. They had barely said hello. Now they had to say goodbye.

Naomi was smiling her little smile as he came over. Colin could feel his heart rate increase. He told himself it was from being cold, wet, and from being burnt with coffee. It had nothing to do with Naomi. Colin held on to that lie as Naomi pushed the button on her fob to unlock her car. The doors unlocked. Looking at each other with stupid childish smiles, knowing what was ahead of them, they both started laughing as they ran the ten steps from the front door of the coffee shop through the rain trying unsuccessfully to get into Naomi's car without getting too wet.

Chapter 6

Except for brief navigational instructions on how to get to his hotel they didn't say much during the drive. Naomi wanted to ask Colin all sorts of inane questions, but she already knew all the answers. They talked all the time on the phone. They shared their personal triumphs. They dumped their personal problems. They knew each other. Instead of noise, Naomi again, appreciated just being next to Colin. In his presence. Just being quiet. Suddenly, Naomi found herself wondering why her hands were shaking.

Was it because of being chilled from the rain?

Or because Colin was sitting in the passenger seat of her car?

Naomi was glad it was only one stop light, two stop signs, no police, and ten minutes to get to the hotel where Colin was staying. The rain picked up again. It struck her car with a loud, heavy drumming as she turned into the parking lot.

Naomi parked in a spot by the side entrance, the door Colin said was closest to his room. It was only another quick walk, but the last quick walk through the rain from the coffee shop to the car had taken all the lift out Naomi's hair. Or course her hair had been the perfect super-cute that morning. When she agreed to coffee, Colin had told her not to worry about wearing anything other than her normal work clothes. He was there to see her. He didn't care about what she would wear or how she looked.

Ultimately, he was just a stupid man and did not understand that a woman was always judged by what she wore and how she looked. And even if it wasn't by people around her, Naomi herself always wanted to look nice. It was probably more for her than for him. Even so, even though he was her best friend, Colin would still always be a stupid man. She checked her flat and damp hair in the rearview mirror Now the rain went and ruined all that. And from the sound and sight of the current weather situation, her personal appearance wasn't going to improve.

"I guess we have a couple options," Colin said.

"We could sit here in your car and make-out like teenagers at the old Hub drive-in theater."

Colin raised his eyebrows in a cheeky and suggestive manner while giving Naomi that sly half-smile that almost made her want to take him up on the offer. If for no other reason than to see the expression on his face.

And then he his face became a sad mask. A frown. A reluctant turn of a person who had come to accept the inevitable. And then if by force he started to speak again.

Words he didn't want to say, but words he had come to accept.

"Or, since I know you have to get going. I will leave you here. Sparing you from having to get soaked just to spend maybe another five minutes of bad coffee before you have to go back out into the rain."

Naomi felt the words more than she heard them. Colin was saying goodbye. And she didn't want that either. She wanted to stay. She wanted him to stay. She wanted to spend more time in the intimate silence of his company.

She missed her friend.

Not until Naomi saw Colin walk into the coffee shop, had she realized how much she physically missed him. Talking and pictures were fine, but the actual physical presence of the person was something different. It was a connection. It was real. It was life. Naomi contemplated her next move and chose a gambit.

"Or, since you're already soaked by the rain and coffee, you will run to the door and stand in the rain, holding it open so I can run from the car and into the hotel. Then we will go to your room where you can get me a towel and you can change clothes. After that, we will go find another cup of coffee on our way to visit some of the places where we would hangout after school and on weekends."

Naomi watched Colin. His face wore the expression of an animal the moment before becoming roadkill. She even considered slapping, or even flashing him just to see if he would respond. Colin blinked once. Then again. And finally, a third time as the truck ran him over, leaving a Rorschach deer stain on the road. Naomi was certain she could have lifted up her shirt and all Colin would have done was blink, maybe. The crack of thunder seemed to bring him back to reality. Either that, or maybe he had heard her thoughts about lifting up her shirt to see if he was still alive.

"You,...have to....go, to....work?"

Naomi almost laughed. He sounded like a child who was just learning to form sentences. Still not sure of how to string the words together, or if the words were even the correct choices. Holding and annunciating each letter of each word to finally ending on the up inflection of suggesting they thought they were asking question but weren't sure if they did it right. Naomi decided it was funny. So, she did start to laugh. But not at him, but because of him. Well, like with the rain and spilt coffee, maybe a little of both.

"Besides, it would look tacky for people our age, especially someone your age, mister-six-months-older than me, to be making-out in a car when they have a perfectly good hotel room."

Naomi laughed at her comment. Colin had just started to peel himself off the road as she drove another truck over him. As he put himself back together, she told him it would be okay. She would explain when they were in his room while he changed. Besides, she told him, he was starting to soak her leather car seat with his wet clothes.

"Go! Go open the door. I will be right behind you."

"Okay, here I go."

Colin opened the door and was quickly jerked back by the seatbelt that he had forgotten to release. Colin, for a second time, had just picked himself up off the road only to get splattered again. Naomi burst out laughing at him. He had to laugh as well. When did he become such a klutz!

"I blame you."

Colin laughed at Naomi as he quickly shut the door from the incoming rain and moved to release the seatbelt clip from the lock.

"Me? How am I to blame for making you forget to release your seatbelt?"

Naomi answered while still laughing at Colin.

"You render me stupid-silly. When I'm around you, I'm just that goofy silly kid from all those years ago. I think you're some kind of witch."

They laughed some more.

"I suppose you could put me on a giant scale and see if I'm the same weight as a duck."

They laughed some more.

"Alright, let's try this again."

Colin opened the door. This time successfully making it out of the car. As he ran to the door the rain, once again, soaked him to his skin. During his run to the door his right hand fumbled in the front right pocket of his jeans for his key card to open the door.

As his feet sloshed through the small lakes forming on the poorly draining sidewalk, Colin managed to get the key card out and placed it against the black plastic sensor panel keeping any non-guests from slipping into the hotel from the side entrance. Amid the background noise of the falling rain, Colin heard the metallic magnetic click of the door lock releasing. Colin reached for the wet and worn metal door handle and opened the door.

In the time it took for him to open the door, to step back and move out of the way, while still standing outside before being able to take that first step into the side entryway, he heard a click and slam of the car door, the rapid splashing sounds and pure gleeful-like giggling of a schoolgirl running.

Before he could do anything, Colin caught a glimpse from the side of his vision, a flash of a wet streak of black clothes and blonde hair. Accompanying that streak was the audible schoolgirl like laughter. With a smile Naomi came to a halting, skittering wet shoe stop just inside the doorway. Colin realized he was just standing there in the rain as Naomi looked at him with an expression of why are you just standing out there, you goof? But since he was already soaked cap-a-pie, he paused a moment in the falling deluge then casually sauntered inside to join Naomi.

Looking at Naomi, Colin become lost. Her once styled hair was now a damp flat. Her clothes soaked at the shoulders and splatted throughout. But her face was glowing with a warmth and thrill of someone who could find a moment of happiness even during the zombie apocalypse.

"I love rain like this. It's rainy days like these where I could stand naked in it if no one was around."

Colin smiled at Naomi. She was so amazing. She was so beautiful. The thought of her standing naked in the rain; her pale skin, her blonde hair soaked by the falling water, her mouth, pale red lips slightly parted A single drop of rain hanging from the curving edge of her top lip. Hanging, gathering and swelling in size fighting to stay there but building up to much until it finally had to let go and run down the curve of the mouth and down her chin to join with the other drops of moisture to fall from her raised chin. Her eyes closed and raised to the darkened sky over her releasing itself to her taught tight skinned naked pleasure. His painter's imagination already seeing it on his mental canvas. His hands already doing the sketches.

His mental canvas made him forget about the small lake forming around his feet. The water running off his soaked clothes and down his legs filling his shoes. That thought that mental imagined image of the real Naomi standing damp and cold before him made him forget how cold he felt because there was a warmness spreading out from his center. From his heart.

Colin looked at a damp Naomi. A chilled Naomi. And this time he didn't try to look away from her. She didn't try to hide herself from him. Colin could feel Naomi's look as much as he could see her looking at him. They were both, stupidly mesmerized by the past caught in the present. The two of them standing like love-struck soaking wet teenagers in the side entrance to the hotel. It was Naomi with a slight cough who broke the trance-like spell. Colin didn't notice the passage of time as they lingered in the entrance lobby because, as Naomi could see, he was obviously trying very hard to not look at her chilled nipples.

"So, we gonna stand here all wet and shit? I think you said something about changing clothes and some really shitty hotel coffee?"

Fortunately, Colin was as cold as Naomi and the blush to his cheeks caused by her catching him admiring her could pass for chilled skin, probably. Colin looked at the somewhat wet Naomi. Her hair was a dark wet blonde instead of the golden blonde it had been in the coffee shop. Her light jacket was beaded with water, and soaked on the shoulders and arms. She was right. They were here for a him to quick change, for her to dry as needed, while she explained why she could be late to work.

"Right. Sorry. Changing clothes and you probably need a towel. Right. Sorry. Okay. Up three flights and the second door on the right. Stairs okay?"

"Stairs are fine. You first since you know where you are going. Plus, I can stare at your ass as much as you stared at my nipples."

This time Colin knew he was couldn't hide his blushing. Naomi had noticed him looking at her. Colin on one level of thought told himself he was just appreciating her—after all Victoria's Secrets had built an empire on the concept of appreciating a woman's body—but on another level, a more ethical one, he understood he had been objectifying his friend.

"Okay. If you want to punish yourself like that, and possibly never want to eat again; start staring at my ass and follow me."

They walked up the three-flights of stairs. Colin marked each step with a wet squishy sound. While behind him he could barely hear the gentle, almost ballerina like, prancing steps of Naomi. Reaching the last several steps, Colin intentionally started to sway his ass and pop his hips in an exaggerated manner. Naomi's laughter echoed in the stairwell.

Before he could take another step, Colin felt a delicate hand grab his ass and then give it a friendly slap.

"Can I get some fries with that shake. Yowzah!"

"Hey, hands off the merchandise. Don't make me say Pineapple."

He turned, looking down at Naomi. Wet, beautiful, amazing Naomi with her sparkling blue eyes, her pale skin, her damp blond hair; his heart wanted to say so much, but his brain wouldn't allow it.

"Shut-up and move that ass before I slap it for real!"

Naomi laughed and her smile warmed his cold body. Colin really wanted out of his wet clothes. He also wanted to know what was going on with Naomi. Why she wasn't worried about work. They walked the final several feet in a squishy silence. Colin with put the key-card into the door slot and with a portentous loud metallically clanging sound, once again the metallic magnetic lock released and the green light indicated the door was open. Colin reached his hand forward and opened the door and they walked into his hotel room.

Chapter 7

Naomi found Colin's hotel room to be a clone of every standard hotel room in every chain hotel conglomerate across America. It was bland. Through her various trips, both personal and business, Naomi already knew what the room would be like, from the décor to the smell.

What she wanted to know was, what was Colin like? This was Naomi's admitted voyeuristic tendency, she liked to look in other people's homes. If she were out running an errand and saw an open-house sign, she stopped. She just had too. She wanted to look. Naomi hated that she loved it so much.

Now that voyeuristic curiosity was starting again, and Colin was the focus. Was he tidy or messy? Did he straighten the bed after sleeping in it or leave the sheets and blankets all pushed back? Did he unpack his suitcase and use the dressers at the hotel, or did he spend his stay living out of his carry-on bag? Those little details, those questions, Naomi just had to know the answers. She had to know because to Naomi, those were the little details telling her what Colin as really like.

When she had previously asked, he replied he was a neat guy and liked to keep his life somewhat organized, but sometimes chaos would win. Then he would finish his projects, and take several days to push the chaos back and reorganize. Now Naomi would find out if Colin was gaslighting her with his answers. Because if he was, lies, especially to a friend, those could never be forgiven. A nervous anticipation, similar to all those open houses, came over Naomi as she stepped into the room. What would she see? This excited her imagination more than watching than an episode of the television show Hoarders. What was she about to see? How bad was it?

The bed was almost made. Colin had obviously slept in it, but he had sort-of made the bed before he left that morning. He put the sheets and blankets back into place, but did not tuck them in. His single carry-on piece of luggage was closed and sitting on the hotel provided luggage stand. There was a leather briefcase-slash-shoulder bag on the desk. If it weren't for the bed and his luggage, Naomi might have suspected no one was staying in the room. A quick glance in the bathroom as she walked in reveled only a single bath towel hanging from the rack. Colin didn't even leave his tooth brush out. They walked into the main part of his room.

"Hang on. Let me get you a towel."

Colin went into the bathroom as Naomi looked about the small single hotel room with its small desk and roller chair. Its single lounge style chair over in the corner next to the window. The hideous orange-brown carpet. The standard white linens peeking out from under the coarse brown comforter on the bed. This was the sterile but don't-shine-a-black-light-in-there filthy environment of a hotel room. Colin returned from the bathroom with a large heavy weight white bath towel for her.

"Here, you can wipe off your arms, face and hair."

"Ooh, you think there's something wrong with my face?"

Naomi gave a smile as she teased him. She was relaxing. The anticipation anxiety was wearing off. She was becoming comfortable being with Colin. This wasn't a phone call. Even the coffee shop worked as a barrier. Now it was just them, and it was comfortable. Naomi was happy about that.

"Besides being too beautiful, no. I just figured you wanted to dry off a bit. Smart ass."

They both smiled. Naomi liked his smile, it was easy. "Well thank you. My hero."

"Anytime, my wet maiden in distress. Now if you will excuse me."

Colin walked to his carry-on bag and took out a set of dry clothes. Naomi, still curious about his habits, mentally noted his clothes inside the suitcase—all were neatly folded and organized. Colin, clothes in hand, crossed to the bathroom and closed the door behind him. Naomi thought Colin might try talking to her, continuing their conversation through the closed door. He did not. She was happy about his choice.

Naomi thought having a conversation with someone with a door in between was generally rude. Unless there were mitigating circumstances, a situation which forced the necessity of such a conversation, otherwise just pause for several moments then resume the conversation when all parties were once more together. Naomi used the time while Colin changed to think about the morning so far and to dry her wet hair.

Naomi grabbed the generic hotel lounge chair and sat down. Outside there was a sharp crack of lightning and Naomi out of an ingrained childhood habit started counting. The seconds between the lightning and thunder was supposed to be how many miles away the storm was. One. she gently held her damp hair with the towel—two—trying her best to blot it dry without messing it up more than her gleeful sprint through the rain already had. Three. There was a slow, window shaking roll of thunder. Hmmm, three miles away thought Naomi as she carefully dabbed at her face, trying not to blot the light layer of blush and mascara she had put on that morning. Naomi wondered if the storm three miles away and leaving, or three miles away and getting closer? She would have to wait for more lightning and thunder.

While she waited, Naomi slid her feet out of her wet shoes. Naomi was glad she had decided to wear her dress sandals that morning. It would make it easier for them to dry, sandals also made it easier to get her feet in and out of the wet shoes. As she dried her toes, the door to the bathroom opened and Colin came out barefoot and in dry clothes.

Naomi thought he looked rather stylish and also strange. Colin was wearing pleated black dress pants, with another loose linen shirt. Naomi was a little disappointed that the new shirt was black instead of the semi-transparent cream color that she could almost see through. And although she knew she couldn't see through the black linen, it didn't matter because Colin hadn't fully buttoned the shirt. He only buttoned two of the lower ones, his warm chest lightly covered with shortish black hairs was clearly visible.

Naomi looked at the clothes—they didn't match. The very casual shirt with the very dressy pants, although both black, they didn't go together and Colin looked just a little absurd, as if he didn't know how to coordinate clothing. Naomi was sure he could, he had sent her pictures of him all dressed up in his suit and tie with the caption of "Bring out the Gimp." But now, dressed like he was, and trying to distract herself, Naomi thought Colin looked like a fashion reject, he really did. Naomi couldn't help but laugh.

Colin, standing just outside the bathroom door instantly understood what she was laughing at, it wasn't hard. He had packed simple and light for the trip. Since it was only going to be for barely three days, he only brought two casual shirts and one pair of blue jeans. His only other shirt and pants were his dress ones for the gallery show. Since his jeans were soaked and needed to dry, and he couldn't go walking around in his underwear, Colin was forced to wear his dress pants. He knew why Naomi was laughing. He knew he looked stupid.

"What, don't you like the new California clothing style? We call it "casual formal" it's a little bit like a fashion mullet. Party up top; business down below."

Naomi began to laugh harder.

"Fashion mullet is exactly the term to describe how you look."

"Still better than Porky Pig and Donald Duck, they only wore clothes up top."

Their laughter continued, it was light and refreshing. Colin took out the desk chair and slid it opposite of Naomi, he sat to face her.

"Ok. What's going on? I thought you had to go to work?"

Naomi blushed at his direct question. She didn't want to admit her deceit but ignoring it or trying to deny it would only make the situation worse. Besides, she was sure Colin would understand. And, if he didn't, well then Naomi knew what she would do.

"Bottom line up front: I took the day off. I don't have to work."

That was easy enough, Naomi thought, just rip the Band-Aid off. Colin's expression was that of not quite understanding her answer. It was the moment it took for the brain to process and compare what it just learned to the previous information. It was the expression of coming to understand he had been intentionally lied to, by a friend.

Before he could say anything Naomi, as the expression of contemplation became an expression of what's going and why did you lie, Naomi began her defense. She explained how she wasn't sure how the morning was going to go. Sure, they were friends, they were good friends. They were very good friends. But they were very super greatest best friends who hadn't seen each other in a very super long time.

The last time they actually had any physical interaction was when they were eighteen. Saying those words, since they were eighteen, caused her voice to carry an edge of sadness and regret. She tried to hide it, nor was she surprised by it. Saying those words, to him as they sat there forced a realization of how distant their lives had grown, and of so many experiences they didn't get to share. And never would.

Naomi took a brief, reassuring and cleansing breath and continued. She explained, not knowing how seeing each other again was going to go, Naomi thought the best course of action was to take the day off work.

By doing so, several aspects of her day became easier. First, she didn't have to worry about work. Instead, she would enjoy a pleasant three-day weekend. Second, depending on how the morning coffee went she had options. If they found seeing each other was nice, friendly and all, but nothing in a manner that would suggest spending no more time than a hello, a cup of coffee, and then a nice-to-see-you and goodbye; well, then Naomi had already planned to go to the Minnesota Institute of Art for several hours. From there she knew of several stores with sales on spring clothes. She would have treated herself to a day of art, shopping, and all-around relaxation.

Or, if they found themselves lost in conversation, as they could when drinking gin n tonics and talking on the telephone, well then, they could sit and enjoy the morning and each other, reconnect and enjoy a conversation that didn't involve a time delay. And, if they felt a need to not talk, to just sit, to just find solace in the fact that they were still friends despite the years and distance; that moment wouldn't be broken by one of them saying, "you still there?"

Colin leaned back in the chair, slouching, pushing out his right foot, tapping Naomi's leg.

"So, you decided to cover-your-ass just in case I was still the freak I used to be."

Naomi, about to respond, watched a sly smile warm on Colin's face. He understood. His self-deprecating comment, nothing more than a jab at her. This Colin was still the same younger Colin, but this Colin had more confidence to him. Naomi liked this Colin. She was glad the day had worked out and the two of them were still the very special, super bestest friends, smile face emoji, exclamation point they always had been. And still were.

Lost in her thoughts Colin, Naomi missed the next crack of lightning and the two seconds it took for the roll of the thunder.

"What happened to us?" Colin asked.

Naomi blinked, bringing her thoughts back to the room. Looking at Colin she patted the coarse towel on her wet feet.

"What do you mean?" Naomi asked back.

Colin straightened himself in the chair and rubbed at this lower back. Slouching was not good on the spine. Colin brushed his front top teeth against his lower lip, a little habit he did when thinking. He visualized his thoughts on his mental canvas and began.

"When I saw you sitting in the coffee shop. When I first came in, started walking towards you. With each step closer I started to remember all of the shit we did as kids. All the seemingly endless phases we went through. All the good and bad. The drifting apart. The coming together. Thoughts about everything between us. In just those couple of seconds, all of you and me came crashing back."

Naomi paused from drying her feet. Colin said he had thought of them as he walked to the table. Naomi wondered if he believed in telepathy or ESP? She had been doing, thinking the same thing, the same thoughts. She now understood what his question meant. In her way, Naomi had thought the same thing. What had happened to them?

They were obviously still comfortable with each other. In fact, Naomi thought she could lean to her left, rip a fart, and all they would do is laugh like little kids. But there was something different. Maybe it was time? Experience? It was life. Life happened between them, for good or bad, probably equal parts of each.

"I understand. I guess life happened to us. We moved forward, either by desire or necessity. What's the old saying, you can never go home again."

Colin smiled at her answer.

"Yeah, I guess. But maybe it would be nice to visit it once or twice. If for nothing else than the great Saturday morning cartoons and the sugary cereals."

They both laughed, exclaiming almost at the same time, "Bugs Bunny and Road Runner cartoons!"

"Favorite Cereal?" Colin asked.

Naomi thought a moment. She doubted Colin would know it. He looked like a Cap'N Crunch guy, or maybe Trix.

"I doubt you'll know it." She replied.

Colin's face became a mix of laughter and competitive.

"Try Me!" he challenged.

"Quisp."

"No!"

"Yes." Naomi asserted.

Colin started laughing. His face lit up with

"I loved Quisp!"

"Hmmm, maybe."

Naomi wondered if Colin was agreeing with her to just agree with her, or if he honestly meant it? The skepticism must have come across, been expressed on her face. Before she could test Colin, he defended himself.

"The box had that weird alien guy with a propeller on his head. The cereal looked like little saucers and tasted like," Colin hesitated. Naomi understood. She could, right at that moment, hold the memory of that taste in her mouth, but she couldn't describe it either. Colin tried again.

"It tasted like processed corn combined with a year's worth of sugar."

He was right. Naomi knew he was a Quisp guy. Funny world she thought. They grew up together and it took several decades into adulthood to discuss their favorite childhood cereal and Saturday morning cartoons.

"Yes!" Naomi exclaimed.

"All that sugar combined with watching the Road Runner, my parents would force me to go outside and burn it all off. I think I would run or ride my bike for hours without tiring."

They laughed. They remembered. The rain continued to fall.

Their laughter subsiding, Naomi casually lifted her leg, putting her foot on her right knee, took the towel and absently started drying her toes. Being there with Colin was so easy, almost too easy, Naomi thought. She glanced at window and the rain; drops splattering with heavy watery thuds against the glass. The rain was still coming down and she didn't feel like another wet run to the car, at least not yet. Naomi turned her attention back to Colin. He was still smiling. His shoulders giving occasional jostles of almost contained mirth. Their eyes met, then for a moment Naomi felt the possibility of an idea; not sure if it came from Colin or if it came from her. Either way, it made her feel something different, somehow connected.

Colin wasn't sure why, or if there was a why, a rhyme or reason for the immediate and inexorable need to do something. Holding Naomi with his eyes, Colin realized he was moving from his chair to the edge of the bed next to her. Colin felt parts of him, rational and sane and pragmatic parts start to shut down. While other parts, the nostalgic and fearless and simplistic parts came forward.

Naomi, the girl, the woman, his one true friend who had always been there and now she was right here. Colin looked at her delicate, small feet with dark purple polish on her toenails. His heart started to do funny things to his brain. Here she was and he was feeling as nervous as he had when he first said "hello" to her in the adolescent bustle of that school hallway all those years ago. When they were younger. When life was just as simple and as complex as it was now.

Colin tried to keep his voice from shaking, cracking. He took a calm breath and he took the chance he had always wanted to take.

Colin looked into Naomi's ice blue eyes. "I want to ask you something."

Naomi looked at him her expression serious honest open. Colin was sure she had picked up on something in his voice. Was it the hesitant nervous cracking? Was it the tense scared look of his eyes? Naomi stopped drying her feet. She put the towel on the desk next to her and looked at Colin with a serious expression of her own.

"You can ask me anything. You know that."

"I know, I just wanted to warn you."

Naomi's expression changed again; Colin could see it. She was wondering if something was wrong? Colin tried to ask, but took a breath first. Naomi gave him a reassuring smile. A smile telling Colin know it was okay, she wasn't going to be offended. After all, what he wanted to ask her was tame, it was nothing when compared to some of the conversations; the things they had said and asked each other. But this was different. This was real.

"Go ahead. Ask."

Colin swallowed a small breath; it was all his tense nervous body would allow.

"Can I kiss you?"

Naomi looked at Colin. That was something she hadn't expected. Someone, well not just someone, but Colin asking her if he could kiss her. Naomi felt a new clutch of pterodactyl's hatch in her stomach.

Colin wanted to kiss her.

Colin no more than two feet from her.

He wanted to lean forward.

He wanted to bring his face next to hers.

His body close to hers.

His hands resting on hers.

He was asking her permission if he could press his lips against hers.

Now it was Naomi's turn to have her heart do strange and funny things to the brain.

Her heart started beating little faster.

Her throat suddenly went dry.

She never imagined him asking or saying anything like that, "can I kiss you?" Naomi thought she would have preferred Colin asking her something intimate and personal like her favorite sexual position.

But of course, they had already talked about that along with how their opinions on oral sex. He could have had the decency to ask her if she like anal. That answer would have been an immediate hard no. She was a normal woman, not a male porn fantasy. But no, he couldn't ask something so simple as that. He had to ask for something even more simple yet so complex. Can I kiss you? Because the thought of saying yes, Naomi knew what saying yes would mean. Or did she?

Afterall what was one kiss? She had casually kissed other guys in greeting. Generally gross yes, but not a big deal. Of course, that kiss was always on the cheek and Naomi always hated the greet-and-kiss type of people. But this was different. Naomi knew Colin. And knowing him was more than being familiar, being friends.

Naomi knew if she said no, he would respect her decision.

If she said yes, just a single kiss, for just a moment, he again would respect her decision.

That was Colin.

What scared Naomi, making those fluttering, crashing, nervous tremors cascade through her body, in her heart the real question that needed answering was not if Colin would stop with just one kiss, but could she stop?

Naomi needed a moment before answering. Another one of those infinite slow-motion moments when the world instantaneously slowed and an entire lifetime could pass by in a heartbeat. Naomi adjusted her position in the chair which and suddenly become too small, closing in around her. It was too close to the bed. It was too close to Colin. She turned away from him. Her eyes drifting down to study the arm of the chair she sat in. The chair that was too confining and too close to everything in the room. Naomi thought maybe she would find the answer on the arm of the chair.

Like the time traveling poem on the table in the coffeeshop. Maybe a previous guest, knowing in the future Naomi would be faced with this question, left the answer for her. But there were no words waiting for her there on the arm of that chair. There was only the faded and worn fake brown leather.

Naomi turned her head forward slightly until she could see his legs on the edge of the bed. His neatly trimmed toenails. His toes. His bare feet. The errant sprouts of dark hair. He had nice feet for a man. Those nice feet were twitching and moving in a contemplation of their own. Their nervous movement the physical expression of Colin's inner anxiety.

Naomi was sure if she said "Just a kiss.", "Just a single moment.", a simple intimate expression between the two of them, Colin respected her enough to make it just a single kiss. Naomi hesitated to say yes because it was not Colin she was worried about.

"I don't think that would be a good idea."

"I know," said Colin. "It's just that I've never kissed you. We have never kissed. In all the years we've known each other. Sorry I didn't mean to make this uncomfortable."

"You didn't. It's just, just, well you know, we probably shouldn't. That's all." She said.

"I know." He replied.

Naomi tried to distract herself. The crack of lightning sounded. She picked up the towel to dry her hair. She started counting. The time measured by the hard slapping pitter-patter of rain against the window.

Naomi trying to lose or at least change the one thought in her head that was refusing to leave. It was an emotional earworm, but instead of a song, it was the simple yet complex intimate expression of a feeling. *One*, Naomi counted in her head. But then the emotional earworm interrupted, Colin was right there, sitting on the bed his shirt half open bending over to put his socks on.

The windows loosely shook as the thunder, now almost a booming bass drum sound, rolled over the hotel. Naomi concentrated on her hair. It had looked so nice that morning, it started as a perfect-super-cute hair morning. Naomi tried to keep herself focused on how she would fix her hair, make it nice again. And then the idea of Colin's hands, his nice-looking hands reaching up and wrapping themselves in her hair. Naomi pushed that thought away as the echo of the thunder faded away. Colin had accepted her answer.

Colin, Naomi was sad to see, buttoned his shirt, picked up the shoes next to him and bent to put them on. Naomi finished blotting her hair, there was no way it would become perfect and super-cute, but the rain did bring out the floral scent of her shampoo.

Naomi continued focusing on those simple thoughts—well-controlled and well-defined. Each aspect of her life, even what to do with formally perfect super-cute hair that was now wet, each aspect contained in its appropriately labeled box.

He didn't push her. He didn't try and wheedle or manipulate or pressure her. Naomi knew for Colin that a kiss would have been just a kiss. He wouldn't have tried to do anything else. Naomi also knew, because she had told him no, he wouldn't, probably, try again.

The probably thought was not supposed to be there. It was supposed to be in its box.

Colin, about to push himself up from the bed, caught her eye. Breaking the momentary unresolved internal organizational struggle.

"Well, it's still raining pretty good. I will leave it up to you, but if you want, there is a nice little lounge area down by the lobby. They have coffee, a fireplace and some comfy chairs. We can go there, have a cup or two and continue our conversation. Maybe after a while the rain will let up enough for us to go someplace, or if you really wanted," Colin paused making a pouty, sad face expression, "if you want to go home because you're all wet, I would understand."

Naomi watched as he pushed himself up from the bed, then reached his hand to her, a gentleman's offer to help her out of her chair.

His hand. There it was again. So nice looking. The fingers long and delicate in a masculine way. The nails a little rough, maybe from nervously picking at them.

Naomi put down the towel, reached up putting her hand on his. As Colin gently wrapped his hand around hers, Naomi looked at her hand, thinking it seemed so small, swallowed up, surrounded by his. That feeling, the sight of it, her hand so small compared, contrasted, juxtaposed against Colin's hand.

Suddenly Naomi felt small. Not just her hand, everything about her felt small both physically and emotionally. And in that, in that sensation of smallness, Naomi, maybe, even, just a little bit, felt vulnerable. Colin's hand applied the perfect amount of pressure that it cradled hers, a tender embrace which was neither crushing or suffocating, or weak and leaving doubt if it was secure. His hand and grip was able to endure.

In that perfect embrace of hands Naomi found herself connected to Colin. She could feel the warmth of his skin. His skin was soft yet callused just enough to let her know he used his hands, and they knew physical labor.

She could feel his muscles tense as he provided her support to lift out of the chair. Then Naomi felt his heart. Her fingers on his wrist rested on the exact spot, his pulse, feeling the beat of his heart. The strong, steady pulsing and through their connection his heartbeat was now part of her. The initial feeling of vulnerability, albeit small and fleeting, was now replaced, suffused with the knowledge that not just her hand, but she was safe, would always be safe, in Colin's embrace.

They both stood, looking at each other. Naomi didn't try to remove her hand from his. Colin didn't try to remove his hands from hers. Naomi wondered if he felt the same connection. That what she felt coming from him, he also felt coming from her. Without a word Colin smiled his silly lopsided grin. His mouth, lips moving up on the right, somehow going downward on the left side, a glimmer of teeth in between.

"Ready?" He asked.

"Ready." Naomi replied.

They both turned to go. Their hands still together. The connection still intact. Naomi wanted to hesitate. She wanted to somehow indicate something she didn't know how to say or do. The warmth between their hands grew. She could feel his heartbeat, so strong, a deep vascular beat with a depth and strength. They had taken no more than three steps towards the door. Naomi knew that once past the door it would all be normal again. And that was the problem. Because at that moment, her hand in his, the connection between them felt normal. It felt natural. It felt right.

Two more steps and then they would pass through the door, from the room in to the hallway. The storm now over the hotel. The pitter-patter of the rain now a driving squall of intensity, rain against the window and wall of the hotel drowning out all other sounds.

Then the connection intensified. Naomi felt his hand tense, the muscles of his arm tighten, the beat of his heart so strong his entire hand resonated with it, and therefore so did hers.

Colin paused, looked at the door. Naomi thought he would let go of her hand, hoping he would not.

Instead of letting go, he turned to look at her. His face was a blend of several emotions she could feel being physically expressed in his hand. Then in an instant it was resolved. He became relaxed again. His eyes were no longer serious and dark, but back to their playful light brown. His jaw relaxed, but his mouth still seemed tense. His hand held hers, it firmed slightly, she felt muscles tense and indicate she was to turn and look at him. Naomi wondered what was wrong. She turned her body to him. The entryway of the room was narrow forcing them to stand close to each other. Naomi found she was close enough to Colin that she could now hear his heartbeat as she felt it. She wondered what was going on.

"I'm sorry. I know I'm not supposed to." He said.

Before Naomi thought about what Colin was talking about, what he meant, or even how to respond, Colin's free hand brushed lightly down the side of her head and neck as he leaned forward and kissed her.

At first, out of sheer surprise Naomi didn't know how to react. She had never thought Colin would kiss her after her saying it probably was not a good idea. And as his lips held her lips Naomi found she did not mind. Maybe this one kiss was what they needed. Because after Colin had asked to kiss her, the thought of kissing him was impossible to remove from her imagination.

She felt his mouth relax against hers, it opened slightly, invitingly, and to her surprise, Naomi found she responded in kind. Their tongues coming together, a light touch and dance. Then as if through a mutual understanding, they withdrew. Their mouths closed, their lips lightly, slowly moving away.

This time it was Naomi. Something changed in her. Their kiss was supposed to be just a kiss. She was willing to yield to that moment. Afterall it was just a kiss. But that was the problem. Just like holding his hand. Just like every conversation they had with each other. Just like every secret shared. Just like seeing him that morning in the coffee shop— with all of those were a brief initial awkwardness that quickly became a normal routine, as if each of those actions were something they did daily.

The first kiss should have been beyond awkward to the point of uncomfortable. Like kissing a stranger for the first time, like it had been when she kissed her husband for the first time. But it wasn't.

There was no wondering what way to lean to prevent bumping noses. There was no accidental clacking of teeth. Their lips met with ease.-The kiss felt more natural, more-right, then any other kiss Naomi had ever had. It felt easy. It felt relaxed. It was the sensation that the two of them had been that intimate all their life. It was the idea, the feeling that they were right, it was the world that was wrong. And before she could think or rationalize or try to define the situation and put all of those feelings into a nice neat organized box to be properly placed on the shelf next to all the other well-organized feelings and thoughts in her life, their lips only a breath apart from each other, Naomi let go of Colin's hand, placing both of hers on each side of his whiskered face, she let go of all her inhibitions, listened to her heart, and kissed him back. Uncomplicated.

Chapter 8

Colin did not know if he would have been able to walk out the door.

To leave the room behind.

To go down to the lobby.

To sit across from Naomi.

To just drink coffee and talk.

Maybe if he could hold her hand again as he was doing now. Her hand in his. Her hand was so warm and soft. It felt so small in his.

She was exploring his hand, her fingers moving back and forth. They would trace across his palm, up each of his fingers, then back down across his palm and over to his wrist and back again. Even though her fingers were moving, her hand somehow stayed constant against his, holding on, not wanting to lose that solid contact of her against him.

Colin knew what Naomi had said, "It probably wouldn't be a good idea for them to kiss."

Yet, Colin wondered what if he did anyway?

What if he took a leap?

He knew she wouldn't hate him for it. They were too close for that. There had been recent times between them when they were actually pissy with each other. As if they were a married couple and he had messed up somehow and she was mad at him for it. Then they would talk, and it would all be worked out. They were always going to be friends. Nothing was going to change that fact. Not time. Not distance. Not a lack of constant contact. They were friends. They always would be. The end.

Naomi's hand was now steady. As if she somehow knew what he was thinking. Somehow through their hands they were connected. Through that simple physical contact made them one mind and heart. Maybe that was the reason he was thinking those thoughts and deciding what he was going to do, because Naomi was thinking and feeling it as well. At least that was what he told himself.

Stopping just two steps from the door. He gave Naomi's hand a light squeeze, a suggestion that she should turn to look at him. Colin could feel his heart beating. His body resonated with the nervous energy of each pulse. He was sure Naomi could hear it as clear and loud as he did.

She was looking up at him. Her face so beautiful. Naomi was beautiful to him because he knew she had a beautiful soul. She was filled with a gentle kindness and compassion towards the world around her and that inner beauty reflected outward.

Naomi was there with him now. She was there next to him. How many times, years ago, when they would go to movies, shopping, just hangout and she had been that close to him and he never did anything about it. How different their lives might have been if he could have been brave for once, instead of always afraid. Always the coward. Colin knew he wasn't that boy anymore. He had come to terms with his life. With his past. He also knew he wasn't going to let another moment pass by, another opportunity to be lost. Life was meant to be lived and chances needed to be taken.

Totally oblivious to the storm outside, the thunder, the rain, Colin's hand moved up and brushed her hair back from her face.

He heard himself saying, "I'm sorry. I know I'm not supposed to".

Colin leaned forward and kissed Naomi.

Not knowing what to expect, her reaction, Colin initially was going to give her a simple and brief, but more than just a friendly kiss. His lips pressed to hers, hold for a moment, then move away. That had been his original intent. But as his lips touched her lips, something happened.

In a brief mental flash Colin heard the saying, the heart wants what the heart wants.

Their mouths met.

Their lips pressed together.

Their worlds shifted into a mutual orbit.

The simple and comfortable bond they shared in holding hands was replaced. It exploded with a fiery passion demanding to be released before it would acquiesce. The intensity of the feelings surged through Colin like the lighting burning across the storm clouds outside.

His mouth and lips moved against Naomi's and hers moved against his, responding with an equal intensity. That was a shade of color Colin had not been sure of, Naomi's reaction. A part of him had remained aware of Naomi and was waiting for her reaction. Had he gone too far? Would she pull away? Would she pull away and slap him? Would she forgive him for violating her response, her suggestion that the two of them kissing probably wasn't a good idea?

And as Colin felt her lips hold tight to his, as her mouth opened to his, Colin had his answer. What Colin hadn't expected, what he had only dreamed of, came when the kiss ended. He had done it. He had taken the chance that he had been wanting to take since the first time he found the courage to talk to Naomi. The first she acknowledged him.

The kiss had been as perfect as every imagined and fevered scenario.

The kiss had not been even close to any of those imagined and fevered scenarios.

In those flights of erotic mental fancy Colin had to be Naomi as well, imagining how she would react, respond to him. Now Naomi was really here, and he had no idea what was going to happen.

Their faces inches apart.

Their lips barely separated.

Colin could still feel her warmth.

He could still taste her.

Before he could think of anything else. To move away or to kiss her again. To say some trite, fumbling, apology like I'm sorry. Before any of that, suddenly there were hands on both sides of his face. Fingers moving across his beard and into his hair, holding him. Then her mouth locked against his as another surge of lightning burnt through the storm clouds to light the heavens above and the earth below.

Colin kissed her back. Now there was no hesitation. There was no wondering how Naomi was going to react.

There was no thought. There was only the building of the intense physical desire between them. Their tongues danced, moving across the dancefloor of their mouths.

Naomi's fingers moved deeper into his hair. Colin felt his hands move down and across her back. Both of them pressing and pulling themselves closer together. To impossibly try and physically occupy the same space, and yet somehow succeeding. Naomi made soft light moans as Colin moved his mouth down along her neck.

Kissing her soft white skin.

His lips feeling the beating of her heart.

His tongue tasting her.

Her fingers wrapped tighter into his hair. And not even aware he was doing it, Colin bent his knees, lowered his arms down around Naomi's waist and picked her up. At the same time his lips left her neck, only to trade places as her lips locked against his. Her soft moans of pleasure increased and Colin was surprised when he found himself involuntarily responding with his own.

She was amazing.

What they were doing was nothing and yet like everything he had imagined and fantasized. The last crack of lightning had broken open the storm clouds and the rain pounded against the window like a tympani drum, driven by the rapid tempo of the wind. Colin carried Naomi to the bed. There was no hint of protest. Her lips, mouth, tongue still exploring his neck.

If anything, her passion intensified. Letting him know she was aware of what he was doing. She knew what his intentions were. That she wanted it as much as he.

In the four steps to the bed, Naomi had unbuttoned his shirt and her lips and tongue were moving from his neck to his chest. Then she stopped kissing him. She leaned forward resting her head on his chest, nestling into him. Her damp hair, a fragrance of flowers brushed against his chin. And for the first time since he kissed her one of them finally spoke. Unprepared for what she said, Colin almost dropped Naomi.

"I can feel your heartbeat. I can hear it."

Colin thought his heart might have exploded from hearing those words. Naomi's voice was quiet and seemed to be filled with a tender wonder, as if hearing his heartbeat was the most amazing sound she had ever heard. His body was suffused with a warmth, starting from where Naomi's head rested and radiating outward.

Colin came to the bed. He kneeled as he lowered Naomi, set her on it.

Her arms relaxed and her hands began unbuttoning his shirt.

His arms moved to her waist, hands sliding up under her top, brushing up her back. Her skin so soft and warm. His fingers brushed across her as if she were a canvas. Colin felt his shirt come open. Her hands moving across his chest. Fingers weaving into his meager chest hair, curling it around each digit. Her mouth moved to his nipples, tongue circling each one. Back and forth, exploring, tasting.

His hands found her bra, and to his surprise because Collin always had problems with unhooking bras, with a simple pinch and push it came undone falling loose. His arms, hands moved down, reluctantly moving back from Naomi's kisses, his hands found the bottom of her top and gently started lifting it up. Naomi knowing his intentions, moved back just enough, raised her arms and let him undress her.

Before the top had cleared her head and arms, her face still covered, Colin paused leaned forward and kissed her breasts. He felt Naomi's reaction, her body tighten, goosebumps raising across her skin, nipples rising up in response to his touch. Her breath quickened and once again Colin heard her quiet moans and sighs.

She felt his hands, his comfortable and warm hands press harder against her back, holding her, moving over her, then back down to top of her pants. His fingers slipping, sneaking just inside, underneath, moving around her waist, to the front, to the button catch. Naomi caught her breath; she couldn't help it.

Colin's touch, the feel of his hands on her.

Naomi's body was responding, a slow burning warmth was building inside her.

As his hands came across her waist, she couldn't help it, she tried to fight it but couldn't.

It tickled.

Out of reflex Naomi tightened her abs and pulled her hands back off Colin's chest, from exploring his chest hair; her elbows moved in and locked side by side together to further block Colin's hands. Her own hands going down to take his from her waist as she slid back on the bed.

"I'm sorry. I can't help it. That tickles!"

"I noticed."

They both smiled and laughed. It was funny. Naomi thought it might have broken the mood. Changed everything, made them step back from where they had just been headed, from what they were about to do. But her bodies reflex hadn't. She could tell from the front of

Colin's loose-fitting dress pants he was certainly still in the mood. And from the warmth and humming inside her own body; if anything, that tickling touch had made her even more turned on.

Colin stepped from the bed and slid his shirt off his body. Naomi looked at his chest. He was still a skinny guy and she thought that as a good thing. Colin was never going to be a big broad chested, wide shouldered stereotypical hunk. He just wasn't built that way. But what he had, his body wasn't soft or weak looking.

His chest, and arms were lean and solid and defined. She could see the strength in him, she had felt it in when he had just been holding her. His abs were flat, with just the hint of some middle age belly above his pants. Naomi wasn't going to judge; she was fighting the same thing. His sparse dark chest hair had some strands of white mixed in. The hair she had just been running her hands through. And wanted too again. The chest she wanted again to kiss. Pants she wanted out of the way of her appreciative eye and searching hands. Naomi's eyes went back to Colin's face, and he was standing there watching her. This time he had caught her looking at him, staring, longing.

And in her heart where those brilliant burning white shooting star words had landed, where several minutes earlier the slow-burning warmth of desire had gone cold, suddenly there was a fire burning so bright and hot Naomi thought it would consume her.

"Colin—"

"Yes."

"You take my breath away."

The storm sounded overhead. A sharp metallic crack of lightening, the tympanic roll of thunder shared in the same instant. And the hesitant hands that before were covering the front of her open pants, the front of her panties, were suddenly alive again. They were filled with the heat of her hearts fire, fueled by it.

Now it was Naomi's turn to make the little sounds, the purrs of pleasure as his hands cupped her breasts, nipples tightening as his thumbs floated over their top, the tip. She moved to kiss his chest again, her hands moving down; he moved before she could. He was lowering himself, kissing her mouth, his tongue with hers. Then he moved down to her neck, warm and firm kisses, finding that spot under her ear right before the shoulder, her purr now almost a moan.

His fingers finding her pants already unbuttoned. Those hands began to push her pants down as his mouth followed. Now on her breasts. His breath hot against her nipples, his tongue the perfect soft stimulation she wanted. Her hands clutched at his head, her breath almost a gasp.

Naomi leaned back on the bed and as her pants went down so did Colin. This time he didn't tickle her as his mouth moved over her stomach. His kisses were firm and Naomi had no time to be ticklish, her body was busy with other stimulation. Her pants now down around her feet, as were his. His hands gliding up the back of her legs, his mouth over the front of her simple black panties.

She wanted that mouth right where it was.

His mouth was hot against her, she pressed herself closer, harder against him—if only her panties weren't in the way! Naomi thought, then she would be able to really press against him, to feel him.

Naomi wanted those interfering panties out of the way. It seemed Colin had the same idea. As he laid her back on the bed, the hands that had been holding her ass now moved up, fingers curling inside the tops of her panties, she lifted her hips.

Despite his obvious arousal, Colin didn't rush across her body. He didn't make cursory or brusque token gestures of trying to please or arouse her. He took his time. He explored and appreciated her body. Her panties however were still stuck around her knees as his mouth again on her breasts and nipples. He was studying her with his mouth and tongue and hands Naomi felt herself, her body melting, building, the fire in her spreading.

Colin's touch made Naomi feel like she was his canvas, and he was painting her body with his. She relaxed into the bed, arching her back again as he kissed his way down her stomach and again the firm kisses. She wanted to kick her panties off to some unknown location but for some reason Colin held her legs in place.

Colin's tongue moving down her body. Naomi let her purrs become catching moans accompanying each breath. The rain coming down. Colin now sliding her pantie around her ankles. His lips kissing down past her belly button.

Naomi thought she was going to catch on fire or melt or both. She decided to help Colin, to hurry him along, and slipped the panties that had been keeping her legs together from around her feet. Colin didn't push or rush, he just seemed to glide across the top of her, over her legs and back across her heat.

She knew what he wanted to do.

She knew what he was teasing her with.

What he was slowly building her towards.

Seducing her with his mouth.

She certainly wasn't going to refuse him, not now, not ever.

Colin brushed her legs with kisses and with those panties finally out of the way Naomi opened her legs to Colin's waiting mouth. The soft movement of his lips and tongue across the intimate flesh of her body. Naomi could feel her body responding.

Colin had always said he enjoyed oral, but now he was proving it. Her body was responding. It was building, releasing, the flow of honey as Colin's tongue glided inside her. Naomi couldn't help herself. She had to experience him this way. She didn't care if wanted it or not. But from his enthusiasm he obviously did.

Her hands. She had to hold his head. To put her hands on him. In his hair. Over his ears. Her body tightening from the touch of his fingers and mouth. Holding his head. Bracing him against her in just the right way. Her breathing tight with small quick breath. Giving voice to the sensation her body was currently feeling. What it was building towards. Then holding the last breath, Naomi held Colin's head as his mouth covered her. His tongue moving inside and over her. Naomi let out a deep gasp as her body trembled from release.

Naomi lay there on his bed. Her body humming. Purring! Colin with the lightest touch she ever felt again moved over her. He kissed his way up her body. He paused at her breasts.

He looked at her with questioning eyes, would it be okay to lick her nipples, was she still too sensitive? Her answer was a coy smile and a glimmer of *go ahead*. He spent several minutes once again kissing, licking her breasts.

Naomi relaxed under his touch.

Her body calming.

Her body recovering.

Her body once again building.

He paused from his actions and reached down under her legs still hanging over the bed. He slid another arm under her back and lifted her up. Naomi felt like a fairy tale princess as Colin lifted her like that, being caught in his strong arms, carried away on an adventure. However, as she far as she knew, Prince Charming had never kissed the sanitized Disney version of Snow White like that.

How sad Snow White.

He carefully put her down on the bed. Her head coming to rest gently on a pillow, just like a porn version of a fairytale princess. And like that porn version fairytale princess Naomi had a porn version fairytale prince. And his kiss had certainly awakened her. Now he was kissing his way up her body. Moving from her breast to her neck. Kissing her until he found that exact spot. The one that made her catch her breath, to start purring again. To start melting.

After several minutes, she could take it no longer, and she knew he couldn't either. She wanted him in her. She wanted to feel him in her in a way the two of them becoming one. She moved herself under him. Before he could question her actions, help her in any way, she took hold of him and placed him against her. Still wet and open from his earlier oral techniques he easily slid down and entered her.

She came again.

It was quick.

Hot and wet and he felt it.

She knew it.

She could see his face. So close to hers. His smile. Knowing that just that simple act, the two of them coming together, becoming one, was enough to cause her body to react that way. She wanted to grind her hips against his. She rolled him over. She wanted to be on top this time.

She straddled him cowgirl style.

Naomie let her hair sway back and forth over his face. His hands were holding her breasts, with soft squeezing. She controlled the speed and movement of their gyrating hip. Colin raised his head up and licked and kissed her breasts and nipples. Naomi thrust their hips together. She could feel another orgasm building.

She pushed him down, holding him, grinding her pelvis hard against his. One hand on his chest, her fingers in his chest hair, her nails tasting skin. She moved her other hand to her clit and started rubbing it. She shifted her hips slightly, positioning him inside her to hit just the right spot. She could feel it. Inside her, she could feel him growing harder. She knew he was close.

Her grinding now faster. Her body building to a heightened passion. A moan that couldn't be contained. Breathing tight and fast—then the release! She shuddered. Pushed hard against him. Her body tensed. Her body relaxed. Her body quivered. Her orgasm had been enough for Colin. Inside her, deep, she felt his hardness. Colin's hands held her hips and ass with a firm determination. He positioned her. His motion increased. His action fueled with a passionate intent. Naomi's body still tense. Still resonating with a low humming of her orgasm began to respond to this new stimulation. A new wave growing, buildings. Then behind Colin's hardness she felt a swelling release. Naomi gasped from it and then there was a warm wet sensation mixing with her own as she once again quickly came. They stayed like that as their bodies emptied themselves, mixing together in her, flowing out over him.

Chapter 9

Naomi lay on Colin. Her arms tucked in against his chest. Her hands holding his shoulders. Fingers moving in little circles against his skin. His arms were across her back. One higher, the hand resting against the side of her breast. The other stretched long, the hand cupped and holding her ass.

Their breathing a quite slow rhythm. Their bodies sated. They looked at each other, eyes locked together. Each looking deep into the other's soul. Looking for any sign regret or a sad resignation that what they were doing. That maybe what they just did was somehow wrong. Instead in the labyrinth of life and emotion and choices that were made or not made. All that confusion was juxtaposed by the simplicity of their mutual love.

Colin lay there in a state of euphoric exhaustion. Naomi was still there. She was still on top of him. She hadn't disappeared. This wasn't like waking from some fevered, sweaty erotic dream only to find he was alone in bed. Naomi was still there and they were together. Her eyes were half closed and she had a relaxed and contented smile to her mouth. Colin could feel her warm breath on his chest. Her hands and arms and her delicate little fingers gently caressing his shoulders. Colin wrapped his arms tighter around her. He had to make sure she was there. He had to make sure that she couldn't somehow slip away.

"What's wrong?"

Naomi's voice broke into his thoughts.

"You're shaking" she said.

Colin hadn't consciously realized it, but yes, he was shaking. His body realizing and releasing all the emotions it had contained for years. Feelings buried so deep, never thinking they would rise from the from those crypts and be felt again.

Naomi!

He was in bed with Naomi.

This was a moment he had waited for. This is what he had dreamt about for most of his life. Since after the first days he had gotten to know her. When he built up the courage to talk to that blonde Norse goddess. That beautiful, amazing Valkyrie who would walk the same hallways with him back in middle school.

Colin thought of a line from a Cowboy Junkies song. *"Two are born to cross. Their paths, their lives, their hearts. If one should turn away. Are they forever lost?"* Colin wished he could express such beautiful thoughts in words like that. The words of Bruce Springsteen also came to mind, *"Is a dream a lie if it don't come true or is it something worse?"* Colin felt his life up to the moment had been like those words. He and Naomi fated to cross and then he turned away. The something worse, the dream of he and Naomi that had never come true. And now it had. Now he held her body; their bodies pressed together, the heat between them filling the room. Colin shook because a dream that had been something worse was now something else. They were not forever lost.

Explaining the complexity of these thoughts was more than he knew how to do. More than he wanted to try. So he distilled them all of that down to one simple vapid sentence.

"I'm fine. I'm just happy." He said.

"Just happy?" She replied.

Colin tightened his arms around her. Buried his face under her long, now messy, blonde hair and kissed and bit her neck. She purred again. Moved his lips to her ear and whispered.

"Yes, happy. That kind of happy."

"I'm that kind of happy too."

Naomi felt the Colin's light shaking ease and stop. She admitted to herself, some of the shaking might have been hers. She understood when Colin said he was happy. She was so many things, so many emotions all at the same time, but happy was their essence.

Reluctantly she eased herself off of Colin's perfect body. Colin's body was perfect because she fit on it comfortably. Her head could rest in the crook of his chest and neck. Her arms tucked in against her, while still being on top of him.

He was long enough that even her feet rested on his legs. His body contours shaped to match her contours. Naomi imagined how nice it would be to have him around when she wasn't feeling well or was sad or cold. How nice it would be just to crawl on top of him, cuddle in, his arms gently rubbing her back and butt. The sense of security and comfort it brought. The healing energy coming from contact with another person's body. Colin was perfect. He was a living man-pillow.

"Could this ever work?" He whispered.

Not sure if he was asking her a question or thought out loud. Colin's voice was quiet. Everything now seemed quiet to Naomi. Before, when they had been together embraced in their passion as the large wind driven drops of rain sounded like hail bouncing off the window; now reduced to a quiet splatter. A gentle gathering mist.

Naomi was lost in the glow and warmth of the feeling of her body pressed against Colin's body, her living man-pillow. Her head lying on his shoulder. Her lips so close to his chest she again wanted to kiss. Not a passionate desire driven kiss, simple tender, just an idea of a kiss. His free left hand was absently brushing fingertip circles on her hip and leg. Naomi knew what Colin had just asked but right now she didn't want to think, to contemplate. All she wanted to do was lie there in the silent poetry of the moment.

Naomi didn't know what to say, how to respond. She wanted to lie there. It was so warm, so comfortable. Coffee —how had their morning gone from coffee to this? Naomi knew how. It was that kiss. Colin had kissed her. She never imagined something as simple as a kiss igniting such a passionate need in her. No other kiss had done that before and she was sure no other kiss ever would. And it wasn't just the kiss.

No one goes from zero to sixty because of a single kiss. They had history. The chemistry between them was something unique. It made her sad thinking about all the fun they had missed, all the years lost because of the stupid immaturity of youth and not seeing the person standing in front of them. Colin's question hung there, suspended in the breath between them like the mist floating just outside the window.

This was never supposed to be what this became. It was ever supposed to become a question like "Could this ever work"? It was never supposed to be something in her heart she had wanted to have happen. But it had happened. It had definitely happened. Naomi found herself smiling her body relaxing into the recent memory, the thought of them together. It had in fact, Naomi thought, happened several very pleasant times. What Colin was now asking, thinking, understanding the question, the sentiment, the feelings and the possibilities. Naomi understood why Colin was asking it, because in the emotional recesses of her heart Naomi's thoughts were the same.

"I suppose. But usually men need to rest for a few minutes before going again. Especially men your age."

Naomi smiled, lightly laughing at her quip. She could feel Colin laughing lightly as well. She thought it was clever and it also helped to deflect from Colin's question.

"Not, that. And yes, give me a couple minutes. I'm not a young man anymore. My turn-around time isn't what it used to be."

"Oh, that's okay, because I'm guessing your, shall we say long distance stamina, is better than your youthful sprints."

They both laughed. It was good. It deflected.

"Sorry. That question, that thing is said sort of fell out of my mouth. Let's forget I said it. It was just heat of the moment romantic nonsense."

Colin, sweet hopeless romantic Colin trying to reverse course, steer them from the collision with the iceberg of consequence he had set them upon several breaths ago. The question, his question wasn't asking if what they had there in the hotel room was going to work?

Naomi knew in her heart that Colin's question was more than just a cigar. She knew what he meant because in her own post, and just a little illicit which somehow made the sex even hotter sexual thoughts, Naomi had wondered if it could work. If they could work? If there was a possibility, winning the lottery jackpot chance, that somehow, she and Colin could make it. Naomi knew the answer and she was sure Colin knew the answer as well. Caught up in his own post crazy sex fueled thoughts is where the question came from. Naomi could tell he already knew the answer.

She knew it from the way he asked it. He knew it. He knew the answer as soon as the question fell out of his mouth. That was why he tried to take it back. That was the problem with saying something out loud without thinking about it first, Naomi thought. Once it was said out loud for the world to hear, the world never forgot. The other problem was she now knew it as well.

Sure, she had been privately thinking it. But Colin gave his emotions voice and she had heard it all the way down into the emotional recesses of her heart. Colin lay silent, having taken his question back. All that there was between them, and the silence of the room was the sound of Colin's hand, moving of its own volition, brushing back and forth across her back and thigh and the and the forgotten patter of the rain.

Naomi wondered if Colin realized he was painting her? She wondered what he was painting? Naomi contemplated giving him a quick kiss on the side of his chest, her lips were already so close. Before she could that, Naomi knew she needed to answer the question currently sharing their bed, their moment. Her brain knew the answer; now if Naomi could only get her heart to agree.

"Can we both accept and agree that for today, for as long as we stay here and the rain is coming down outside, yes Colin, for just this one rainy day it can work. Agreed?"

Naomi felt Colin's arms tighten around her, the painting paused, his legs sandwich hers, their bodies embracing. His embrace was warm and strong and through it, through the intimacy of that embrace Naomi could feel the hundreds, the thousands of emotions going through him. The light trembling of his body. The light trembling of her body. She felt each one because those were the same emotions, she was sharing with him.

Naomi knew he understood. He didn't like it, but he understood. She didn't like it either. But there was a lot of things in life she didn't like. What was it her parents always told her? "Life is never fair, it's just life."

Her parents were right. Understanding life was just life and then embracing that understanding. Just the two of them in the bed and the sound of the falling rain moving in step to the music of the storm dancing and dipping against the window, swirling and twirling in the streets below. In distant heavens, a sharp crack of lightning as the rhythm changed. Naomi didn't feel like counting this time.

"What if I refuse to let you go?"

Colin's voice soft, just above library quiet became light and blithe, and Naomi knew they were just them again. "Well, lots of things would happen. But most of all what is going to happen is everything is going to become unpleasant for both of us because I want to pee. So, unless you want me to be embarrassed and really angry that you made me pee the bed, I suggest you let me go."

"Oh, sorry."

Colin's arms relaxed, hands letting her go. Naomi started to laugh.

"Ha. Gotcha!"

Colin hesitated several seconds. Naomi had played him. She was watching a myriad of emotions run across his face. From the socially awkward topic of telling someone you want to pee; to the polite understanding that Naomi wanted to go pee and he had been holding her, keeping her from going; to realizing, after her exclamation stating he had been played.

The problem was, Naomi realized, that now she did in fact have to go pee when several seconds before making any mention of it, she didn't have too. Stupid psychosomatic response. Before Colin could move back towards her, Naomi took the initiative.

"Okay, now I do have to pee. So, you go clean up and then when I will. And while I'm in the bathroom—do you have anything to drink? I would love some water, and if you wanted, we could share some coffee. Not a lot, I don't want it sloshing around in my stomach because I believe you said something about being ready again soon."

While trying to untangle themselves from each other as well as the sheets, they paused and they smiled at each other. For the second time that day Naomi felt her heart stop from just a smile.

"Okay. I don't have anything up here, but I know back down in the lobby there is some water and coffee. I will grab some of each and be right back."

Colin stepped into the bathroom and shut the door. She could her the water starting. Several minutes later he came out, and started to dress. Naomi watched. She had to pee, but she liked watching men dress. It was sexy to her. As they lifted each leg to put on their underwear. She never met a man who sat down to do it, they always stood. Some men sat to put on pants, or socks, or shirts, usually shoes; but she had never known a man who sat to put on their underwear.

Colin also wore loose fitting boxers. She would have thought him for the trendy boxer-briefs. Or if not those, maybe just the traditional tighty-whities. But the loose boxers, she hadn't expected those. Maybe because she never imagined him wearing them. In her self-fulfilling fantasies of Colin which she admittedly sometimes indulged; he rarely wore underwear.

Usually, they were already in a hot tub, or shower. Her favorite fantasy imagined being in bed with him. He was sleeping and she had a special way to wake him. Naomi knew how to wake a Prince Charming. Colin slid his boxers up, adjusted the elastic band and the legs, then picked up his dress pants from the wrinkled pile on the floor where she had pulled them off him, and again still standing, Colin slid them on one leg at a time. Again, the underwear adjustment.

Naomi started to forget about having to go pee. She started to forget about being thirsty. She started to wonder how much more time Colin needed before he would be ready again.

Finally, Colin put his shirt on, covering up his chest. The skin she just minutes before had been kissing and biting; his man skin. Naomi found herself moving to the edge of the bed, next to where he was, next to his still exposed man skin. She tried to fight it, to not want to do it, but she couldn't help herself.

Colin turned, looking at her with a *what are you doing* expression on his face. Before he could move or respond in anyway, Naomi on her hands and knees moved up and put her lips against the exposed top part of his chest and neck. She kissed and lightly bit at him again. She felt playful, teasing; then she felt his hands on her arms, a firm embrace of her body.

Naomi's fun teasing kisses began to become more fervent. Colins hands started to lift her, her own hands going around his waist, her lips up to his neck. Naomi forced herself to stop. Which actually she so much didn't, it was her bladder. Stupid bladder. She pushed herself back, as she lightly pushed Colin towards the door.

"Go now! Before I don't want to stop and then it will be my fault about peeing the bed. Which, ick, go. Run!"

Colin flashed his stupid sexy making her hotter lopsided smile at her.

"Okay. Be right back. And by the way. After what you just did; I've rested enough."

He gave her double eyebrow raise and a wink and he was out the door.

Chapter 10

After Colin left, Naomi freshened up, the polite euphemism for whore-bath—pits, tits, and pussy. Then she brushed her hair, and touched up her lipstick. After the freshening up part was done and Colin still wasn't back, Naomi busied herself with tidying up the bed a bit.

It had become rather messy, which was fine, she enjoyed the way it became messy. But the same compulsive behavior that suggested she touch up her makeup, also suggested she straighten the bed. Because, after all, a tidy bed just begs to be messed up again. And she really wanted them to mess it up again.

Naomi looked at the disheveled bed. It certainly hadn't taken them long to destroy it. Of course, it wasn't supposed to get messy in the first place. It was supposed to have been just coffee. But that kiss. Colin's kiss! It wasn't awkward. They did not bump noses or clack teeth. It wasn't weird, like kissing a relative. Instead, it was electric. It was an atom bomb — KraaBoom! The instant their lips met was pure chemistry. Naomi was unprepared for her reaction.

Can a single kiss be wonderful? Can a single kiss be so wonderful that it has the power to change a person's perspective? That Hollywood kiss between two characters that is so perfect, so wonderful it changes the direction of the story.

Naomi contemplated that question as she made the bed. It had been a really good kiss. No, thought Naomi. It was that perfect wonderful kiss that changed the direction of her story. From that first kiss to all the other kisses and everything else. They were all equally as wonderful. They were equally as perfect.

Still, the kiss was the catalyst. Sure, it was an amazing wonderful kiss, but it was Colin's kiss. The guy who had always been there for so much of her life, other than relatives. Naomi realized she underestimated her feelings for Colin. She did love him. But she compartmentalized that love, putting it into friendship box. That's where Colin had been for too long, compartmentalized, filed away as a friend. Apparently, all they needed was a good kiss.

There was also something different about Colin. He had never been like that before. He had never tried to kiss her, especially like that. Something was different with him.

He was stronger, more open then when they had been kids. They were both different since all those years ago. Naomi's heart hurt at that thought. Because of that action, that emotional file structuring, they had missed so much life together. So much of what they had just did, and Naomi smiling coyly knew they would be doing again. And was it so bad, Naomi asked herself? Naomi, smoothing the comforter, paused and thought about the answer. No, it wasn't so bad. It was something she, in her own way had wanted as much as Colin.

She knew she was fiercely loyal to her marriage but there was so much history between her and Colin. There were too many feelings, complex emotions, a myriad of connections. All of those were reasons why there was no fumbling and awkward foreplay.

They were experienced, mature enough to take some time, to know what and how to pleasure each other. Naomi found her body warming from the thought, apparently it could work in life like it did in the movies. She usually didn't cum as many times as she had, not that she was complaining.

Naomi tried to identify the catalyst. Was it the years of intimate friendship between them? The titillating illicit idea of what they were doing, like errant children excited by the thrill of misbehaving when no one was there to catch them? Maybe it was the rain and it did have some hold on her she couldn't quite explain? Maybe it was fate?

Collecting the pillows, putting them back on the bed, either way, it was certainly too late now, Naomi thought, smiling. For one day it was okay to let herself free from all her rules, to let down her guard and take off her emotional armor. As Naomi finished arranging the pillows, making them comfortable to sit against and slipped back into the now tidy ready to be messed up again bed she heard the door unlock and open. Colin came in carrying two bottles of water and a cup of coffee.

"What took so long? I was starting to get worried you had forgotten about me. I was about to get dressed and come and look for you. Of course, once my clothes are back on, they probably wouldn't come off again. So, it's good you came back when you did."

Naomi smiled at Colin. She was smiling a lot today. She wanted to hate being so happy. Which Naomi found begged the internal contemplative question of; was she always that sad because she didn't always smile like this? Watching Colin walk into the room, slip off his shoes using his feet, hands still holding the coffee and water, Naomi thought about it. Was she always sad?

No. She wasn't always sad. She just wasn't always happy. She just *was*. It *was* life. It was just how it *was*. There were times when the *was* of life was good and she felt free and open like the birds in the park where she took after work walks.

There were times when the *was* of life was worse and she imagined she was a deep ocean shark, drifting, barely swimming in the cold dark depths of the ocean. But mostly the *was* of life was just what it was, neither good nor bad, it just *was*. But now, what she was feeling was something she hadn't felt for a long time and her body and her heart responded, making Naomi smile. Naomi felt young.

Colin was barefoot his shirt untucked, the top button open. His hair still a little messy, because he hadn't taken the time to brush it better before leaving the room. His smiling face was still a stupid expression hopeless romantic goof. Naomi knew she wore the same expression on her face. He was walking over to her with a bottle of water, looking at her and the bed.

"You've been busy while I was gone."

"I don't like a messy bed. Especially when I'm alone in it."

Naomi made a sad, pouty face at Colin after telling him she didn't like being in bed alone. She took the offered water, opened it and had a quick drink. It was good, refreshing. She wanted some more, but she didn't want it sloshing around in her stomach. Because right now, looking at Colin, she definitely wanted to do something that would cause some sloshing. And going from zero to sixty always caused sloshing.

"Besides, everyone knows a made bed, all nice and neat, is just begging to be messed up again."

This time it was Naomi's turn to the do the wink and cheeky double eyebrow raise. Then she pursed her lips and made a kissy face at Colin as her hand patted the bed and pulled back the nicely folded sheet. Colin took her hint. In a matter of seconds, he had put down the coffee and the other bottle of water and was unbuttoning his shirt.

Like before, when Colin was dressing to leave the room, Naomi moved to the end of the bed where he was standing and undressing. Once again so close to him. She could smell his man-skin, and again she felt not just the need, but the wanton desire to feel it, to taste it. Not bothering to ask, knowing he wouldn't care, as Colin removed his shirt, she unbuttoned his pants.

Pulling them down, she made sure to take the boxers with, she saw the man-flesh she wanted. Naomi put one arm around his waist, the other held him and she leaned forward and tasted him.

Colin hadn't expected Naomi to take him like that, not that he was going to complain. Still partially dressed, shirt hanging from an arm, pants around his feet, his heart picked up the pace as the blood coursed through his body, his skin warm and flush, coming to life again, responding to Naomi. He was still trying to get his shirt off when Naomi had pulled down his pants and began doing what she was doing.

Now with her in front of him, her one arm wrapped around his waist the other helping, not that Naomi needed that hand to help, thought Colin. He relaxed into Naomi enthusiasm, while trying to steady himself. It was amazing and also a little awkward. He managed to get his shirt off without stopping Naomi from doing what she was doing. Much like their first kiss that morning, Colin once again didn't want to move, just like he didn't want to open his eyes lest it break the moment.

Her hands and mouth going over him, holding him. Colin wanted to put his hand on Naomi, to touch her skin and hair, but he didn't move, he just lost himself in the moment. Besides, Colin wasn't sure if he could move without falling or stumbling. His pants were around his ankles and he knew if did anything he was going to stumble about. Then after one great movement Naomi leaned back away from him.

"I think you're ready again."

The look of pure uninhibited desire on her face was how Colin was feeling. Not caring if his dress pants for that night became wrinkled, like his shoes, he pulled them off with his feet and climbed onto the tidy straightened bed with Naomi. He moved to return the favor she had given him in kind, but instead she took hold of him, one hand on each head, she pulled one in for a kiss, and guided the other inside her.

Once again, they were locked in passion. The undulating movements, their bodies responding, the splattering of the rain becoming lost in the silent thunder of their breathing. Colin knew the spot and once again kissed and lightly bit Naomi's neck and shoulder. She responded with a pleasured moan and moved to wrap her arms and legs around his back. Then her mouth was on his ear, kissing and biting at him. Her hot breath against his skin. Bodies tense, rubbing, pushing against each other. Then Naomi's whispered in his ear.

"I want you from behind."

She unwrapped her legs and arms, and Colin with a slow reluctance removed himself from Naomi. She turned to her side, her back towards him, and angled her ass up and against him. Colin turned to complement her actions and then he felt Naomi's hand on him, once again positioning, once again inside her.

Instantly Colin knew Naomi liked the change in position as he felt a wet warmth around him. He kissed at the back of her neck, his free hand cupping and kneading her breast. She pushed back against him. His hand moving downward from her breast, finding her heat and with a firm gentle touch he began a tight circular massage. Colin felt Naomi respond, her skin getting hotter, her body becoming tight around him. Then her free hand came over and grabbed at his ass, pushing him against her as hard as she was pushing back against him. She was forcing him against her, grinding her flesh harder against his. Before he could do anything about it, for the second time that day Colin felt himself releasing. He tried to hold back, but his mind and body were to connected to the heat of Naomi.

"Keep. . . going. . ." Naomi's gasping whisper.

Colin kept his moments going —"There!"—and then he felt Naomi's body tense and shake against his—"Yes!" — the catch to her breath—mmm—the feel of her around him—"haa. . mmm. . . yes.

He removed his hand from her velvet heat and brought it back up to lazily caress her supple breasts. He kissed the back of her neck as they held each other while the heat washed over them.

Chapter 11

They lay in the once again messy bed. And once again Naomi was comfortably nested into the crook of his arm as if she belonged there, had always been there. Colin felt impressed with himself; twice in less than two hours. Knowing it was a stereotypical guy thing to think, but he didn't care. Naomi certainly seemed to think so, or at least she told him so somewhat vocally about five minutes earlier.

Colin mentally admitted that Naomi inspired his performance. She was enthusiastic, aggressively enthusiastic. Well, they both were. There was something there between them, and for lack of a better definition, Colin called it the cliché term, chemistry. From the kiss to now. From all the years of always being friends and never drifting apart as he had with other people and friends in his life. There was something between she and him.

Colin also knew the other word for it, besides chemistry. Colin loved Naomi. It was just that simple. It was love. Whatever defined the idea, the emotion, the action. Whatever love was, Colin loved Naomi. He wanted to tell her, as she lay there in his arm her breathing quiet, matching his own, he wanted to tell her he loved her. He didn't ever want her to leave. He didn't want the day to end. But he knew that wasn't how their day was going to go. There was nothing to do but lie there with her, and for Colin, to just lie there with Naomi, even if it was for just one day it was enough.

Colin knew it had to be enough. He came to Minnesota for one day. This was all they were going to have. Had Colin known he would spend his day in bed with Naomi, he might have planned on staying longer. But he never expected this to happen. It just, sort of, did. Colin tried to distract himself from those thoughts, the Naomi thoughts, because they made his heart ache.

He drifted in thought to the coming evening. The gallery show of his new paintings and drawings. And as he imagined how the show would go, Colin realized somewhere along the way in life, he had become arrogantly cynical. At his first show he thought he had died and been asked to open for the Rolling Stones. It was exciting as people asked about his work. He was enthusiastic as he explained the techniques and the expression, his emotions when painting. Slowly after doing more and more shows, excitement's veneer soon wore thin as life's reality kicked him in the balls.

Colin would find himself stuck sipping wine while making small talk and listening to the moronic ramblings of the people who came to those events. Those people whom Colin once found so sophisticated because they dressed in such nice clothes and drove expensive cars. Under their veneers they were nothing more than people Colin knew he would never want to be around.

The men, the husbands, were usually middle-aged or older, they were stock-analysts or high-powered businesspeople, founding member of some high-powered legal firm, or some specialist doctor who could work medical miracles with his hands and of course was well paid for those miracles.

Those men would tell Colin they liked a particular painting and how it would look fabulous in their second home or posh cabin. With snide, vaguely hidden arrogance they said how they thought about taking-up painting as a hobby when they retired or just for fun. It didn't really look that hard, after all that Bob Ross guy made it look easy, even told you what colors and brushes to use. How hard could it be?

The women, the wives were mostly the stereotypical trophy variety. Those women were usually the second, or possibly, even the third wife. The age at least ten or more years younger than their iron-clad prenuptial agreement until death or a younger woman comes along husband.

Those vapid women who insisted they were worldly because their vain and egotistical husbands took them on trips to the bikini-beaches of some exotic place. Colin thought the reason the men went on those trips were to look for prospective wives or mistresses. He was stuck there daydreaming, pretending to listen to some banal topic which was supposed to be as interesting to Colin as it was to the her. Those women with exaggerated vocal fry gushed, with much hand gesturing, telling him his paintings were amazing.

And then there would come at least one inquiry, *what do you charge for family portraits?* Colin determined he would rather cut off his hands than paint a family portrait. It wasn't that he couldn't. It wasn't that everyone had to sit there while he painted. He would just take several pictures and work from those. The problem was no one ever thought the portraits looked like them.

"We don't look that!"

"My hair isn't that color."

"My eyes don't look right."

"It's not like the camera picture."

In the end the effort was never worth the commission.

If it wasn't the request for the family portrait it was the request for the private personal portrait, a nude sitting.

Those bored trophy wives who understood their current status, much like an opened container of milk, had an expiration date. They would see some of Colin's bedroom paintings; women in filmy satin slips leaning against sun-streaked windows; nudes laying on a bed sometimes partially covered with a blanket or a sheet, sometimes nothing at all.

Those expiration date wives wanted to be like the forever young and beautiful women in the paintings. However, what Colin could never explain to those expiration date wives was the fact even the women who modeled for those paintings were not the women in the paintings. A painting was as much an idea, an emotion as it was a visual description and depiction of a scene.

The other reason Colin refused, with politeness and tact, was of course because some of those women placed thinly veiled inuendo into the request. Sure, they said to Colin how they wanted an erotic painting, a special gift for their husband. But behind their heavy eyes, quiet vocal fry voice, and suggestive body language, they were asking Colin to not just paint them but to also have sex with them.

That young, excited, first art show Colin full of bright colors from the initial excitement, became faded and dulled Colin. He was peeled, cracked and wore away, and now cynical Colin found how he hated talking to and dealing with people. However, cynical Colin loved his life. He loved the freedom. He loved the release of his expressions through his paintings. Zen Colin always believed the universe demanded balance. So, to pay the price for the good part of his life, the quiet intimate alone in his studio painting, he endured the pandering to the small-talk-masses at large social gatherings where he was the focus of attention.

All of that and more would be what lie waiting for him at the evening's gallery event. Then it would be wake up tomorrow and take his flight back home.

Home to his own bed.

Home to his coffee maker.

Home to his quiet studio.

Home to his yard where he could sit with his oak tree and contemplate his place in the world.

Home to his bathroom puta who challenged him with her eyes and body every time he looked at her.

Home to Margo his wife of twenty-two years.

Margo.

Margo who had told him to stay in Minnesota longer if he wanted too. Maybe look up some old friends, some of those people he had grown up with, see what they were up too. With Facebook she was sure he could find some of them.

Maybe take a day and drive to West Lake and see how it had changed. Maybe, if he wanted, maybe try to put aside some of the old animosities and pain and consider going to see his family. They might like to see him again after all those years. Margo told him those things with supportive loving eyes.

Margo who was there for him.

Margo who loved him.

Margo.

Of course, on one-point Margo had been correct, because of social media Colin found various friends from the past, or more accurately, they found him. Several people from his high school class messaged him at his mandatory social media accounts. Those accounts he could not care less about, but because of how the world worked he was forced to keep updated and occasionally respond to queries.

There were occasionally messages from the echo-people. That's what he called them, the people from his past. They echo from the past to the present, sending messages wondering if the person on the website was really him? They wanted to know more about his life. Was he really, what they called, a famous artist? Where had he disappeared too? Would he friend them on Facebook?

Those echoes came from all corners of his past. Reverberations from the bullies who tormented him. Doppler's from the friends who had never thought to reach out to him before, but were suddenly interested again when they see him on a website. They all echoed out to him, and Colin let the majority of the echoes reverberate and fade away. Colin did respond to a few of the echoes, bringing the past to the present.

Responding with a hello and yes it was him. His digital responses were a variation of his social function responses. They were always pleasant but not too pleasant. Never revealing more than was already available on social media, just saying it all in a different way. It was a creative rephrasing to sound personal and new. And they of course responded. But it never went further or became more because Colin didn't want more. He liked simple. He liked easy.

Since arriving in Minnesota, Colin had not thought about his home in California. He had not thought Margo. The thought of seeing Naomi again, that thought had consumed him. A restless Thursday night wasn't so much sleeping, rather more of his body forcing the brain to shut down, almost like a coma. Only to awaken an hour or so later, eyes open, thoughts unrestrained, and wide awake, again.

And awake, looking at the clock hoping that hours had past instead of minutes. That it was now time to get ready and meet Naomi. Instead of six am, the clock read two-thirty. Instead of the warm pink and red glow of a rising sun, the dull buzzing hum and orange glow of the parking lights filtered into the room.

Again, the routine, Colin lying there, a brain busy with a hyperactive imaginative scenario of seeing Naomi, until once again the body shut down, forcing another hour of so-called sleep. Stepping into the coffee shop had been stepping back in time, into another place, another reality.

The instant Colin took the first step, blinking the rain drops from his eyes and seeing Naomi, Margo ceased to exist in Colin's new world. There were only thoughts of Naomi as they drove back to his hotel so he could change out his clothes soaked by rain and coffee. There was only Naomi when he kissed her there in the doorway of his hotel room. And there was only Naomi as their first kiss led to another first between the two of them. Now, at this moment as Colin held Naomi—Naomi! Colin found his mind drifting back to the reality of Margo.

Margo.

Margo the woman he loved.

Margo his companion.

Margo his wife.

Margo.

As the reality of life pulled at him, Colin pondered the question: if he loved Margo, why did he and Naomi have their own secret life? Why was he here with her now? Colin knew it wasn't because he didn't love Margo. He was there because he loved Naomi first.

Never in his life would Colin have let another woman come between him and Margo. Colin was certain of that fact. He just wasn't built or programmed that way. Maybe it was part of being a hopeless romantic, the trope description which was Naomi's favorite taunt. Colin didn't care. Maybe he was a hopeless romantic. There were worse things to be. He had grown up with those worse things.

As for cheating on Margo, he had had his chances. He could have had his pick or opportunities. From the vapid trophy wives insinuating they wanted a special painting for their husbands. The models he hired who were trying to get ahead, flirting with him, suggesting they would be *very grateful* if he would help them out with more work or extra commission money. The random women who would flirt with him at various places around town when he was alone.

Those times when Margo would be gone on a business trip and Colin would go out for supper by himself. Sitting at the Blue Moon bar, his favorite local place, quietly reading and passively people watching. He would be drinking a beer, enjoying a burger, and depending on how busy the place was, he would have random and always interesting conversations with the bartender Mike.

Between those moments there would be the interruption of suddenly finding his personal space violated by a random woman pointedly taking the seat next to him with a "Anyone sitting here? Mind if I join ya"? Or, if he were sitting at a table over in the corner, they would look for one in the same area, or worse, they would ask if he were alone and could they join him. All the options began and ended the same—tedious.

Those women always seemed to be a cut-out stereotype of each other. The all wore an overly revealing easy-on and easy-off dress, the of *out on the town* perfume as they leaned close, shoulders back, giving a preview, a sneak peek at what was being offered. Colin had no interest in those women and they soon discovered it when he didn't respond to any of their attempts to engage him in conversation. He had no interest in them. He was flattered of course, but he wasn't that guy.

However, one aspect about the situation, no matter how many times it happened and Colin was both irritated and flattered that it happened more than he cared admit. Colin was amazed at how the world changed. He tried to figure out the point in his life when he went from the dorky, gangly guy no girl or woman wanted to talk to, much less date, to one day becoming the guy who had women hitting on him? When did that happen? Colin thought of that along with all those other thoughts, and then he came back to thoughts of Margo.

Margo.

Margo who would be home Sunday from her business trip in San Diego. Margo, who Colin knew would be calling or texting him tonight just before the show was scheduled to open, like she always did. She wished him good luck and told him she loved him. Colin thought of all that as he shared his hotel bed with Naomi.

There was a light breath on his cheek; a gossamer touch to his lips. His focus reversed, Margo shifting out of the frame, then back into and through the falling rain, then into soft blue eyes, gentle blushed cheeks covered with errant locks of blonde hair, and the red lips of Naomi.

"Where did you go?"

She could tell he had left, even for that instant, she still knew his heart.

"Her."

Chapter 12

At that moment, Colin couldn't bring himself to say Margo's name. Hoarsely, he was barely able to whisper "her." Margo's name was impossible to say while sharing a bed with Naomi.

"Are you okay?"

Naomi's voice quiet, an almost whispered concern.

Naomi understood. Colin could see it in her eyes, so blue, so open to him. Naomi who had never professed any deep feelings for Colin in the past. Naomi who had instead of stepping back away from Colin's kiss, embraced him and returned the kiss with an ardent desire. Colin kept his head, his eyes turned towards hers, his heart and soul open for her to see. He took a long, slow, quiet, breath.

In.

Then.

Just, as, slowly.

Out.

"Yes."

Their souls still open, looking at each other. Because as Colin had faced something about himself, about his life, Colin also wondered about Naomi, after all they were in this together.

"Are you okay with this? I mean not just about me and her, but him?"

Colin wasn't sure if was supposed to ask, if it would be crossing one of the boundaries, the rules he and Naomi had established months ago, those simple mechanical rules to protect themselves and their other relationship, their parallel lives. Now those parallel lines had crossed. Colin didn't know what happened when parallel lines crossed, what it did to the universe?

Colin decided if he wouldn't say Margo's name out loud, he also wouldn't say the name of Naomi's husband. Colin knew it was stupid and childish, but in his mind, he thought if they didn't say the names, then neither of their spouses existed. And as long as the rain was out there, washing, cleaning, revitalizing; then for this breath of time it was only the two of them. There was no one else.

There was only Colin.

There was only Naomi.

There was only a realized moment of an infinite love between them. Just them. The lines had never crossed, the rules of the universe were still intact.

Colin felt the slight reflex of Naomi's body tensing, the subtle possibly unconscious effect of skin and muscle that if he and Naomi hadn't been holding each other like they were, Colin never would have known his question had evoked a response. And maybe that was one of the ways Naomi had detected the change in Colin, it was the feel of his skin, the small subtle change that told her he had gone somewhere else. His thoughts following the crossed parallel lines out in the storm.

It wasn't brain surgery. Colin knew Naomi loved her husband, just as Naomi knew he loved his wife. Colin now mentally switching back to third person pronouns. Back to where the lines didn't again try to cross. Back to where the lines were still parallel. They were both committed, heart and soul and love to not just some other people, but specific someone's with whom a life together wasn't just some imaginary piece of fiction. It was a reality laid out before them.

And because Colin could feel those intimate subtle tensing and relaxing of the individual muscles of Naomi's body as she thought about her answer, Colin knew she was as aware of his body and his thoughts as she lay pressed against, touching, intertwined with him. That morning when he arrived at the coffee shop. He thought he had made his decision. He thought he was confident in his resolve. That was before he stepped out of the rain into the coffee shop. Before seeing her sitting there.

But at this moment did he regret? Could he live with what had happened? He had already given his answer. It was time for Naomi's.

"Do you believe in fate?"

Naomi's question as an answer wasn't as simple as Colin had hoped for, he knew she was leading to something. Colin thought about it, the question. *Did he believe in fate?* Was this moment preordained? This day had been decided when the universe came to be; some cosmic design from the beginning of creation? That Colin couldn't believe, or could he?

Lying naked in bed with Naomi, having her body wrapped around his, feeling the warmth of her skin pressing against his, her soft breath moved across his chest; talking philosophy and the meaning of life was not really high on Colin's priority list.

"I suppose. Maybe. Yes. Sure. Does it matter?"

Naomi gave him a quick pinch on his nipple and lightly dug her nails into his skin, teasing, drawing him in. Her not-so-subtle way to get his attention.

"I'm serious."

Colin gave her question a longer, more thoughtful contemplation. Did he believe in fate? There were times he would say no, it was just more of that hippy crap he heard from the burnt out, old flower children living out their days in the valley. But there had been so many times in his life where *things* just seemed to happen at the right time. And all those *things* just seemed to fit too well together as if they were leading the person, him, towards something undeniable.

"Yes. There are times I do believe in fate."

She smiled at him and Colin felt like the Grinch after he came to understand the meaning of Christmas; Colin felt his heart grow ten sizes too large. She was looking at him from the crook of his arm, and propped up on the pillows he could see the soft turn of her face and blushed cheek; Naomi had dimples. Looking at her now, this close, this intimate, he could see them. They were subtle but there. Her mouth stretched, happy inviting. He wanted to kiss it again, he wanted to kiss it forever.

"You were offered a show here in Minnesota. She," Colin noted Naomi had chosen to use pronouns as well. He relaxed a little. "She couldn't come along because of work, and in fact told you to stay longer, maybe lookup some old friends. So, you asked me if I wanted to meet you for coffee or something. I said yes. For some stupid reason I thought it would be nice of me to bring you back here so you could change out of you wet clothes.

And then you had to be stupid and kiss me.

You will never know how hard I tried to not kiss you back, but I could not, not kiss you. It was a perfect kiss. It wasn't supposed to be perfect. We should have bumped noses. Our teeth should have clacked together. You were supposed to try and shove your entire tongue into my mouth. Instead, it was perfect and from that moment I knew what I wanted."

Colin liked the way Naomi presented her case and he understood why she was in the legal profession. She could pick apart the details, look past the minutia, and get right to the heart of the situation. She emphasized her salient points, making sure he heard and understood them. It also made her nose sort of wiggle when she spoke. It was so cute. But he understood what she was explaining to him. Even he wasn't that obtuse. Even though sometimes it took the entire universe to hit him over the head with something before he got it.

"Do you understand what I'm telling you?"

He forgot about the cute wiggling of her nose because she once again playfully pinched his nipple to get his attention. Because as Colin was thinking about how cute Naomi's nose was, how it sort of wiggled when she was talking, his hands started to drift over her body again, casually brushing their way back to some of the more favorite areas. Also, his brain was determining that the way Naomi's nose wiggled when she was speaking to him, it wasn't cute, it was adorable. The light pinch on his nipple paused his hands and brought his attention back to what Naomi was saying to him.

Colin thought about it, and yes, he did understand. Just like when Colin was younger and trying to make it as an artist. How one of the people at a student art show, some strange old man, loved Colin's paintings and bought one. He asked if Colin would do commissions? That young and excited Colin, who at that time was barely able to afford his share of the rent naturally said yes.

What that younger Colin didn't know was that strange old man happened to be the owner of one of the largest vineyards in Napa Valley and the commission turned out to be several paintings for his vineyard and home. Was it fate or dumb luck? Colin didn't know. But if it was fate, then it seemed fate once more had chosen to put him on a path to something.

Fate.

Maybe Fate might occasionally at least have the courtesy to consult with him before doing this type of thing. But no.

"Yes. I get it. But you've avoid answering my question."

"I just did. You artist types really need to learn to understand the fine print."

Colin's heart skipped as Naomi smiled at him. She owned him. At that moment, she owned him.

"Yes. To be more obvious. Yes. For today only. For our one moment that Fate never gave us before. Yes, I'm okay with it."

Chapter 13

Her right arm across his chest, her left arm tucked under her, the hand against his ribs. She squeezed him, tight. She held him. And in return he wrapped her tightly against him. Together they lay there, feeling the rise and fall, the filling and emptying of air in the lungs, the soft breath on their faces, the sweet smell of their bodies filling the room.

Again, Naomi lay there in Colin's embrace. It was after eleven, and for the second time that day she found herself physically satisfied. Not that being physically satisfied was a problem. The problem was Naomi also found herself becoming emotionally satisfied when she had no right to be.

Her life was supposed to be what it was; work, home, weekend, repeat. That was life. Then Colin had to go and wreck the illusion, the fantasy of the day by talking about their spouses. She understood he wasn't doing it to be mean, or wreck the moment, what they were currently sharing.

Colin always looked at the emotional side of life, which was why she always teased him about being a hopeless romantic. Telling him he was a walking-talking version of a Lifetime or Hallmark movie. Colin wanted to make sure he hadn't forced her in some way to do something she didn't want to do. Naomi understood what motivated Colin to ask. He didn't want her to be hurt.

He didn't want to hurt her.

Yes, as she had told him, she was fine with what was happening between them. For their one day it was just the two of them. But what Naomi didn't confess to Colin or even to herself, was her personal sense of disloyalty to her husband. She had given him her word –her oath– to be loyal to him. Naomi tried to tuck those feelings away, compartmentalize them until later. Like her feelings of love and passion for Colin, her feelings of loyalty and commitment to Brad refused to be simple.

She was on an emotional merry-go-round and those dizzying thoughts and feelings kept circling back around. Brad was a good man. They had been introduced through mutual friends a year or so after her divorce. They hit it off, and soon they were seriously dating. At that time, he was low-middle management in the purchasing department for an electronics manufacturing company. However, after years of hard work he was now the manager. He had a strong enthusiastic energy to him. After a lazy stoner ex-husband, Naomi had found that outgoing personality as attractive as his physical looks.

He was decent and honest and most importantly Naomi thought, he could tolerate her. He provided for them as much as she did. He had his bad points as well as his good. Naomi knew in her heart she loved Brad, which then raised the contemplative question, *"why was she in bed with Colin?"*

Was it the idea of Colin and who they once were? Did she get caught up in the emotion of the past, all those feelings and the romantic ideas? A simple selfishness and lack of compassion and consideration? Or was it boredom in her life? The monotonous soul-crushing routine which she had passively accepted because that was just how life worked. Did the idea of an illicit tryst with someone—well not just someone—fulfill some psychological desire to break the pattern?

In her head Naomi knew what she meant and she also knew she would have had trouble trying to describe it in a clear and concise manner. Naomi also knew what she felt. And that was something she didn't want to admit to herself, much less say to Colin. Because if she did admit it. She would be forced to feel it. That was a complication to her reality she did not want to deal with. She had enough going on in her life without that emotional shit-show.

So, Naomi decided to keep it buried, deep, forever. Naomi had already told Colin she loved him. In her heart she meant it. But what she didn't want to face was the idea of her without him. Naomi knew there was a part of Colin, probably smaller than he let on, but there was a part of him that when he asked her to run away with him to those various places, Naomi knew he was serious. And that scared Naomi. It scared her because there was a not so small part of her, probably larger than she wanted to admit to, that wanted to run away with Colin.

The room was filled with their aroma. Naomi felt her body fit so perfectly against Colins, as if they were matching puzzle pieces that completed a picture. Her head resting on his shoulder and chest. She could smell his man skin. When she turned her head just a little, she could lightly kiss and taste it. She felt the slow rise and fall of his chest and heard the subtle sound of his breath going in and out. She could still feel and hear the strong steady beat of his heart. That sound along with all the other sensations and emotions flowing through her, all of that made Naomi's heart ache.

Caught in all of those feelings, especially the ache in her heart, Naomi started to feel the weight of the room. Their actions, no matter how they perceived them, no matter how the two of the them justified spending this time together, they had both violated other parts, other commitments and promises in their lives. Naomi started to feel the weight of the room and it was starting to become too much for her. She had to do something, she had to get off her mental carousel ride. It had started to turn to fast. It was becoming off-balance and wonky. It was making her dizzy and anxious, and she had to step off of it or else she was going to jump. She he had to move.

"Don't take this wrong but I can only cuddle for so long."

Colin tried to feign being upset about it, but as much as he loved the feel of Naomi against him, lying like that with arms wrapped around each other, Colin was also feeling his arm go numb. As Naomi moved away from him Colin felt the blood returning to his arm. He watched as she moved away, not much, but far enough that they were no longer touching. In an almost deliberate manner, Naomi arranged some of the pillows behind her and sat propped up in the bed, next to him, but again, not touching. Colin couldn't help but notice a strange expression on her face, a tightness that hadn't been there before. To Colin, Naomi looked like she didn't know if she wanted to laugh or cry.

"What's it like living in California, in Sonoma wine country?" she asked.

Colin adjusted himself on the pillows. As he considered her question, he propped up next to Naomi but respected her unspoken request for space. He never really thought about where he lived all that much. It was just where he ended up, sort of a default setting.

As for talking about where he lived, as a personal rule he didn't like to tell people where he lived, he didn't want people bothering him, complicating his life. The only people he actually had a meaningful conversation with were the people he knew, the people already living in the area. Colin started to think maybe he wasn't such a good neighbor. He didn't know much about the lives and interests of the people he waved to across the street from him.

Even those few people he did socialize with, Colin never asked them personal questions. Any information they brought to a conversation, they offered of their own volition. Colin always did his best to avoid those intimate conversations. Those interchanges required sharing feelings and emotions and telling stories and history about who you were and how did you get to where you were. Colin didn't like those conversations. Those conversations only led to complications and complications were not simple. In that line of meandering mansplaining thought, Colin realized he never thought about what it was like to live where he lived.

"I don't know. Nice, I guess. Sort of expensive, but it's not as bad as all the news articles say it is. I like the north over the south. They're all crazy down there in L.A. and San Diego, the big city life. I guess I'm still a small town, rural country boy at heart."

Naomi laughed at his small-town comment. Not a funny story laugh, but a small sharp sardonic laugh. He glanced at her. She still seemed a little distant about something. Colin wanted to ask. He wanted to let her know he was there. Not just right there in bed with her, but always there in her life.

Then the possible answer came to Colin, did he have the right to be *there* for Naomi? What was he to her? He had never been her boyfriend. He wasn't her husband. They were two friends that because of an amazing kiss ended up in bed together. *What about Margo?* The thought no sooner was formed than Naomi's hand drifted across his arm.

"Why didn't you ever come back? Come back home, even to visit?"

Her voice was quiet and small; the question was loud and big. Colin took a breath, a big loud breath. He had told

Naomi some of the shit about his life growing up. The constant tormenting, the threats, the random acts of violence all of which were juxtaposed by supportive nurturing, friendly enthusiasm and lavish gifts. It was a vicious form of love. Naomi knew about it, but that wasn't what she was asking.

"I don't know. I guess I didn't know how."

"I understand."

"You do? My answer was a little cryptic."

"You didn't know what was waiting, if there was anything here for you. There was a big unknown and don't take this wrong but I think besides all that, you were scared."

Colin turned to look at Naomi, she was passively looking out the window. She knew he had just turned, his body reacting to her statement, ready to challenge her. So, instead of facing him to defend her statement, she turned away and left him to face it on his own. Colin looked at her profile of her head and wanted to be upset. He wanted to deny her the satisfaction and prove her wrong. Colin wanted Naomi to face him.

Even though they were inches from each other, Naomi was no longer there and Colin was alone. Colin tried to think of something to say and then wondered why his hands hurt. He looked down and realized he was clenching the sheets and blankets, his knuckles white.

Naomi had just cut him. No, she didn't something so simple as to cut him, she ripped him open. She knew how to do it. He had never held back from her, told her more, the intimate details, things even Margo didn't know because Colin knew Naomi would never tell anyone, or use the knowledge against him. Or so he thought until just that moment.

Scared!

Colin wanted to leave. He was done. He could just leave. What was here for him anyway? Naomi? Naomi was never going to be his. He dreamt about it. He had lived his teenage years in the lie of pretending that one day she would just look at him as he looked at her, that she would somehow know, even though he had never told her, she was supposed to know how much he had loved her. Because why wouldn't she know? They were together all the time. Why did he have to say those things back then; those words and feelings he so openly shared now. And if he did say them now, when once again they couldn't do anything about it except have an affair. Why didn't he shout those feelings to her back then when his fantasies could have been their world?

Colin felt the weight of everything life had given him. All the weight he had been given to carry and instead of putting it down, dropping it and saying he was done with that shit, Colin found himself adding more and more to his burden.

He was no longer able to carry it.

He knew why he had left.

He knew why he had never come back.

With Naomi's comment Colin found he couldn't carry the weight anymore and he felt everything crash down around him. The emotional wreckage lay around him, never to be completely picked up and put back on his shoulders to continue to carry around. Colin looked at all those broken damaged memories and found the one he was looking for, the defining moment.

"Once. I think I was eight or so. My father came home a little drunker than usual. A little angrier than usual. I forget all the details, so many of those times just blended in together. Maybe I just don't want to remember? I do know, from that night, I can still see and hear it all. I still feel what it did to me. This time my father came home from the bar in his authoritative man of the house mode. When he was in that mindset he always felt the need to teach someone, anyone in his way, a lesson on who was in charge. That night it my mother. -Yell!- She needed to remember who the boss was. -Push!- Who brought home the paycheck. -Shove!- Who paid for their food! -Slap!- Who put clothes on their backs! -Hit!- Who was in charge of the house! -Punch!- Mother needed to know who the man was! -Slam!-"

Colin felt his hands clenching the sheets again, the bed shaking around him. Colin kept his eyes locked forward, the million-mile stare through the walls and out into his past. He wasn't sure if Naomi had turned back to him or not. He hoped she was still looking out the window at the rain. It was easier without having to see her eyes. But as his hands gripped harder onto the bed, the sheets knotting between his clenched fingers, he felt a small, warm soft hand on top of his right one, resting there, covering it, being there.

"Naomi, I can still hear her screaming."
Colin found a sardonic and effacing laugh come from his broken voice.

"This may sound funny considering my height, but I used to be able to get into really small places."

"Mother yelled at us, my older brothers and sister and me, to run and hide before father went after us, before everyone needed to be taught a lesson. I had found a special place in the basement. Back behind the clutter of basement crap; the various boxes where holiday decorations were kept; old clothes that no longer fit, but had yet to be gotten rid of; miscellaneous toys and junk and life packed up and stored for another day. I had made a secret fort down behind all of it. I'm sure it wasn't that secret, but it was to me, and it was that night. I hid in there for hours. Even after the screaming and yelling, the swearing and the pleading, the anger and the anguish, when all of it had stopped and the house lay wounded and silent; after all that ended, I didn't come out. I wasn't sure if I could. I wasn't sure if I knew how. I was so afraid."

Colin felt numb. He knew Naomi's hand was on his, but he no longer felt his hands. He no longer could feel his body. All there was, the only sensation was the warm wetness moving down his cheeks.

"You're right. I didn't come home because I was scared. I left because I was scared. That's why I never told you anything about how I felt. I never shared my feelings, my love for you. I was so confused. So conflicted. I didn't know if was more afraid of telling you I love you and possibly learning you didn't love me back, or maybe even worse, finding out you loved me as much as I loved you. Because then you would have learned all the shit about my family. What went on. What it had done to me. If you would have told me you loved me, I think a part of me would have died because back then there was a part of me that just wanted to leave. And if you would have told me you loved me, I never would have been able to leave you. I was never going to be able to get away."

The hand resting on his squeezed so hard. It was holding him, grabbing on and pulling him up from the emotional wreckage piled around him. Pulling him free from emotional wreckage piled on him. Naomi was there with him and once again proving what she always told him, she was stronger than he was. Colin felt her arms around him, drawing him against her. Colin's head found that place along her shoulder and neck, that place where it was meant to fit and her hand held his head, as he held her. She was warm and strong.

"I'm sorry. I wish you would have told me. We would have figured it out. I would have helped you."

"You're right. I am scared. I'm still scared. I've lived my life that way. I don't think I ever really came out from behind those boxes."

"You didn't have to tell me any of that, but I'm glad you did."

Her lips were warm and soft against his forehead, the numbness forced back from her touch. His hand pushing back against the tears catching on his whiskers.

"It's okay. I wanted to tell you. I've tried to tell you several times. All those recent times when we talked, and I would say stupid things to you that I knew I shouldn't. When it was just us and I felt safe. Like I do now. I needed you to know why I didn't try harder back when it mattered. When we could have had more than just this."

Colin moved away from Naomi, her embrace softened, moving with him. He brushed away the errant tears still finding their way down his face. Colin looked at Naomi. Her eyes. Her blue eyes the shade of winter ice surrounded by the summer brilliance of blonde sun. Colin felt his heart break and mend in the same instant.

What had Hemmingway said about love? When two people love each other there can be no happy end to it. Colin thought about that, love and happiness, maybe Hemmingway had been right? Colin mentally looked at how much happiness love had given him. Then again, what did Hemmingway know? He felliated a shotgun.

"Naomi?"

"Yes?"

"Would it be alright if I kissed you"?

"Shut up you goof."

Once again, the kiss was perfect. Naomi's lips were soft and warm and like before, their kiss held everything that was good in the world. In that kiss as the rain and storm slashed against the hotel, Colin found he wasn't afraid anymore.

Naomi hadn't meant to go that far with her accusation against him. In her heart she never meant to try and hurt him. She wasn't a vindictive person. Naomi hadn't realized her verbal jab landed so hard. She had never known Colin's life had been that bad. Not that Colin was the only one with a shitty home life. There were other kids in their school that lived in similar situations. Possibly even worse. But she didn't care about them. Naomi only cared about Colin.

He had suggested, implied, but never directly described what those moments of his life were like. She hadn't expected the haunted edge in his voice. Some of those memories that still lived with him as if they were fresh and new. Still filled with all the sounds and smells and emotions as if they just happened.

Now Naomi felt bad for what she had said. She tried to never speak in anger or with inflamed emotions. She didn't like to talk at those times because she knew from experience there would be consequences to what she was going to say. Those words were coming from her internal defensive mechanism. When she started feeling vulnerable. When she let someone get to close and she felt herself losing control of her emotions. When that happened, which was rare because Naomi always did her best to always be in control of her emotions, but when it did happen, Naomi started putting up her hard edges.

Naomi hated her hard edges. Her defensive armor. She forged it on the day she decided to leave her first husband. It protected and insulated her. It let her face the coming future with a cold hard courage. It was a promise to herself to never end up in a situation like that again.

When she and Colin talked on the phone and Colin would joke about the two of them running away on a cross-country road trip, stopping at all the stupid and touristy roadside attractions, like the largest ball of twine, or biggest cast iron skillet; Naomi warned him he would grow tired of her before they made it a hundred miles. That he thought she was soft and all warm and cuddly like a puppy. She told him, warned him, she had hard edges and she wasn't soft and fluffy like a puppy. She had hard pointed quills like a porcupine except she didn't have a soft vulnerable underbelly. She was completely covered in quills. Or at least that was what she told herself.

The problem was, she did have a chink in her armor. She did have a soft underbelly. And Colin without ever knowing he could, he knew how to exploit her weakness. He did it by just being honest with her. He openly shared his thoughts and feelings. He never tried to exploit her feelings. He never tried to gaslight her. He was just being her friend.

And because they had become so close, Naomi found herself doing something she wasn't supposed to do. She fell in love with Colin. He was in her head as much as he was in her heart. And maybe that was why Naomi had just said what she said. She was trying to push back. Trying to get control of her heart again. So, she confronted Colin. She pushed him. She told him he was scared.

The stab of accusation at Colin, was just as much a stab at herself. Naomi was scared of Colin. She was scared of her feelings for him. She was scared because he could always get past her defenses. He could melt her icy heart and get to her soft underbelly. Colin knew how to make her feel vulnerable. And being vulnerable was something she had promised herself she would never be again. She would never be a victim.

Naomi relaxed into the bed. Letting the sound of the rain soothe her. Letting the warm comfort of the room envelope her. She relaxed into Colin and lowered her defenses.

"I understand. Rick, my first husband, you remember him?"

Colin nodded. His eyes and mouth subconsciously tightening.

"Rick would push me. He never hit me. He would physically move me around. He would manipulate me. He knew how to gaslight me. He could make me think I was the crazy one. That I was seeing things that weren't there, or what I was seeing wasn't what I thought it was. I was a stupid little girl with a head full of stupid little girl fantasies. Because of that, it was easy for him to manipulate me to make me feel small and weak, keep me off balance and unsure of myself. And if I started to wake up, to see the world I was really living in and start to take back my control, he would push me."

Naomi saw the tightness around Colin's face become more pronounced. She knew he had never liked Rick. The few times the two had met was always an unsteady and tense situation. Rick would become overly protective to the point of acting like he owned her. Colin would glower and play the part of Naomi's friend because she knew Colin didn't want to make her upset.

"One time he was pretty high, and I was mad about something, probably how he once again wasted money on drugs when there wasn't any food. I yelled at him. We yelled a lot. But I guess that time I yelled harder and louder and stronger than usual. I was opening my eyes and seeing past my self-imposed little girl fantasies to the see the realty of my life. I had started to feel confident again because I was getting tired of living like we were living; like poor white trailer trash. He came at me. He started yelling accusations and started pushing me again. Except that time, he pushed me harder than usual, and I fell backwards over the couch, hitting my head and twisting my wrist."

Naomi found it still bothered her to talk about it. What it took for her to realize she needed to finally get away from that life. Everyone around her, well not everyone, but enough people around her had told her to leave Rick before it came to that moment. They kept presenting facts to her, but Naomi didn't want to see the facts. She only wanted to see what she thought she wanted to see.

Then came the day she was forced to look at her life. From that day forward, she made a promise to herself to never be manipulated or used that way again. No matter what, her life was once again going to be her life. She was going to see the facts and not be swayed by emotion or easy talk. That was when Naomi first started finding her quills, her hard corners, her armor.

"He tried to make me think it was my fault. I had forced him to do it. He had to push me. Even angry and high he knew just what words to say and the tone of voice to use to start to sway my resolve, like he was hypnotizing me. The sad part was, before that day I would have let him. There I was on the floor, hurt and scared and crying and he was trying to convince me all of that was my fault and he needed to push me before I hurt him. That I was about to attack him and he was defending himself. Through the pain and the tears, I realized I was nothing to him except a puppet to be used and played with whenever and however he wanted. The next morning when he left for work, I called my friends and I left."

Naomi put her hand on Colin's hand as she looked at his angry face. He still wanted to be her hero.

"I didn't tell you that to make you angry, or for any reason other than to let you know I understand. I know what we can do to ourselves. What we let others do to us and what it takes to let it go. Together, here, we can let it go."

"I'm sorry," he said.

"About what?" she replied.

"About not trying harder. About not being there. For leaving you."

"Colin, you were always there. Even when you weren't, you were always here."

Naomi pointed to her heart.

Naomi felt a stillness come between them. It was that moment, the pause in the rain, as one storm cloud diminished, emptied, a new one drifted down to take its place. His eyes were so brown. But there were also flecks of green in them, buried. Naomi wondered what he saw in her eyes?

"Colin?"

"Yes."

"Can I kiss you?"

"Shut   up   you   goof."

Chapter 14

They didn't kiss. They laughed. Naomi felt it come out of her, uncontrolled and uninhibited. Naomi laughed so hard she thought she might pee. And that made her laugh even harder. For the second time that day Naomi had thought about peeing the bed and now that was funny too. The laughter became cathartic and soon they didn't know why they were laughing and they didn't know how to stop. All of the pent-up emotions and feelings were coming out. Naomi thought of the saying, something about if ya didn't laugh you would cry.

And instead of crying, they were laughing. Then for some reason Naomi thought it would be both funny and fun to hit Colin with a pillow. He returned the favor. The laughter continued along with their naked pillow fight. Several minutes later, tired, their laughter subsided, they sat on opposite sides or the bed wearing fatigued smiles. The rain had started again. It was all good.

"I need some water. Colin you're closer. Gimp, bring your mistress her water."

Naomi tried to take a stern expression and tone, as if she were a dominatrix. But her face was still tired from all the laughing. Her mouth seemed frozen in a smile and she had to work her jaws and rub her cheeks to get her face to relax.

Doing that made her want to start laughing again. Not wanting to start all over, she distracted her thoughts from being silly and instead looked at the naked figure of Colin. It worked. It worked a little too well. Naomi found herself for the third time that morning wondering if Colin was in working condition. She decided to test the situation.

"You're the strong independent woman. You get the water."

"Fine, I will."

Colin watched as Naomi dramatically stood and sashayed from the bed over to the water bottles on the dresser. Placing both her hands on the dresser, she slightly bent forward and pushed her ass out, flashing her bare butt cheeks at him. With a flick of her hip, she took a bottle of water from the dresser top.

Colin thought about quickly moving over and playfully biting her on one of the lean, pale cheeks. Instead, he just watched. Watched as she flashed him. Watched as she hinted at him with little shakes and twists of her shoulders and hips. Colin watched as Naomi slowly, seductively, erotically, almost pornographically lowered herself onto the bed, sinking into the mattress.

Watching as she slowly curved and turned her back. Her left leg coming up, her left shoulder turning, her soft, small round breast with a small pink nipple now seen as the arm moved around to hold herself. Then Naomi lowered her left side onto the bed. The front of her body coming to rest against Colin's right side. Naomi was warm. Her skin was so soft. Colin, again, felt his heart start to hurt. He knew what he wanted to do, but it seemed a few more minutes were needed. Getting older had its advantages as well as disadvantages.

"Can I have a drink of that?"

"Okay. Open your mouth."

Colin watched with disgust as Naomi took a big drink of water, held it in her mouth and looked at him while trying not to laugh.

"No! Gross. I'm not a baby bird!"

Naomi swallowed the water as she started to laugh and cough. She found the expression of disgust on Colin's face to be priceless. In a disgusted way, Naomi almost wished he would have let her do it. Naomi thought it would have been funny to dump the water all over his face. Trying to control her laughing and coughing she passed the water bottle to Colin.

"After what we've done today. You think that's gross. Do you know where your mouth has been?"

They both smiled at her comment.

"Yes, yes I do know where it's been. I also know where yours has been. But I'm still only drinking from the bottle if that's okay with you?"

"Says the man who still kisses me."

"Says the woman who still kisses me."

They laughed again. Naomi didn't know how he did it? He always seemed to be able to get inside her defenses. He knew how to melt her icy heart. Maybe he didn't know how? Maybe she let him? Either way Colin had once again found his way back under her defenses. He did it without even trying. Looking at him, she could feel herself becoming lost in all the emotions and Naomi felt her heart start to hurt again.

"Tell me something amazing. Something about where you live?"

Taking another drink, Colin turned and looked at Naomi. He handed the bottle back to her. Taking the offered bottle, Naomi noticed on Colin's lower lip hung a final, single drop of water. Naomi moved to moved to lick it off. She thought she would not just lick it off, she would bite as well. That lower lip definitely needed a good, but gentle, bite.

Positioning herself to spring forward, Colin ruined his soon to be fun by errantly wiping the drop away. Disappointed at the fun Colin had missed Naomi drank some water. She hoped a drop of water might hang from her lip and Colin would notice. Maybe he would do something similar as she would do to him. Before she could get to far in her imagined scenario of Colin licking and biting her lip, he disappointed her by responded to her question.

"Like what?"

Naomi knew Colin was now distracted by her question and even if there was some water hanging from her lip he would not notice.

"Something amazing. Maybe something special no one knows about?"

Naomi took another thirsty drink. However, even if Colin had failed to notice the water on his lip or the possible water on hers, it didn't matter. Naomi had seen his, and the thought of it was still with her. Knowing they still had some time, Naomi eased her drinking, she didn't want a lot of water sloshing around. Colin's eyes became distant, drifting to look upward. His face thoughtful, eyelids narrowing as he searched through some old memory files, moving stacks around, looking for the one particular special piece of information for Naomi. His face tightened as his lips pursed; the searching was becoming intense. Naomi could see Colin wanted to find something special for her, maybe it was something he had almost forgotten about. She became excited to know what he would find for her. The silent stillness hung between them as he thought.

"Okay. I've sent you pictures of the mountains around the area, right?"

Naomi thought about it. Yes, he had sent her pictures. The pictures Colin had sent were of grassy green mountains with a few trees and some rocky outcroppings. She liked the pictures. The reminded her of hiking around the Superior National Forest up along the North Shore of Lake Superior. Except Colin's mountains were not covered by trees and rocks and waterfalls. They were gentle slopes rolling upward to grass covered vistas of the surrounding vineyards and fields.

"Yes. I remember them."

"Okay. Something no one knows about and something amazing. I climbed one of those mountains once."

Colin smiled at her, nodding his head as if to suggest what he had done was something amazing.

"I can leave ya know."

"I thought it was funny."

Naomi started to get up. Intending it to be a joke. But moving from the bed, acting like she was going to leave, Naomi started to think she should. The action drove the thought process. She did have to leave. She had to get home. There was stuff there she could do. There was always something at home she needed to do because no one else was going to do it. Afterall she and Colin had had their fun, their moment, what else was there? Mixed in with those thoughts Naomi also understood why she was feeling that way, the *I should leave now* feelings.

Colin was still inside her defenses. He was too close. And maybe, thought Naomi, that was the most important reason of all why she should leave. Even with that moment of sarcasm, the veiled threat which she initially had no intention of going through with, in that moment, her defenses instinctively started to go back up, to close her off from the world.

Naomi stood, her resolve, her armor becoming stronger as she took a step away from the bed. Then she heard Colin's voice. Out of reflex—maybe—Naomi turned to look at Colin. He was sitting there on the bed. His waist and legs covered by sheets, his knees loosely crossed, half up, making a sort of tent. His upper body, leaning forward, his left arm loosely resting on his knees, his right hand patting the bed, the spot she just vacated. His stupid lopsided smile, the little flash of his teeth, the flash of light off his brown eyes; the sound of the rain against the window.

"Okay, there's more. Sit back. Relax. Trust me."

Chapter 15

Naomi's armor was incomplete. The seams were still open. There were still chinks. Weaknesses she hadn't been able to strengthen, and Colin once again went through her armor as if it wasn't there and found his way into her heart. Naomi wanted to hate the fact she couldn't defend herself against him, maybe. Naomi knew part of the Colin situation was that he trusted her. He held nothing back. He didn't try to sweet talk her. He didn't try to use or manipulate her.

First and foremost, Colin was her friend. Because of that friendship she trusted Colin absolutely. Because of that friendship and trust Naomi knew her defensive quills, her hard corners, her armor was useless against him. And Naomi was comfortable and accepting of that one weakness, but she could never let Colin know about it. As long as the rain was coming down, this day was theirs and theirs alone. Naomi had said it to Colin several hours ago. It was her decision to make. It wasn't anyone else's, it was hers. In her decision, Naomi felt strong again. Even if her armor was useless against Colin, it didn't matter. Naomi was stronger, and the decision was still hers to make as she wanted.

Naomi would return, not unwilling, to the bed, to Colin. But she was also going to reward herself and punish Colin by giving him what he wanted. Naomi turned to go back to the bed. For fun she once again sashayed as she walked; she knew what it would do to Colin. With a questioned look on his face, Naomi moved her pillows down, and adjusted them; one for her head and one for her feet. She then got back onto the bed and laid face down, her arms tucked under her head pillow.

"For being a smart-ass, you are going to rub my shoulders, back, and butt. If, you try anything stupid with my butt, I leave. No questions asked. You know my feelings about the porn fueled stupidity that causes men to think women like things up their ass. They don't. At least not me. But I do like to have my ass cheeks rubbed. Along with the shoulders and back. So, get to work and start talking."

Naomi relaxed as she felt the bed shift and then Colin's hands were once again on her body. He was once again painting her skin. It was nice. Colin may be able to get through her armor, but Naomi also knew she could get through his.

In fact, Naomi was pretty sure if she really tried; if she didn't hold back, she could use Colin's feelings for her as a weapon. Naomi knew she could probably make Colin do anything she wanted. In that deviant and manipulative thought that Naomi knew she would never, could never do that to Colin. He really did love her that much. He trusted her that much that. He didn't even try to put on armor against her. Naomi suddenly felt like crying again. She couldn't understand why someone would love her that much. And although she didn't understand why, Naomi knew Colin did love her that much.

It made her feel comfortable, safe, and warm.

Like when she was a little girl and on a cold snowy day she would lay on the floor. Positioning herself between where her father was sitting and reading and just close enough to the wood stove to be warm, but not too hot. There on her blanket, in the perfect spot, she would read or draw until lulled by the warmth of the fire and the safety of her father she would fall asleep. Oh, to be a little girl like that again. Naomi's body relaxed under Colin's touch, and she found herself hoping by the time he was done with his story, rubbing her body, he would be ready to do something else with her body. If there was still time.

"Okay. Let me know if the pressure is too much. And, so I won't be penalized for straying too close to the off-limits area, how about a little warning sound?"

Naomi gave a little snort. It seemed men could learn. They just had to be motivated to want to learn.

"Oh, you'll know."

"Thanks."

Colin pressed into the little knots along her neck and shoulders. It was almost better than sex, almost.

"So, yes, one day I climbed one of the hills. I had always wanted too. I thought it would be fun to look down at the valley. There was a specific mountain I wanted to climb, it's part of what's called Sugar Loaf Ridge."

Naomi made a little, "ahmmm" sound to let him know she was still listening. Which she was, but his hands moved with a practiced ease and her flesh was responding.

"Anyway, in the fall the weather can get cold at night and temperature inversions happen. Cold air blows in from the San Francisco Bay and mixes with all the hot air raising from the sunbaked floor of the Sonoma valley. That situation causes clouds to form over the mountains. From the valley floor you can stand and watch it happen. The clouds form so close to the top of the mountain, as if you would be able to reach up and grab them. I watched it happen so many times and I always wanted to be up there to experience it. So, one day I did."

The massage suddenly no longer mattered. How good it felt became forgotten. Naomi turned to look at Colin as he sat propped up next to her. His arms and legs and other parts so close. But the idea of sitting in clouds appealed to Naomi. She loved the rainy foggy days. Many times, on her way home from work, Naomi would stop at a park not far from her home. Over the years she had come to spend many hours, probably several years' worth of time walking that park. She had spent so much time there, knew every trail, every side path probably better than the park maintenance staff. Naomi came to think of the park as hers.

Those long tedious, stressful days of work, she could lose all of them in the park. On the weekends the park became a minivacation. Starting in the morning going well into the afternoon, Naomi explored the trails and chose the pathes less taken. Naomi loved being in the park at any time, but she loved the evening walks most of all.

In the evenings when the sun was low and heavy in the sky, the air with just a hint of movement with light breeze, Naomi would walk to the pond. The water surface a liquid reflection of trees and sky shimmered and rippled as life moved over it.

The pond was always busy with muskrats swimming back and forth, working on their home. Ducks would be paddling about, their heads dipping down to eat some grass, their butts sticking up. Frogs croaking their songs. Birds diving through air attacking swarms of bugs circling about the water. Standing there watching all the life around her, Naomi waited for the fog.

As the temperature cooled, she would watch the air over the water thicken, the moisture coalescing and the water's surface reaching, transitioning to something magical. Soon the ducks and muskrats drifted from sight with only quiet splashes of water to signal their presence. And when the fog was heavy enough, thick and full, the slight movement of the air would carry it out to the shore, to where she stood waiting. On a good evening, the pond would become completely covered by the fog, concealed in it. Then the fog would drift up off the ponds and out onto the trails where Naomi stood waiting for it to reach her. She would stand still and let her legs become lost in the mist.

"What was it like, to be there in the clouds?"

"Amazing!"

"Tell me more. Everything!"

Chapter 16.

Colin's lopsided grin was back. His stupid lopsided grin with the salt-and-pepper rough stubble beard. It was no fair that men aged so well, at least he was. Naomi decided to secretly love and hate him for that.

"It was a long time ago. I had just finished art school and was trying to find my place in the world, a job as an artist. I was trying to start a life out there in California. I decided I would climb that mountain and figure it out. So, I packed up some stuff. Some easy quick food and water and other stuff."

"Like what food? What other stuff?"

Colin smiled and cleared his throat a little bit. It was an embarrassed sort of sound.

"Mainly I brought some cheap granola bars and a shitty bottle of wine 'cause they're all I could afford", again the embarrassed throat clearing.

"What?" Naomi smiled at him. "Did you bring a girl up there with you. Did you fuck on the mountain with the clouds all around you?"

As Naomi said the words, she also imagined it, excited by it, became lost in it. She sometimes thought about having sex in the fog, but it was never heavy enough to hide what would be going on from the world.

"No nothing like that. I was alone. I needed to think. Besides I wasn't dating anyone. To be honest I went up there because I was thinking about coming back to Minnesota. I wasn't finding anything there in Valley. And what I brought with were several joints."

Naomi laughed at him as best she could as she lay on her belly.

"You got high on a mountain. Your head figuratively and literally in the clouds."

Colin started laughing. Apparently, it sounded as funny to him as it did to Naomi. She could feel the laughter in his hands as he continued to almost absently rub her back, slowly working his way down.

"No. Actually I didn't even open the wine."

"Liar."

Naomi felt a light slap on her ass. It wasn't firm, it didn't hurt, if anything it surprised and even a little bit, excited her. Then his hands were massaging her again.

"No, I'm not lying. Let me tell you and you'll understand."

Naomi wanted to say something about his little slap, his spank, but she wanted to hear more about the clouds. Plus, she still sort of liked it. Stupid Colin. Without even trying he still found her weaknesses.

"I'll spare you the uneventful details of my hot, sweaty hike to where I wanted to go."

Naomi thought about asking for the details, but did she really need them? She wanted to know about the clouds.

"I made it to the summit of the peak furthest from the trailhead. I knew the one I wanted. It was sort of special in a way and I knew exactly how the clouds would form, what they would do.

It was this peak I would always watch from below, down at the base of the range. I would park in the town of Kenwood, by the stop light on highway twelve. I would wait there in the evening just to watch the clouds form. Sometimes I had a glass of wine, sometimes not. But I always sketched the mountain and the clouds. I had so many drawings and pictures of that mountain I became a little obsessed. One day the woman at the tasting room where I would get the glass of wine asked me why I didn't go up there and draw what it looked like."

"When I stood up there at the top, I looked down at Kenwood. I imagined I could see myself standing down there, like an echo or shadow. The echo me was standing there by the stop light looking back up at the now me. My timing wasn't bad. I found my spot, took out my sketch book and finished one rough drawing when I felt the cold air start move in from the bay."

Naomi wanted to ask more questions about it, what Colin saw, what he drew, she wanted the intimate details, but he seemed far away and as he was telling his story Naomi found he was bringing her with. He also had forgotten about actually rubbing her back and was now just loosely running his hands over her body, which at this point happened to be her ass cheeks. And that absent movement felt delicious. And the narrative was loose and imaginative. And Naomi felt herself start to melt away into something and someone else.

"Besides the other stuff, I also knew it would get wet and cold, so I brought a sort-of raincoat. I was about to take out the food and wine and the weed and settled in. But before I could the subtle, little changes in air became not-so subtle and big. You can feel everything as it happens. The change in pressure and temperature, the movement of the air. It affects your entire body. Even though I was hungry and thirsty, and I thought about the weed, those thoughts became lost when the clouds came down. I forgot about everything as it started to happen. I guess the term or the idea I'm looking for is, it was spiritual, or Zen. I forgot about everything and there was only that moment. I looked around me and the damp air started settle on the now cooling grass. The clouds started to form above me. Starting thin and wispy, soon they were like a heavy white pillowy fog. They were just above my head."

He stopped. Naomi wondered why Colin stopped telling the story. Naomi decided that she was glad she hadn't left when she had threatened it. She would have missed this moment, the story. She wanted Colin to finish it. She wanted him to finish it for two reasons.

"It's funny." Colin's voice was distant.

"What's that?" Naomi asked hushed. As if her voice would break the silent poetry of the clouds. She didn't want Colin to bring them back from his story, not yet.

"As I think about those clouds again. They were a lot like fog, but yet different. I can't explain it right. It's just, just—I don't know. Anyway, I guess it's something you just have to do to understand."

"I get that. Keep talking. Tell me more, what happened next."

"The clouds started become thick and heavy with moisture, you could feel it. I opened my mouth and I could taste the clouds, breath them in.

Without thinking, excited by the thought of tasting clouds, Naomi interrupted the story. Turing to look at Colin as she spoke.

"Like the reverse of your breath in the cold winter air. Where we pretend, we're smoking when exhaling. The warm breath freezing in the air."

Colin smiled down at her. Naomi thought of how she would love to wake up every morning to his smile.

"Yes, like the reverse of that. So, as they became heavier, they became denser and en mass started to descend. They flowed down around me. Everything became wet and cold, and soon every object around me was gone. I was lost in the clouds. I couldn't see the ground I was standing on. When I was a kid, just a naïve child, my mother would point up at the clouds and tell me that was where Heaven was. That God, Jesus, and all the angels were up there looking down on me and so I had to be good. I had to be very good. I had to be better. I couldn't be like everyone else, especially father. If I wasn't good and behave myself then God and Jesus would punish me. She told me Heaven and God were in the clouds and didn't I want to live so I could go there when I die? As life went on, I came to realize the hypocrisy of that lie."

There Colin paused a moment. He paused talking. He paused moving his hands. Naomi wasn't sure, but she thought he may have paused in his breathing. He became still. His eyes were distant. Somewhere else, someplace she couldn't go. In a personal way, Naomi wasn't sure if she would want to go there. Quietly she pondered if parents really understood what they did to their children. Colin blinked, glanced at her, and with a wink of an eye he was back.

"But that day, it almost felt, it was like if there is a god and whatever god is, well it felt like God was there. The air was still, heavy with silence. The clouds became thicker and heavier as they moved down the mountain side, through the draws and over the fingers. I was soon covered by dew, it dripped from me. I could hear the drops falling from my hair to my sleeves to the ground; a gentle rain like sound. I don't know how to better explain it.

It was like for that moment, while I was stood there silent and still, Nature let me in on its secret. It was just a little peek. In that one moment I wasn't just another human scrambling about trying to figure out how to make lots of money. I wasn't threatening and fighting other people around me. I forgot about all the shit which is ingrained into the soulless dogma of society. I became nothing more than a cloud and it was everything."

Naomi lost in the story, in the imagination of the being there, that she didn't hear the little plopping sounds coming from her pillow. It took her a minute to realize she was crying. She wanted to move to wipe the tears away before Colin could see them, before she had to acknowledge them. Naomi knew if she moved, if she tried to hide how the story affected her, Colin would stop to ask her what was wrong and Naomi didn't want that. She wanted to stay in the clouds. She wanted to stay in them forever. She let the rain come down.

"I know it was only a couple minutes, but I thought it was hours. Then just as slowly as it began, it faded. It was just as strange. I could see everything above me, but nothing below. Even my feet were still lost in the clouds. I imagined that if I really believed, deep in the core of my being, if I held to the purity of the thought, I could start walking across the sky, across the clouds. They would support me and as long as I had the clouds to walk on, I could go where ever I wanted to go. Then the clouds were below me and I stood on the top of an island mountain surrounded by a sea of puffy swirling amorphous ocean of whites. Around me, the world's light started to fade as the sunset and the night sky filled with constellations of stars and all its quiet mysteries took hold. The clouds started to break up and thin as they settled down onto the valley floor. The night sky both dark and bright. I sat there for a while longer. Just looking at the stars, feeling them, the weight of the nothingness of everything."

Colin laughed after saying the nothingness of everything. Naomi took the opening and quickly wiped the tears away from her still glassy eyes. She tried to stop thinking, imaging being there. She didn't want the tears from coming back. She didn't want to let Colin see her when she was weak.

"What's so funny?" Naomi asked.

"That last part really sounded like hippy new-age crap."

"What did you do after that? How long did you stay there?"

"I don't know. It started to get cold and all my clothes were damp. I started to pack up the stuff I carried but never used when I made the mistake of looking up at the stars. They were so bright, they seemed so near, almost like the clouds had been as they formed over me.

Again, I thought if I could steady myself, focus all my energy and believe, I would have been able to reach up and touch one of those stars. I watched them move around me.

Occasionally I would see a shooting star and all I could do was watch it go. The idea of trying to figure out a wish was beyond me. At some point I was trying to figure out why everything was shaking, thinking there was a small tremor I realized I was shivering that hard from the cold. Not wanting to die of hypothermia or be killed, eaten, and pooped out by a hungry mountain lion I meandered my way back to my car and drove back to the house I was sharing with a bunch of buddies."

"What did you decide up there. What did you find?"

"I don't know what it was or where it came from. I just knew I wasn't going to give up on trying to be an artist. The next morning the guys were wanting my share of the rent money. I still didn't have it, so I gave them all my weed and booze and CDs in exchange for another two weeks. I called my instructor from art school and got some of my paintings into a student art show. Several weeks later I was doing commissions for a major vineyard owner in Napa Valley."

Naomi didn't have words. She had nothing. At some point Colin had forgotten about giving her a massage, or even pretending to give her one. His hands were absently moving around her lower back and butt, making small circles, barely touching her skin. Of all those places they would joke about going, like to Alaska, or glass roof cabins in Finland, right then Naomi knew there was one place she needed to go.

"I want to go up there? Up to the clouds? Could you show them to me?"

Chapter 17

"Anytime."

Naomi put her hands under her, pulled her legs forward, kneeling, brought her face next to Colin's. His face, his expression open and honest and Naomi knew he was serious. If she said to him, Let's go, right now! Let's forget about our lives and people and commitments. Let's go to the airport, fly to California and climb the mountain to stand in the clouds together.

Naomi knew in the marrow of her soul that if she said that to him, Colin would have done it without hesitation. His hand came up. The fingers brushed along her cheek, finding, gathering, collecting the loose strands of hair hanging down around her face and put them back behind her ear. She felt those tears again, the ones she lost in the clouds. They were close, too close and no recriminating words or thoughts would hold them back.

"Colin."

"Yes?"

"Hold me."

His arms wrapped around her. They were warm and lean. She hid her face against his neck. His body no longer smelled like Colin. Now it smelled of them. In her feeling of needing to hide from the tears and to hide from the cause of those feelings Naomi felt again the need to have Collin for her own. As her lips found his neck, his arms tightened around her. As her teeth found his ear lobe, his breath quickened. As they came together Naomi found the previous primal physical need was gone, supplanted by something new. Their first time they felt that burning desire to know each other in every physical intimate way. The second time, Naomi was still feeling the heat and the excitement from the first intoxicating act. She knew Colin had as well.

This time that initial need was absent. A quite, intimate passion had replaced it. The intoxication was still there, but subdued. By going beyond the physical act to their emotional connection, their honest love for each other Naomi again felt that feeling she hadn't felt in such a long time. Naomi felt young and what it was to be in love.
They did not rush.

They found and explored each other again with a slow easy tenderness. As their heat rose, once again Colin entered Naomi and she responded to his touch. As their bodies came together so did their hearts. As they did, Naomi allowed herself to acknowledge the bond between them was something more than she had ever imagined.

Lying next to each other. The heat from their bodies spilling out, warming the room. Their arms intertwined, holding the hand of the other. Naomi turned her head and looked at Colin. She could see him in profile. The side of his face seemed interesting to her. His nose was strange looking from her angle. Not that it was a strange looking nose, it was just how she was looking at it. It was like looking at a Picasso painting. His left eye seemed to register that she was looking at him and it moved to look at her. But again, it seemed odd, because she could only see the left eye. It was so brown. There were no flecks of any other color, just shades of brown. Colin turned and looked her. His face seemed right again. His nose fit, and didn't seem odd. She could see both his eyes. Both of his soft brown eyes.

"What?"

"Nothing. I was just looking at you is all."

"Why?"

"Because I want to remember you this way. I want to remember to make sure I remember everything about you from today."

Colin moved to open his mouth. He wanted to say the words he knew he shouldn't say. But once said those words could not be taken back. They could not be unheard. Those words spoken by the heart. Crafted in the marrow of his soul. The words his brain kept telling him he was not supposed to even think, much less say out loud. Somewhere in the conflict of emotion and rational thought Collin knew he should not tell Naomi how much he loved her and what she meant to him, he could not. What good would it do them?

Besides, Collin knew he would never speak those words because Naomi already knew them. Just as Collin knew Naomi's feelings for him even though she never spoke them. It was the connection between them, their intimate bond. Rationalizing his feelings, once again memorizing every intimate detail of Naomi she must have noticed. Collin was always told he did not have a good poker face.

"What were you going to say?"

"Oh. Nothing."

Naomi was close to him, her hand in intimate places. Colin felt that hand start to move. He was tired, and although one part of his body reacted, another one did not. It didn't matter to Naomi. She kept finding him, she was coercing him to tell her. Colin wanted to react, but he was so content, so peaceful he settled for an easy compromise.

"I was going to say you could take a picture."

It was a lie. It was a stupid lie. Take a picture? What the hell did that even mean? Of course, it was the best he could come up with while Naomi stared at him with her breasts exposed. However, Colin also applauded himself on his answer because he knew a picture of him was not going to happen. There would be no evidence of their day together.

Just like they deleted all their texts to each other. It didn't matter if their text conversations were just venting about their day or a sick game of "Would You Rather?" Where one of them came up with two horrible options the other had to choose from. Or personal confessions of shared emotions and secrets those times when they opened their hearts and trusted each other. What they shared, what they said to each other was for only them.

So, at the end of each day, before going home, before their individual *other* arrived, they deleted everything. And just like every day before this one, there would be no evidence it ever happened.

"I have a picture of you. You sent it from some big dinner party thing you were at. You were in your suit and tie and looking all dashing. But I don't want that dinner party Colin. He's not mine. He belongs to those people, in that place. I want *my* Colin. The one here with me now."

Colin understood. He wanted *his* Naomi as well. Naomi looked at Colin with a question obvious on her face. Naomi wanted to ask him something. From her expression it was important, it was serious. He wanted to know.

"Go ahead and ask."

Naomi's hand slid from under the covers where it was still touching him, up along his thighs and stomach to find a new resting spot against his chest. Playfully she pushed at him, a reproach for reading her expressions, her thoughts. Instead, after pushing at him, Naomi's hand stayed on his chest. It was warm and Colin was sure it could feel his heart beating.

"Alright. Since for as long as I've known you, and neither one of us are going to mention how long ago that was." Naomi gave Colin a warning smile after saying it. "I always knew you could draw. How come when I would come around, even when I would try and sneak up on you, and somehow you always knew, sometimes you would crumple up or hide some of your drawings and other times you didn't?"

Colin didn't get a chance to answer, he didn't need too. As soon as Naomi asked the question out loud. As she watched Colins face as she asked the question, she knew the answer. It was so obvious. Maybe that was why she missed it. She just thought Colin might have drawing stupid guy stuff like boobs. Of course, Colin's boob drawing would have been better than the standard circle in a circle with a dot in the middle drawn by the usual idiot teenage boy.

Naomi could still remember some of the tattoos Collin had drawn given some of the guys in school. But still, it wasn't like she would have minded if Collin had been drawing boobs. And maybe because the teenage boy bias in her teenage girl brain Naomi had missed what was always right before her.

"You were drawing me. Weren't you?"

Colin tried to turn away. Naomi gathered herself and pushed up onto her elbow, to look down on Colin. To not let him get away from her.

"I know I'm right. You would draw me and you didn't want me to know."

Chapter 18

Colin lay there. He had nowhere to go. He was naked before her. Naomi owned him. Naomi saw him. The brain fought hard to keep the heart from saying those thoughts and feelings it should not. To say those words which would only complicate their already complicated situation. The cold hard rational brain fought hard, but finally the heart won control and the complicated truth came out.

"Yes, I used to draw you. I've always drawn you. I've never stopped."

Colin fought against the tightness in his eyes and chest. He could feel the warm crystalline glaze forming on his eyes. He blinked it back. The heart may have control, but the brain was going to try and keep some level of dignity.

"Why didn't you tell me? Why did you hide it from me?"

"I didn't want you to think I was some creepy stalker like that Every Breath song by the Police. Sitting around drawing pictures of you."

Naomi thought about that for a moment. She wanted to say she would have been flattered. But Colin was also sort of right. It would have been kind of creepy having someone sit and draw you all the time whether you were there or not. They were both kind of right.

"I guess I understand. But what do you mean you never stopped drawing me?"

Colin sat up and looked at Naomi.

"Do you trust me?"

Naomi sat up as well. She didn't hesitate in her answer.

"Yes."

"I need to take your picture. Just your face. I want to show you something."

Naomi hesitated. She was naked and he wanted to take her picture. She trusted Colin. But she didn't trust a smart phone. That last thing she wanted were pictures of her boobs on the internet.

"Just my face and then you delete it. Okay?"

"Deal. As always, delete everything."

Colin pulled back the sheet covering him, sat up and got out of bed. Without any sign of being self-conscience about being naked, Naomi watched him as he went to the desk and picked up his phone. She looked at his body. She liked what she saw. In fact, she was a little jealous; how come men just get better looking as the age and women just begin to sag? It was not fair.

She lost those thoughts as she watched his body as he walked back to the bed and lay next to Naomi. He tapped the camera app open and boxing the lens to just a small portion of her face, specifically her nose cheeks and eyes, he took the picture. Collin lay back and turned to show Naomi the picture.

"See, this is the picture I just took."

Naomi looked at it. All she saw were her nose, eyes and cheeks. Thankfully no boobs.

"Okay?"

"Get your phone and go to the web."

Naomi slid out of bed and Colin watched her go. He couldn't help it. It was Naomi. This was everything he had ever imagined it to be. It didn't matter to him the timing in their lives. It was Naomi and it was as close to perfect as it could be. She took her phone from her purse and came back to bed. She gave him a wink as she got to the side of the bed, turned and seductively climbed onto the bed. It wasn't very far to go, but Naomi was coming over to him, slowly, one hand forward, then the opposite leg, then the other hand, the other leg; one movement at a time.

Her face made almost a pouty seductive pursing of her lips and several torturous erotic moments later Naomi hovered over his face, moving to kiss him. Colin found himself pursing his lips, preparing to meet and return Naomi's kiss. Then right before their lips met, Colin felt Naomi's tongue move over his waiting lips. Before Colin could react, to catch Naomi in an embrace and kiss and lick her back, she moved away and casually, as if she didn't just do that, lick his lips, flopped down next to him on the bed.

"Okay. What am I supposed to look for?"

It took Colin several seconds to get his brain back on topic. Naomi could still turn him into a mindless goof unable to think straight if his life depended on it.

"Do an image search. Use my name with *Strawberry Blondes*."

Naomi typed the words into the search engine and waited. Soon there were a string of websites and images being offered. Several of the options were porn sites, along with several art sites and Colin's personal website. The images popping up were scantily clad women and several paintings. Colin touched one of the images on the screen and it opened to a painting of a woman.

She was beautiful. With green eyes, some light freckles across her cheeks and nose, her mouth just parted as if she was about to be kissed. Her hair was a perfect strawberry blonde color. Naomi thought of her childhood pictures; back when her hair was almost than color. Then, as she matured, her hair had lightened into more of a honey blonde, and now it was going silver blonde. Naomi refused to use the other color to describe her hair. But that beautiful strawberry blonde woman was standing in a field of sunflowers with petals that complimented or matched the color of the woman's hair.

Naomi looked at the picture, studying it. She touched the screen to make the picture bigger, until the image filled the screen of her phone. The picture was beautiful. She found it calming and relaxing. She loved sunflowers. They were so beautiful, so majestic yet lazy.

Naomi also liked paintings. She could look at them for hours as she could with flowers. One of her favorite things to do on weekends, when she could get Brad to go out, was to go to museums to look at all the different paintings and artwork. To Naomi the woman in the picture looked so calm, so serene. She blended in with sunflowers, almost one of them.

"I've never seen that painting before. When did you do it?"

Colin smiled at her. It was a coy, far away smile, as if he was reaching blind into dark closet looking for something, only able to use his fingers to locate it.

"Oh, that was one of my first, a very early painting. I think I started painting those several weeks after I came down from the mountain and the clouds. The first one sold almost immediately, almost before I had finished it, so I did several, a series of them. They helped me to get my start, my big break. They all sold well and I was able to eat and pay my bills that month. If you thought I was skinny back in high school, you should have seen me when I was a starving artist."

Colin laughed quietly to himself as he privately ruminated about those days in his past life. Naomi felt a pang of jealousy. She found she wanted to have been part of that life as well. It seemed Colin was barely able to keep a roof over his head, but his smile, the way he talked about his life back then. He was free. He had found something special. Something most people searched for their entire lives for and few ever finding it. Whatever he found that day in the clouds, it had set him free. She could see it in his expression now, as he looked at the picture. There was something about that picture. Naomi felt her woman's intuition tingling, she also knew Colin. She looked at his expression and she started to breakdown the case set before her.

"Who's the woman? The model."

The tone of her voice, the strength in it. How she had sounded when she spoke made it both question and an accusation. Naomi had caught him off guard. He had been somewhere else, some other time and place in his life, a different *when*. Colin, still looking at his past, paused with long exhale as he tried to find what he was looking for.

"That is Lynde Farrell."

Naomi knew it! Her suspicion was confirmed in the way Colin had to hesitate before saying the woman's name. In that paused instant Naomi found she wanted to hate the Lynde Farrell woman. Naomi wanted to hate Lynde Farrell because at the time Colin would have been painting Lynde, Naomi would have been finalizing her divorce. Her life, their lives, could have been so different if it weren't for that cunt.

"You fucked her, didn't you?"

Colin wasn't sure if it was Naomi's question, or her once again using the word fuck to describe sex. Either way she yanked him back to the present. Back into the room where they were both naked and sitting in bed together. He wasn't going to lie. Besides, Naomi already knew the answer before she asked him.

"Yes. I was younger then and just a little bit stupider than I am now, however, not by much."

Colin smiled as he deprecated himself. Naomi let it pass this time. Colin did that too much, put himself down. She knew he was joking as he said it, but she knew he was also serious. She understood why, but it didn't mean she had to accept it, or let him keep doing it.

"Have you ever heard the drug dealer adage of never do what you deal?"

Naomi nodded yes. She had heard it before.

"Well, that saying can also be applied to painters and their models. It's supposed to be a business arrangement. I call the agency and tell them what I want, and they send a girl over. They stand there, I paint them, end of the day they get a check. Purely business."

Colin paused, feeling Naomi's look. He knew what he had said, how it sounded, how it might make him look. He just said he contacted an agency to send him beautiful girls who would be paid to be naked. Colin wasn't about to try and defend the situation. It was a job. After all, just because someone did or did not take their clothes off for a living, everybody was still being paid by someone to do something for that person. At the end of the day, everybody was the same.

He returned the feel of Naomi's look. Colin knew she understood. He knew she was just trying to make him uncomfortable, to get him again, but not this time. He was on to Naomi's tricks.

"You know exactly what I'm saying. Don't try your legal word-trickery on me."

Naomi made a pouty face and stuck out her tongue at him.

"Spoiled sport. Continue with your story. I'll try and behave."

Colin winked at her and gave her the lopsided smile. She hated him for the now warm feeling she felt because of him.

"Okay, back to Lynde. Being young and stupid, and maybe a little lonely, and Lynde was so beautiful standing there in the sunflowers, the smell, the sun. I blame the sunflowers. After all it couldn't possibly be my fault."

Naomi had a quick—private—laugh at Colin blaming the sunflowers. It sounded so familiar to her for some reason. Stupid Prince. Stupid rain.

Colin took a breath, reached back once again, and instead of staying in the past with the memories he brought them forward to the present room.

"And for your information, Miss Smutty Mouth, it wasn't so much as fuck, but dated. Although, there were times. Lynde was quite—"

Colin thought about it, thought about those days with Lynde. "well, understand she was—"

Naomi was staring at him with dancing eyes, and smirking lips as he struggled to find the right, nice, word to describe Lynde. Fortunately, Naomi saved him the further effort.

"She was bat-shit crazy."

"Yes. Thank you. I thought it would be okay. It wasn't. We made it about two months."

Naomi was now really becoming intrigued by the story. She loved and hated the office talk. She hated the blah-blah, yack-yack stories of her coworkers' family drama sick kids shit. Or sports, she could almost hang herself when someone would come in all loud and excited about how some team won or lost a game. But when someone started getting gossipy about relationship stuff, then she could set aside her work for a moment and join in the conversation.

She had a voyeuristic side and loved gossipy intimate details of people's lives. Especially people she knew. Which Naomi also found strange, because outside of bland pleasantries, what she did over the weekend, what was her favorite restaurant, that sort of shit. Naomi rarely shared anything about her life.

"Do you remember that girl back in school?" Colin's face a mask of concentration.

"Which one. There were a couple of them besides me, if you ever bothered to notice."

"Funny."

"Describe her"

"I can't think of her name. She was a small red head. She would go absolutely crazy at times. Have screaming fits at the teachers or other students if they did something she didn't like and then go running from the classroom crying."

"Jill Donavan!"

"Yes!"

"Jill Donavan was more than crazy. She was psychotically insane! You dated someone like Jill Donavan? I don't know if I want to be in bed with you anymore."

They both laughed.

"In my defense, I didn't know she was insane when we first started dating. Or maybe I just ignored the signs. She didn't go screaming and crying about. Usually."

Naomi thought it was funny watching, listening to Colin mentally, verbally floundering about as he tried to explain his relationship. She understood his reasons and she wasn't going to judge him. She had dated some strange guys in her life and what she appreciated most was not being in the hot seat like she had done to Colin. Then he would be the one laughing.

"Okay, I said I was kind of lonely and she was really, well she was really fucking nuts in the bed. The pineapple safe word would have never worked with her."

"What happened? How did it end? Did she try to kill you or burn your house down. I could have imagined Jill Donavan doing something like that, so this Lynde probably would as well."

Colin turned his head to the left, looked down and brushed the hair back on the left side of his forehead.

"See that scar?"

Naomi looked closely at his forehead. Funny she hadn't noticed it before, or maybe she had, but it didn't matter because there were more important things on her mind, and in her. The scar was old, now more of a faded whitish line, about a half-inch long scar just below Colin's rich thick hair line. Naomi suddenly found herself forgetting about the scar, and wanting to run her hands through his hair and pulling his head down to her. She resisted that urge, for now.

"Yes. I see it. What happened? Did she try to stab you?"

Naomi thought it was funny to come up with crazy things for Colin to have to say no to. Every time she asked if Lynde tried to stab him, or burn down his house, Colin would get flustered all over again and start to once again flounder about. Naomi not only thought it was funny, but also adorable.

"No, she didn't try to stab me. At least not that time."

Naomi expression, her open laughing eyes and smile she wore from Colin trying to defend himself suddenly become an expression of outrageous shock. And Naomi fought, but lost, at trying not to keep from laughing.

"What do you mean that time? Why did you stay with her? She tried to kill you!"

"She didn't try to kill me. Besides it was just a cheap, flimsy plastic knife the restaurant gives you as part of a to-go order. It broke as soon as she tried to stick it in my leg, it didn't even bruise me, barely."

Naomi didn't know if she should be sympathetic, horrified, or shocked. Instead, she continued to laugh. She laughed hard and long until tears were welling from her eyes. Then Colin couldn't resist and he was laughing. Through their laughter the story continued.

"Why did you stay with her?"

"Because right after she stabbed me, she went from being angry about whatever had pissed her off, to being sorry she had become so pissed off that she tried to stab me, to being so horny that she ripped my clothes off and fucked my brains out."

"I think she actually did fuck your brains out!"

The laughter was back they both couldn't resist Naomi's last quip. It was too good. Colin had set her up and she knocked it out of the park. After a several minutes they got themselves under control. They wiped away the tears and even though occasional bubbles of mirth still rose up, they were over the laughing fit. Naomi relaxed as Colin continued the story of psycho Lynde.

Chapter 19

"I was painting a nude series. I called it *In Vogue*. The house I was renting had a warm and soft afternoon light in the bedroom. So, I posed the woman on my bed. If you can find an image of the picture you will see one of the many shitty little rental houses and bedrooms I had in my early vagabond starving artist years."

Naomi tapped opened a new internet window and searched for the picture. Several different options came up, including another porn site. Then she found it. Colin glanced and nodded, confirming that was the one. Naomi opened and enlarged the image. Once again Naomi was amazed by Colin. His skill was—mentally she fought against using the word amazing again—but his paintings were truly amazing to her. Mentally Naomi made a note to buy a thesaurus and work on her vocabulary.

The picture was of a bedroom, Colin's bedroom. On his bed was a naked woman, stretched out on her stomach. Her legs were bent at the knees, her feet up in the air, crossed at the ankle, the upper body propped up on her elbows. On the bed in front of her was a magazine. Naomi could only make out vague fashion like shapes on the page and inferred from the title of the painting, the model was reading an issue of Vogue magazine.

The light spilled through the large bedroom windows onto the simple bed, across her pale skin. The bedside table looked like an aged and weathered wooden fruit crate a person might find along the road. The curtains could have come from a second-hand store. It was a patchwork quilt hung over a simple metal pole for a curtain rod. There was a medium sized plant or tree in the corner.

The room didn't look like much. But it gave the impression of someone dreaming of something more, of someplace better. Dreaming about a life seen in a magazine. Naomi forgot about psycho Lynde. She forgot about Colin's scar. The sense of peace she found looking at the picture, she started to think about the clouds again.

"I love that one too. In fact, I like it more. It's so quiet and peaceful. She looks free."

Colin leaned closer to look at the picture on her phone. His warm breath was once again against her ear. This time Naomi didn't find it erotic, instead she combined it with her imagination. It wasn't breath. It was the warm valley air coming up the mountain side. The clouds gathering above her.

"Yeah. That was a good one. I might still have some of the rough sketches somewhere."

He leaned back and just as she had imaginatively left for the clouds, he was now mentally rummaging through memory, his collection of work, wondering if there were any sketches of that painting. Wondering about his life. His breath now gone, the warm valley air no longer coming up the mountain, Naomi turned and looked at Colin. She wanted to say so much, to ask so much of him. The thought of those words caused her heart to again hurt. Instead of saying those feelings, she distracted herself by running her finger along the scar on his forehead.

"So how did this happen? And why did you take a picture of my face?"

Colin came back from his going through is mental inventory of painting, drawings, of a warm afternoon in his old bedroom and smiled.

"Oh, yeah, the face thing. Sorry. ADD. First the scar."

Naomi moved to lean back again the bed's headboard and Collin cuddled in next to her and continued telling her the origin of his scar.

"Lynde would only stay with me once in a while. She preferred her place because my rental was barely five-hundred square feet and wasn't that nice. The furniture in the painting, that was the nice stuff."

Naomi looked critically at the furnishings in the room and decided to have some, not much, but some sympathy for psycho Lynde. Naomi understood, women like clean bathrooms and a tidy closet. She didn't think it was being sexist to feel that way either, because it was true. She couldn't understand how men could so easily tolerate a dirty bathroom. Or their ability to keep their clothes in small unfolded piles. Naomi did have some sympathy and empathy for Lynde.

"Lynde came in while I was painting that picture. Of course, her timing was perfect because I was at that moment adjusting the pose. I was holding the models' feet, crossing them so the sun shone just across her calves and feet."

Naomi couldn't control the smile coming to her face again. Augh! Another stupid smile. Stupid Colin making her smile so much in one day. Maybe that was why she had smiled so little in the past, she had been saving all of them for today. Naomi also couldn't control her eyes getting wider. She looked at the picture again, and imagined Colin at the end of the bed holding the woman's feet, looking right down at her ass and coochie. Naomi could understand why Lynde might have freaked out.

"Okay I can see from your expression you are thinking something happened, it didn't. Nudes are just nudes. I had painted nudes before and still do. Every artist has, except maybe Terry Redlin and Bob Ross. Nudes were part of my art class. We had nude models all the time. Sometimes if there wasn't a model available a student would volunteer. And before you ask, yes, I did volunteer once. Nothing happened. It's all very clinical. Sort of like a doctor's exam."

Now the clouds were gone. Replaced by the imagined image of Colin standing naked on a table letting people draw him. Naomi thought she would like to have one of those drawings.

"Anyway, Lynde walked in and freaked out and accused me of sleeping with the model because I was sleeping with her. Which is why you never date your models, especially the crazy one.

Anyway, the first thing she did besides yelling and screaming, was to pick up a small wooden bowl from off the dresser. It was where I kept my loose change and keys and miscellaneous stuff I dumped from my pockets. She grabbed that bowl and with the force and rage of a steroid-junkie baseball pitcher, threw the bowl directly at the painting. My response was like that of a secret service agent. I had to take a bullet for the President. In this case the president happened to be my painting. As luck would have it, the bowl missed the painting, but hit me solidly on the head."

Naomi couldn't stop the burst of laughter. The woman had stabbed Colin with a plastic knife which left a bruise and maybe some broken skin. The woman threw a bowl at him, that obviously had hit him and cut him open. It was too funny.

"She must have been really good in bed!"

Collin sheepishly hung his head and tried not to also smile. After a brief pause, he was able to continue with his story.

"The edge of the bowl cut me open. Lynde had an arm on her. The other model remained calm the entire time, like she had been in such a situation before. She just got off the bed, didn't bother with a robe, just walked to another room with the issue of Vogue and continued to read. Blood started to run down my face and Lynde went from insane jealous rage, to overly apologetic, and then to horny sex monster. She came over and started rubbing against me and telling me she was sorry. And maybe we should see if my new girl wanted to join us?"

Naomi continued to laugh at Colin's story. It was a soap opera. If he ever failed as an artist, he could go write for any of the afternoon shows. All Colin would have to do is write about his life. Naomi tried to talk through her laughter.

"No, that didn't really happen, did it?"

Colin smiled, quietly laughing with Naomi, at the present memory of his past.

"Yes. Yes, it did. Needless to say, the first thing I did was to carefully cover the painting and move it away from Lynde. Then I excused myself to go wash the blood running down my face and put some kind of dressing on.

Naomi's eyes were now wide with a wild question. She needed to ask it. She needed to know.

"So, did you do it?"

Colin looked at her with odd expression. He either didn't understand the question or he was too embarrassed to answer it.

"The three-way? Did you guys do it?"

There was a voyeuristic excitement to Naomi's question. An enthusiasm that caught Colin off guard. He wasn't ready for it, so he was unable to stop the unwanted expression from appearing on his face. Stuck in his flummoxed state, he didn't say anything. Naomi's eyes got wide and she saw the answer written all over the stupid expression he couldn't keep from his face.

"You had a threesome with your models!"

Naomi turned and got up on her knees on the bed. Leaning over she started poking at his stomach and ribs, laughing and chanting at him.

"Colin had a threesome. Colin had a threesome."

Colin tried to fight back. He tried to make his face not look like, like, well; look like he had a threesome with two models. But he couldn't. Not with Naomi taunting him. Making him feel stupid about it. All he could do was laugh along with her.

"Yes! Yes, we did. Stop!"

"Colin had a threesome."

Colin grabbed her hands to stop her from poking at him. Her arms still trying to reach at him, to poke and tickle him.

"So, did you like it? Did the girls get into it?"

Colin tried very hard not to blush. It didn't work. He could feel the heat rise in his face. Before today, he had never told anyone about that afternoon. No one, not even Margo. Especially not Margo. She wouldn't have thought it as funny as Naomi. Margo didn't really have a sense of humor about that sort of thing. She still became a little pissy when he painted nudes even though she knew nothing would happen.

Colin suddenly found a liberating sense of relief to talk about it. To share one of his secrets from his life. Naomi now knew so many of his secrets. Some were good, some were bad and Naomi was learning them all. Collin started to feel light. Like in flying dreams. All he had to do was let go and trust he could fly and he would fly. This secret was not one of the bad ones This was a good one. It was funny. It had happened and the entire episode was in fact, pretty damn funny.

"I'm a guy. Of course, I enjoyed it. As for the girls, they sort of got into it."

Naomi rolled back onto the bed, sitting and looking at him. Apparently, she loved hearing about his life. Even in the dimly lit room with the gray raining day in the background, Naomi was glowing. Her ice blue eyes were melting from the warm laughter Colin fought against asking the one thing he knew he couldn't. The one thing his whole being ached to ask.

He fought against it, and drug his present desire kicking and screaming back to the past, to a previous one.

"I came out of the bathroom and the two of them were naked on the bed together. I don't know what was said between them, but I certainly wasn't going to say anything. One of them, I'm guessing the model, had raided the 'fridge and opened a bottle of wine. Another one, had to have been Lynde because she knew where my stash was hidden, had lit a joint. And before you ask, because I know you want too—yes."

Colin could see Naomi's mouth thinking about forming a question, her eyes whirling.

"As for the actual physical stuff? The model, I couldn't remember her name if my life depended on it, she sort of got into it, or maybe a better answer would be, after a glass of wine and several hits off the joint, she was tolerant of Lynde getting into it."

"Psycho Lynde got off on it?"

Naomi didn't mean to use the moniker she had mentally given Lynde Farrell. But she couldn't help but imagine some weird porn-like scene. Colin frolicking naked with a blood-soaked gauze on his head with two women.

One woman, the model was all casual, mellow, and just trying to have a little fun. The other one some kind of psycho, now getting high and drunk and was trying out for a part in a porn movie. Naomi, for the umpteenth time that day, once again had to fight to hold back the laughter.

"So, what happened after you decided that getting drunk and high and having a threesome with two women was better than going to the hospital for stiches and being checked for a concussion?"

"About a day later Lynde and I went our separate ways. I guess maybe she had finally crossed a line with me. It seems it literally took a blow, or in the case a bowl, to the head for me realize it. I guess it was something about respect. Throughout my life, from growing up to becoming who I am, I'd become so use to being emotional food for other people, being used and fed on, I had just come to accepted a certain amount of abuse in my relationships. To a certain degree I still do. I'll do it tonight at the show. I have to sell myself as much as my work. I have to be food for people in order to make a living. That however is my choice, which helps a little bit. But when Lynde tried to damage or destroy that painting, I don't know, something changed, something like being in the clouds. In the clouds, I found a sense of peace and place and purpose.

When Lynde tried to wreck that painting, she attempted to take that day in the clouds, that self-discovery away from me. I learned something about myself once again."

Chapter 19

Naomi understood. She and Colin were alike in many ways, but one in particular. They were introverts. The idea of crowds and people and making bullshit small talk, just thinking about the idea of it was sucking all the good energy from Naomi. She often thought she walked around with a sign around her neck, she couldn't see it but everybody else could, all the extroverted ass-wipes who would come up and start talking at her, forcing her to listen to them. The sign said *Free Food* and she had been fighting her whole life to get rid of that sign.

The first step came the day her ex-husband pushed her a little too hard, a little too far. Instead of bowl to the head, Naomi was pushed backwards over a couch. From there it was making all the other changes in her life. From deciding she wasn't going to spend her life in a bullshit job like the other broken people working in the call-center. Naomi reached inside herself and found the strength to enroll in college courses.

The more she tried, the more she grew. Naomi who had hated school suddenly found a renewed joy in learning, seeking all the knowledge life had to offer. Dedicating her spare time and strength to studying and several years later graduating with a Doctorate of Law degree.

Sure, she was still working a bullshit job, in a bullshit office, but for the most part, it was on her terms. Just like Colin, it took an act of violence to make her find the strength inside herself to do something about it. And when she did, Naomi found she was stronger than she ever thought. But found she still wanted her inner peace.

"What happened to her, Lynde, after you guys broke up?"

I don't know where she went from there. I know she never made it out of the modeling business. I would occasionally see her in advertisements. You probably have too, you just didn't know it. Why would you?"

Naomi pondered what Colin said, that she might have seen this Lynde in advertisements but wouldn't have known it. Naomi thought about it. She looked at the picture of *Strawberry Blondes*, at Lynde and mentally started going thought make-up and fashion catalogs. Naomi thought she could see a resemblance, a familiarity between some of the adverts and the Lynde from the painting, but something didn't quite fit.

Chapter 21

"So, what's up with the pictures and your drawings?"

Colin picked up his phone and opened it back to the picture of Naomi.

"Go back to *Strawberry Blonde,* and zoom in on Lynde's face."

Naomi did. Colin looked over and watched until Naomi had what he wanted.

"Okay. Stop there."

Colin then put the two phones next to each other. Naomi looked from picture to picture. Her breathing paused for several seconds as the proverbial light bulb started to go on over her head.

"They look the same."

Colin moved his phone away from Naomi's, touched the screen and deleted the picture of her as he promised. Naomi noticed he didn't look at her. Instead he moved away. Instinctively trying to hide from the world. Naomi wouldn't let him, for both their sakes, she would make him stay there. She forced him to look at her. Putting her hands on either side of his face, holding him. His brown eyes frantically darted about trying to look to something, somewhere else, but there was no place to look except at her. Finally, the darting stopped and his eyes locked with hers.

"They are the same. Pretty much every portrait I've done, every model has almost the same exact facial features. The set of the nose, the angle of the eyes. The curve of the mouth. I don't know why, but they never seem to notice. I guess they don't get paid to critique, they get paid to look good. Either that or I guess they must think I'm just a bad artist or something."

Naomi looked at Colin, she now understood everything. She understood why he would crumple up his drawings when she would come up behind him. She understood why he had never truly pursued her back in school. She understood why he never came back to Minnesota. And now she understood the depth of his feelings for her. No mere words were adequate to describe those feelings.

"Every woman you have ever painted, you added me to them. They're all a little bit me, aren't they?"

Colin once again had to fight back the clenched feeling in his throat and stomach. Holding his face with her hands. Holding his eyes with her eyes. She could feel and see those deep buried emotions breaking through out into the world for her to see. She let him go. He turned away, wiping at his eyes.

"Yes. Excuse me."

Naomi watched as Colin turned and rolled out of the bed. He needed a moment. She had to give him all the time he needed. Naomi knew his confession to her had gone further than he had intended. She now knew his secret. The secret he probably did not want admit to himself. The depth of his feelings for her. Naomi now knew all his secrets.

Chapter 22.

Colin leaned against the corner of the wall not far from the bed. He mentally chided himself. He never should have done that, telling Naomi about the paintings. That secret was nothing like the sex thing with Lynde. That secret was stupid. It was nothing more than a type of war story and drinking tip. He was sure Naomi had stories like that and if he asked, she would tell him.

But the paintings. Telling her he had been painting her his entire life—he told himself he should have just lied. Lies were safe. Lies kept him living in a world he understood. Now those lies were gone, and he had to face the truth.

The truth about Naomi knowing exactly how much she meant to him.

The truth about her knowing the depth of his love for her.

All of those thoughts stormed through his mind as much as the current rainstorm soaked the outside world as he walked to the desk to get another bottle of water. It wasn't that he was thirsty, he just needed to step away for a moment. He had to get control back. He had to the let the ground soak up the emotional water before it started flooding out again.

The heart had been in control for too long. The heart and its truth and its feelings. The emotional catharsis may have been good for the soul, but it was also hell for the rest of him. Colin had told, had convinced himself, he would have been happy just to see Naomi again. He would have been happy to just get a cup of coffee. They would have talked and laughed. They would have had the safety of the coffee shop chaperones. There would have been no inimitable acts of physical passion. There would have been no intimate confessions of the heart. Colin told himself he would have been happy with just coffee. It was the safe thing to say. Lies always were.

Except for the rain.

Except for a loose lid.

Except for acting on his feelings and kissing her.

It would have been just coffee.

Colin heard Naomi move out of the bed. Her body sliding across the sheets. Her bare feet quietly crunching the tight weave of the hotel carpet as she came up behind him. He took a drink of the water. It wasn't cold, it was barely even cool. Considering the bottle had been sitting there for almost five hours or more, Colin thought he was lucky to get cool.

He tried to get his mind to think about that, the stupid water that was no longer cold, or even cool. Colin wanted the water cold. Cold water to freeze his heart. Freeze the warmth he suddenly felt as Naomi's arms with a soft, slow tenderness wrapped around his waist. To chill and numb him from the amazing feel of her body pressing against his back, as she held him. Colin wanted the water to freeze him in that moment forever.

"Come back to bed. Please."

Colin took another drink. Screwed the cap back on the small, thin-walled plastic bottle, setting it on the desk and turned to face Naomi. He looked down at her. Her ice blue eyes had once again started to melt. She pressed her head against his chest. Her arms locked around his waist.

Why couldn't the water freeze them like that forever?

"Okay. Let's get back in bed."

They smiled at each other. But there was none of the earlier bright and frivolous happiness in the smile. Now the smile was a sad smile. It was a smile conveying the depth and understanding of one person's love for another. And in knowing and sharing that level, that type of love, came the twisted juxtaposition, when two people found a love like that, there could never be happiness.

They moved apart and climbed back onto the bed. Naomi picked up her phone and looked at the time. Their day was moving forward. Their moment would be coming to an end. She set the timer to go off in an hour and turned back to Colin.

"Would you just lay next to me? Just hold me and let me know you're here?"

Colin answered by pulling the blanket up over them, arranging the pillows and positioning his body to fit next to Naomi. To make a seamless blending of the two of them. They stayed like that as their bodies lulled by the gentle warmth, the low rhythmic rise and fall of breathing, the slowing fall of rain lulled them into sleep.

Chapter 23

There was a chiming sound. Naomi heard chimes. Why were there chimes? She had been dreaming, but now couldn't remember it. The chimes had robbed her. They had scared the idea of what she had just been doing back into the nebulous ether of her subconscious.

Naomi woke up. She was in bed with Colin. Her day of just coffee was over. She had to go. She felt him stir next to her. The chimes had woken him as well. There were soft warm lips on her neck, a gentle rubbing of her back. Colin knew how to wake a girl. He also knew how to make a girl want to stay in bed.

Naomi couldn't.

She had to go.

It was almost two in the afternoon. It would take her almost an hour to get home. She had stuff there she needed to do. Stuff that needed to be done because no one else would do it. Plus, there was shopping to do, supper stuff to buy. Naomi thought about all that stuff. And in thinking about all that stuff, that stuff started becoming shit. *Why?*

"You just left me, didn't you?"

Colin had felt her body stiffen. They were still next to each physically. She had been thinking about what needed to happen and he heard it. They were still connected emotionally. There was no place they could hide from each other, not right now, not today. Naomi wiggled away from him so she could turn and face him.

"We need to go. I need to go."

Colin felt Naomi's body stiffen. As they woke Colin could feel Naomi's sleepy warmth and softness fading being replaced with cold hard reality. He had to know that time would end, didn't he? Did he and Naomi somehow forget, this was just one rainy day and now their day was done. Even the sky seemed to agree. The storm had passed. Through the flimsy white sheer curtains Colin could see the clouds breaking up and the sun starting to shine.

Naomi had gotten out of bed and gone to the bathroom. He could hear the water running, the sounds of splashing. Colin looked at the time. It was a little after two. The gallery show started at seven o'clock that night. All the gallery shows were in the early evening. Of course, no one started to show up until around eight. It was social suicide to be the first person at any type of event.

Naomi was leaving. She was going home. He would have hours to just sit there in the room before he had to go to the show. To make his appearance as one of the *Artists-of-the-hour*. To smile like a jackass and whore himself and his paintings so he could afford to live. He tried to push the cynicism aside. The reality of living in that kind of world robbed him of self-indulgent luxury of cynicism. The true reality of the world was the sound of washing in the bathroom.

The reality of the world became a numb slowness growing inside Colin as he forced himself from the bed and ambled around the room trying to find their clothes. The soul crushing, heart breaking, motherfucking reality of a world where he would have to walk Naomi to her car. Then standing there beside the car he would have to tell her—no! He stopped himself there. He wouldn't say those words. Not until he had too. Not until he was forced too.

The water stopped and a moment later Naomi came out of the bathroom. Her hair, finger combed back into place. A quick touch up to lipstick and eye shadow. The wet cloth to try and wash away their day; his smell from her body. Still naked as she came out of the bathroom she moved with a reluctant quickness to her clothes. Silently, without word or expression, she started to get dressed. From deep inside, a small cramping pain detonated in the marrow of Colin's soul. It slowly built, expanding outward, consuming everything in its path, like an atom bomb in slow motion.

They both did their best to dress without looking at each other. They stayed on opposite sides of the bed to avoid bumping into, brushing past, or touching. No words were spoken. No words could be said. There could only be the silence. In the silence, they were safe. All they had to do was remain silent and get out the door. Once they were out the door, the room closed to them, they would be safe from themselves.

Colin felt the slow motion atom bomb continue on its unstoppable emotional destruction. Colin felt like a marionet as he tried to move, to dress himself. His body now under the control of some invisible manipulator who was jerking him about, not letting him do or be the person he wanted. As though feelings of frustration grew in Colin, he spared a look at Naomi.

In the moment of a glance, he saw her fumble about, trying to dress, seeming to have forgotten how. As he watched Naomi struggle to latch her bra Colin realized when Naomi's phone alarm sounded, two bombs had been detonated.

Colin finished dressing first and made small busy activities on the other side of the room. From the corner of his eye, he saw Naomi had finished dressing. She sat down on the bed, slipped on her shoes and picked up her purse.

She walked to the door and as she did, that action brought an end to their time together. Colin always knew she was the stronger of the two of them.

He knew he never could have done it. He always waited for Naomi to make the first move. Well, he had almost always waited for Naomi to make the first move. It was he who had kissed her that morning. It was he who had set this day in motion. And now it was he who would have to be the one to see it through to conclusion. Colin watched Naomi walk to the door and take the handle. The strings attached to Colin forced him forward with mechanical jerks and jumps. The door opened. They had made it. The silence had not been broken. The consuming explosion inside each of them continued.

This time there was no easy frivolity between them as they passed through the hallway, down the three flights of stairs and out the side door. The sun was now out and shining in the parking lot puddles. Colin held opened the outside door and Naomi walked out of the hotel, out into the warm afternoon sun.

Still being forced forward by his strings, Colin noticed, or thought he noticed Naomi walking the same way. Watched her try and turn her head towards him several times. She tried to open her mouth only to abruptly stop.

Each time going back to looking forward and down. Colin didn't know what would happen if one of them were able to speak, to say anything. To complete an action other than a suffering silent walk.

Now at her car, Colin forced against his strings and took a small, hesitant seeming step forward. Hands previously limp at his sides, trying to move up and reach for her. Naomi's strings took her a step back, away from him. Colin knew why, he understood the reason.

Colin let his arms go back to his side. He could not do it, not this time. This was not the room. This was not something as simple as a kiss. This was a goodbye. The emotional detonation, the soul consuming fire of that internal atom bomb had made its way from the marrow of the soul out to the heart. With unstoppable force that fire rolled over the heart and when in the wake of the destruction lay a black charred piece of carbon. Strings jerked Colin forward in small shuffle steps, the strings to his arms remained slack.

Naomi's car was right there. She took the key fob and unlocked the doors as he watched. She shuffled around, head still down, eyes avoiding him, avoiding his eyes. Her movements mechanical, from an action she had done hundreds, thousands of times before, Colin watched as

Naomi opened the door to her car and sat down into the passenger's seat.

It took Colin a second longer than Naomi to understand. Seeing Naomi's reaction of reaching for the absent steering wheel and realizing what she had done. The absurdity of the act which broke their safe silence. Neither could keep from laughing. And once the laughter started, so did the tears.

Colin standing on the sidewalk, laughter and tears breaking him from his strings. Through the tears there was Naomi now laughing and crying, still sitting in the passenger's seat of her car with the door open. She brushed at her face, and got out of the car, shutting the door. Her body still shaking, still trying to deal with the emotions. Colin in front of her shaking, and laughing, and crying. They each took a hesitant step towards each other. The emotional bomb had completed its destruction and now they looked at each other, both standing in the aftermath.

Both tried to talk. Neither one could. There were only sounds, garbles of thoughts too mixed-up to make sense to anyone else, but not to them. They held each other, but they knew their time had passed, it was over.

Colin forced his words out first. Just like he had kissed her first. The simple kiss that ignited a nova and consumed a universe.

"This is it, isn't it"? He asked.

Naomi looked up at his face. His stupid, tear-stained face. She could feel her own warm tears trickling down her cheeks. She wiped at them and nodded her head yes. Naomi swallowed down the ashes from the emotional destruction and found her voice.

"I don't know if I can do this. I hate this." She said.

"I guess this is why it was supposed to be just coffee." She said.

Nodding in agreement, Colin wiped at his face. Naomi knew she was right, but she also knew she was wrong. Colin was about to say so. He was about to tell her why she was wrong. She was sure he was about to tell her so, tell her why she was wrong, but stopped.

He stopped because what their mouths, their voices could not say, their eyes did. Her melting ice blue eyes held his muddy brown eyes and between them passed an understanding of the awe-inspiring depth and breadth of their love. But hidden along the edges was something else.

Naomi knew what it was and as she held Colin with her eyes, she saw he did too. It was the lie they both needed to believe. The lie that just coffee would have been better than what had happened that day. Just Coffee would have made it easier to part, to say goodbye. That was the safe lie they both needed to believe in order to let go of each other and continue to live and breathe.

With reluctance Colin blinked first. Naomi let him go. He now understood. They both now understood. They understood the pound of flesh they had to pay. There would not be a drop of blood. Only tears.

"I guess we should have stuck with coffee."

They both laughed. They could let go of each other now. They held the safe lie instead. They could breathe. Colin held the lie to him and smiled as Naomi open the driver's door got into her car and smiled at him as she pointed to the steering wheel. The engine started and she backed out of the parking spot and drove away.

Colin carried the lie back up to the room with him.

Naomi barely made it a block before she had to pull into some random parking lot of some random business office. The lie had allowed her to make it that far, but no further.

It was just a lie.

It was not the truth.

The lie could not keep her.

The lie could not hold her or touch her.

Not like the truth.

She leaned her head against the steering wheel of her car and give herself to the truth.

Colin managed to open the door to the room before the lie fell from him.

There in the closed car, Naomi could still smell him. On her arms and shoulders, in her hair, she held him now instead of the lie, and her body shook with the truth as the explosion consumed her.

Colin moved to the bed; the bed that still smelled of them. She was still there. He sat down by the edge of the bed, in the same spot they had started their morning together, put his head on the mattress as the truth consumed him.

Chapter 23

Colin watched Naomi drive away.

The late afternoon sun reflecting off the trunk and mirrors of the car as she turned out of the hotel parking lot. Her black car turning left and moving onto the side street to take her to the main road. As her car became just another car lost in the movement of the other cars, then Colin let himself feel the weight of the lie, the fiction of life.

It had become heavy, and he needed to let go of it. It had become too heavy for him to hold. He had made it to his room and there in the quiet he let go of the weight. And then the heart took control.

It took Colin time to come to terms with what was part of him. What had always been a part of him. What he felt. What he knew. What the heart had been trying to get him to realize since seventh grade. What it had been trying to tell him. Colin realized he was finally able to find the courage to listen.

Once the emotions finally eased and he was able to think again, Colin found he needed sleep. Sleep was easy. It was easier than picking up his phone and calling Naomi and asking her to come back. Sleep would let him slip from one fiction of life to the realm of dreams. Sleep was what the brain told the body it needed. And in a moment of truce the heart agreed. Colin was on the verge of completely shutting down, and if he shut down, so did everything else. So, the brain and the heart decided sleep was needed.

Cutting it close, Naomi arrived home at four-thirty in the afternoon.

Brad would be home from work in an hour or so, and she had her chores; her self-imposed house work to do so it looked like she had done something that day, instead of doing what she needed Naomi opened the car door, reached across the seat picking up her purse and the lie. She had managed to carry the lie from the car to the house. She carried the lie instead of groceries. Walking into the kitchen through the back door. Naomi walked into the house and fought back the tears.

It was her house.

It was her house?

What was a house?

Naomi had tried to stop for some basic groceries but failed to find the strength to turn the car off the freeway. It, the car, seemed to have a mind of its own today. The car had moments like that sometimes after long days at work. Sometimes after a gin and tonic at the bar after a long day at work. The car knew what it was doing and where it was going. Naomi appreciated that about her car.

However, today it was supposed to stop at the store so she could get some shit for supper. That was sort of how she saw it, the food she was supposed to get for supper, it was all shit. She didn't want to cook. She didn't like cooking under normal conditions, even more so today. Food was something she needed, not something she wanted. What she wanted was something she would not allow herself to have.

Naomi walked through the kitchen, not putting the lie on the counter like she did her purse. Like she would have done with the groceries. She slid her shoes off and put them in their place on the rug next to the door. As she leaned down to reposition her shoes to make sure they didn't block the door, her hair fell across the left side of her emotion painted face, obscuring the ochers of red and tear stains. Naomi sighed and made her way to the bedroom. She wanted to fall on the bed. She wanted to shut down. The lie didn't fall from her. It dropped like her purse sliding off her shoulder, her hand absently catching the long strap handle, the body and weight of it to be dragged across the floor behind her like a tin can tied to her swishing tail.

From the living room to the bedroom were the images of her life framed and put on the walls and coffee tables and the dressers. The moments of breath caught and held in the instant inhalation, never to be released. And that is what Naomi needed now, but she refused to give herself such a luxury. She would not exhale. She would become like all those pictures, holding their breath and forever caught in a single moment. Forever in stasis. Forever static.

She looked at her bed. The one she shared with her husband Brad. She looked at their bed. The one where there had been so many memories made, both good and bad. Weekend mornings spent drinking coffee and reading papers and watching television. Nights spent in sleep and dreams. Moments in between of shared mutual passions and release.

Dropping everything, Naomi crawled onto her bed, and just for now, while it was just her and no one could see or ever know put down all her defenses. She stopped trying to hold back. She let the emotional weight of the day crush her.

It was close to the time Brad would be home. She had to put herself together. She would have to wash her face and brush her teeth and change her clothes. The clothes that still smelled of Colin.

She still smelled of Colin.

Naomi felt the cramping sensation again, the tears. She fought back against it. She knew how to control it. But did she want to?

Or did she want to feel it?

Every emotion that life intended

Feel all of it.

Naomi held on and took control. She was strong. She refused any weakness trying to break her. Several minutes later she had washed and brushed and changed and was waiting in the kitchen looking through the meager collection of cans and boxes and other miscellaneous food items trying to figure out the combination that would yield supper. The answer was simple enough.

There in the freezer was a frozen pizza. Later that night after twenty minutes at four hundred and twenty-five degrees, supper would be served. Satisfied Naomi looked at the house and sighed. A gin and tonic in hand she started a quick cleaning and picking-up around the house.

Chapter 24

It was Friday.

It was six-thirty in the evening.

It had been four hours since Naomi had left him.

Trying not to look at her as she backed her car out of the parking slot, turned and drove away. Trying not to see her looking in the rearview mirror at him standing there holding his hand up, a gesture of goodbye.

Colin tried not to see her glance at him as she turned left out of the parking lot. Trying not to memorize him as he still stood there watching her drive away. Colin was still standing there trying to maintain the fiction that their lives could go back to being as they were before this day.

The lie that would allow them to go back to their lives and pretend what had happened that afternoon was nothing more than just a fling. Something that was just physical and meaningless. It was just an afternoon of some physical intimacy, some orgasms and nothing more. Life was just fiction anyway, wasn't it? Afterall, a person did not own life, they only rented it for a while. Maybe that was the joke to all of it, the fiction of life.

Colin thought about the lie as he stood there at the art gallery looking at the negative space on the wall filled with paintings. The empty spaces between the collection of works by several artists being featured that night. In that negative space Colin took the first sip of his first drink. His eyes moved from between those negative empty spaces to look at the face of the woman from his new picture.

At seven-thirty in the evening Colin finished his first drink. The gallery show officially started at seven. The text from Margo arrived about a minute later. She always felt the need to check on him and make sure he had made it to where he was supposed to be, as if he were an errant child who needed to be checked on. The mother calling the friend's house making sure he arrived. Colin, at times like these, the shows and social events, would see Margo as another one of the social extrovert vultures who were there to pick some more meat from his carcass. Colin looked at the words and generally ignore them.

Good luck with the show. I know you can do it if you want to. Just relax and let them come to you and you'll be fine. Make a big commission and we can get away to someplace warm and relaxing for a while. Love you.

It was the sting of *Love you* that compelled Colin to respond. A simple, *Here. All is good. Okay. Love you too.* It was all he had.

He looked at the glass of scotch he had put down on the blonde stained oak bench positioned in front of one of his new paintings. This was a spot for someone to come and sit and look and admire his painting. To visualize how it would look in their home. To come up with a reason to give him several thousand dollars for something that evoked an emotional response within them. Colin did not see the paintings. He looked at the glass of single malt scotch.

What he wanted was the opposite of what others would feel when they looked at the painting on the wall. Every person who looked at that painting would see a woman with short brown hair, wearing a sleeveless light blue floral print dress.

She is sitting on a rustic white porch swing her legs drawn up under her, one hand lightly holding the chain.

She sits in angled sunlight, surrounded by pots of marigolds and hanging baskets of Boston ferns.

Her face turned enough to suggest her expression suggests she is looking at someone in the house.

She is turned enough so everyone can see the models face.

The set of her eyes.

The line of her nose.

The curve of her lips.

Everyone will look at the model and wonder who she is and what she is thinking.

Colin did not want to look at the woman. Colin focused on his glass. Colin wanted to see and feel what the contents in that glass offered as it sat there on the blonde stained oak bench.

At gallery shows and other public events Colin usually drank a glass of wine. Wine was easy and it was social. Everyone drank the wine. Everyone talked about the wine. Sometimes they talked more about wine than the they talked about the paintings.

The bartenders and the hostess staff had to know about the wine lest they fall victim to a stern, reprimanding diatribe of education about wine from the shithead drinking it. Colin could, and usually did, socially nurse a glass of wine all night. Maybe two if he felt open to it. But not tonight. Tonight, it was scotch.

Scotch was usually reserved for the other times. The alone times. The silence of an empty world times. The times when he found the pleasure and sensation the taste of scotch would add to those private moments.

In those times the amber nectar helped to burn away the layers of his past and helped him to forget those parts of life that needed to be forgotten. Those parts that needed to be turned to ash. Colin knew it probably wasn't a healthy way to deal with his problems, but it worked for him. Scotch cut the tin cans from his tail.

Colin moved to put his phone back into his pocket. But at some point in time, between not trying to look at his paintings, thinking about a quiet empty world, but before he had actually put his phone in pocket, in that moment of distractions his fingers once again had a life of their own. Apparently, he had typed a text to Naomi. It was waiting to be sent.

Naomi put her glass on the counter. There was a buzzing noise breaking through the drone of the evening news on the television that was on but not being watched. The oven had preheated to four hundred and twenty-five degrees. The oven was telling Naomi it was time to put in the pizza.

Naomi took the paper box portraying the image of a delicious fresh baked pizza From the freezer. She pulled at the perforated tab opening the box. The not so delicious looking frozen plastic wrapped pizza slid out. Cutting the plastic wrap, freeing the pizza from the confines of its sanitary airtight environment, she placed it in the oven to bake. She set the oven timer to twenty minutes.

Another one of the many buzzing noises in her life designed to remind her of task needing attention. Probably designed by men because they didn't want vapid, silly girls to forget what they were doing.

Naomi turned to the counter and picked up her glass. It had left a ring of condensation on the black and white marble countertop. She took a drink from her second gin and tonic.

She wanted to drain the glass. Just take one long drink. Done!

Then put the glass back on the counter. Right back onto its condensation ring. Walk to the cupboard and take out the bottle of gin and repeat. Second verse same as the first. Instead, she took a small sip from her glass and set it off-center of the original ring of gathered condensation there on the black and white marble counter.

Brad arrived home about an hour or so after Naomi. After Naomi had changed into her hanging around the house clothes.

After she had put the clothes that smelled of her and Colin into the wash.

After she had brushed her teeth and cleaned the toilet.

After she had made a quick pass through the house, putting stuff back where it was supposed to be; the shit of life back into place. Making the bed to look like no one had slept in it, even though they would again in several hours, and no one ever saw it anyway.

Brad pulled his truck into the driveway. His work done, returning home to end his day with her. With Naomi to make him his supper. With Naomi there to hear him speak at her about his day. As he, once again, told her that he was going to take care of some stuff in the garage and yard before supper—second verse

Could she get him a beer as he changed quick? Did she do any laundry? If not, he had some stuff he wanted washed if she still had time. Then it was out the side door off the kitchen to the yard and the garage where he would drink his beer and pretend to do something to avoid having to do anything—same as the first.

Naomi wanted to feel the anger, but she couldn't. She knew it wasn't as bad as she was telling herself. It was just not what she wanted or where she had imagined herself to be. *Besides wasn't she the architect of this life?*

The timer on the oven told her she had ten more minutes. She picked up her phone to text Brad. It was easier than walking outside. That was more than she had right now. Without realizing she had even typed it,

"How are you?"

She sent the text to Colin.

Naomi looked at her phone. It buzzed in her hand. Naomi opened the text.

"How are you?"

It was from Colin.

Chapter 25

After the bar had been set-up Colin had given the bartender, name tag James, a fifty-dollar bill. Colin always found a weird pleasure in the expression people gave him when he gave them a fifty.

The bill was odd. Not common like say a ten or twenty. Not the standard large bill, the hundred. It was something in between. A mutant aberration of currency. It was a fifty.

The drinks were free for artists, but Colin had instructions for James that night and the mutant aberrational fifty was for educational reasons. When Colin came to James with an empty glass, Colin would have either two or three fingers presented on the glass for James to see.

Two fingers meant one ice cube, two finger measurement of scotch.

Three fingers meant two ice cubes and three fingers of scotch. James smiled at Colin and told him he understood. Then James joked and asked what four fingers would mean. Colin didn't have a smile, instead he responded in an empty matter-of-fact voice.

"Four fingers will mean no ice. Just top it off and call me a cab or an Uber."

At eleven o'clock that night James fulfilled the final set of duties Colin had asked of him.

The first guests for the show started to show up around seven thirty.

They were the late twenties and early thirty-something hipster types. They rarely ever came to buy. They were there because that was their social thing to do. They had all the apps on their phones telling them about all the events about town.

They would gather together in small groups and follow their social network wherever it took them. This would be their social status evening away from their social status children. In the past those hipster types might have bought something simple and almost within their budget. Just enough to show off to their social clique groups.

Come look at what we bought. Isn't it amazing? Don't you just love it! You bitches should suck our metaphorical dicks because of it.

In return, they were forced by the hipster-wannabe-someone-more-than-I-am code to go to the homes of their friends when those friends made such purchases. And then they in turn were forced to provide oral gratification to those who so recently had performed such an act on them.

That social circle jerk group always arrived first. They were the first to the bar. They were the first to the hors d'oeuvres table and servers. They were the first to not buy anything. Colin had finished his first two fingers, and James had just poured him a second.

Colin tried to eat. Since a simple and unfulfilling hotel breakfast before going to meet Naomi, he hadn't eaten anything that day. Then Colin forced the joke, only he heard and only he responded to it. *The only other thing he had eaten that day was Naomi.* Colin tried to laugh. It wouldn't happen. So, he compensated for the lack of laughter. Scotch was the best there was at what it did.

Around nine o'clock the buyers started to show up. These were the power people. They were the stock brokers and bankers. They were the doctors and lawyers. They weren't the posers wearing trendy clothing, their hair in manbuns, all of them asking to take selfies with Colin in front of a painting they pretended they were thinking about buying.

Now Colin's earlier imagination of the evening became reality. The people coming in now did not care where the bar or the food tables were located or what was being served. They did not care because they knew the drinks and the food would come to them whenever they wanted.

The men were there with their second or third wife. Each younger than the last. Each one better than the other in providing the idea of beauty and physical satisfaction which is all those men wanted from them.

Opposite the men were the former wives of those types of men. They came to the gallery with alimony accounts and woman-squad power support groups. Those women were out to teach their former husbands a lesson. They wrought such a lesson by bringing financial deficit to the bastard that left them for the vapid young sluts that hadn't been born when the first marriage vows had been spoken.

Colin embraced his cynicism as he stared at those various mannequins and marionets and realized why he hated people so much. Or in his scotch-fueled cynicism did he just hate himself?

He looked down into his half empty third glass.

The ice had barely started to melt.

He knew he needed to slow down.

However, at that moment, what he needed and what he wanted were two very different concepts. He pushed at his hair and his hand went across the old scar on his forehead. Lynde's scar. The scar he had forgotten about until that afternoon. Colin wondered what Lynde was up too? Had she found someone worthy of her temperament? Colin still didn't remember the name of the other model, the *In Vogue* model. That afternoon together with the two of them.

The wine.

The weed.

The pleasure they found in the simplicity of just being free without care. A simple life. Colin found himself wanting that again. But he didn't want those two. He wanted someone else. Out of reflex he looked at the face of the model in his painting.

"Here is the man of the hour."

The voice full of enthusiastic zeal, with just a hint of an inflection, was the fifty-something, slightly overweight, impeccably and fabulously dressed gallery owner Steven Krenshaw.

He had approached, *or was it intruded?,* while Colin was lazily floating along in the slow shifting currents of his memories. Colin and Steven had introduced themselves earlier in the evening. Fred had taken care of all the details as soon as the show had been officially scheduled.

Colin knew Fred would make sure what paintings were to be displayed, the lighting and placement and most important of all, the prices. Fred was a good man and Colin felt lucky to work with him, especially tonight when Colin didn't care about any of those little details, not even the so-called most important detail.

Colin arrived a little before six p.m. and there waiting to greet him in the lobby was Steven Krenshaw owner of the gallery. Steven, not Steve, was a short man, heavy set with dark course hair, an aquiline nose, olive skin. He was an enthusiastic and outgoing person, was smart and knew how to talk to people about art and interior decorating, which was probably why he owned a successful art gallery.

Colin privately smirked to himself as he talked with Steven. Once again it seemed he was Fred's wingman. Steven was completely Fred's type and Colin was pretty sure Steven would be into Fred. Colin didn't care. In some ways he thought it was hilarious that Fred used him to meet guys.

Besides who was Colin to judge people for whom they found pleasure and company and love. However, Colin occasionally had to suggest to Fred to pick galleries based on sales and not in the date-ability of the owner or manager. Afterall, they all had bills to pay.

Steven came up and hesitated as he went to clap Colin on the shoulder, realizing it would have looked odd to reach up that far. Instead with smooth elegance, as if that action was the one he had originally intended, he gave

Colin for firm pat on the back as he presented Colin to perspective buyers.

Colin knew it was time to put on his game face. It was time to make some money so Margo could find someplace to try and talk Colin into going to. She would suggest places that she thought would inspire Colin. Although he knew those were the places she wanted to go. He knew this because Margo already knew his answer about going on trips.

"All my stuff is here. Why would I want to leave"?

It wasn't that Colin didn't go places. He just didn't want to go to faraway places. Inspiration was everywhere. He didn't need to go sit on a beach in the Grand Caymans or some other similar place to find it. Colin took a breath. The glass in his hand tried not to shake. Colin once again prepared himself to become food.

The buyer was a doctor. A heart surgeon who was saving several lives a day at the local state university and another hospital Colin was supposed to be both impressed with and humbled by. The doctor who let it be known he was looking for some original art for his second house in the country. He let Colin know he thought Colin's work was nice and had a warm feeling to it.

The older doctor's younger and obviously second wife agreed and batted her long fake eyelashes at Colin with vapid intent. Colin's soul withered as he told the two of them about his latest work. The intimate idea behind it. The two listened with arrogance and ignorance and Colin stood on the sidewalk outside their car hoping to make a deal. He was less than his bathroom puta. She at least challenged the person.

Colin wandered over to James as Steven and the doctor-slash-prospective buyer walked away. Colin took his phone from his pocket. Three fingers later, from across the room the gallery owner caught Colin's attention with a dollar sign smile.

Colin drank another finger.

Colin was doing his best to hang on, just hang on a few more hours. He told himself. He could do it. He took his phone from his pocket to check the time. He looked again at the text from Naomi.

"How are you"?

He had received it from her mere seconds after he had sent the same message to her. His heart told him it meant something. The scotch told him something different.

Chapter 26

Sitting on the couch together, watching the television, Naomi was aware of Brad as he ate pizza. He chased through the channels looking for a show that would finally grab his attention long enough to forget he was holding the controller.

Naomi cognizant enough to see it all pass by in an uncaring blur. Naomi didn't have much of an appetite despite having not eaten much of anything all day. Naomi tried to joke to herself, *all she had eaten that day was Colin*. Her joke was not as funny as it made her heart sad. Earlier in the evening, as the pizza in the oven going from frozen to hot, she did the opposite. Then Colin's text arrived.

They had both text at the same time. The universe had let them know neither one had forgotten about the other. The universe wanted them to know something. The problem was, did they have the courage? Naomi knew Colin was currently at his show. She imagined him laughing and talking with all the fancy people in their ties and dresses. They would be looking at his paintings. They would ask him pointed questions needing further discussion.

They would be asking about settings.

They would ask about the models.

The models with all the same basic facial features.

Every person there would be talking about her.

Naomi forced those thoughts away. She focused on the brown grease-stained cardboard circle the frozen pizza had sat upon.

The same tedious, brown grease-stained cardboard circle the pizza went back onto after being baked.

The same utilitarian, tedious, brown grease-stained cardboard circle she had cut the pizza on.

The same unimaginative, utilitarian, tedious brown, grease-stained cardboard circle that now sat empty with eight cut marks on it.

The empty, cut, cardboard circle sitting on the towel on the coffee table in the living room there in front of the television where there was nothing in particular to watch and if there was something, there was never enough time to find out because her husband kept clicking through the channels.

Did she have the strength to set aside the idea of the love that was in her mind? The idea of love in her heart? Could she forget about the crazy idea of happiness for the complacent life of safe and sure? What was love anyway?

It may start out as eating at fancy restaurants with table linens and gourmet food, but it eventually always goes from number one on the charts to a worn-out, one-hit-wonder. Second verse, same as the first.

And this week's flashback hit from Naomi and Brad. Whatever happened to those two? Here again, and again, and again with that not-so-classic hit, Cardboard Pizza Circle on the Coffee Table in the Living Room.

Sure, it was a vicious circle, but it was safe. Besides, wasn't safe and sure the better bet? Wasn't a simple circle of cardboard with eight cut marks better than—Naomi couldn't think of anything. At least not anything she wanted to admit to. She let her eyes wander between nothing in particular on the television and her phone sitting next to her. The ten-p.m. news was starting. Naomi finished her third gin and tonic wondering why life couldn't just be simple? Why couldn't it be as simple as standing in the clouds?

It was ten in the evening and the gallery was full of people making their Friday night status social outing the event they could tell others about over the next several days. The hipster men and women were feverishly Facebooking, Tweeting, Instagramming, and generally pissing their social media scent on all over their social media friends and followers.

The fucking weekend hipsters wanted to make sure they had proof of their evening out and about on the town. Colin thought he should be happy. Maybe on some level, on some part of his psyche not turned to ash by the scotch he was happy. Whatever the fuck happiness was.

In the context of the evening, happiness was defined by monetary value. It seemed money could be happiness. Several of his paintings had sold and he was a dollar-sign happy painter. His trip back to Minnesota had been finically worth it. He could go home and pay his bills. He could continue to live a life that was more important to others, to the people who bought his paintings, than it currently was to him.

After all, those people didn't want to buy from some artist who struggled to make a living. That wasn't an artist. An artist was someone that no one could afford to buy their paintings. Or at least not just anyone. The art had to be exclusive and be beyond the reach of the average person. Otherwise, what was the point?

Colin thought he should be happy. He had met the definition of the word happy, at least that night's definition of the word. It didn't matter if he currently had several definitions of the word. All those definitions he experienced several hours earlier. What Colin didn't have to think about was the fact that he was maybe, just a little, or possibly even slightly or maybe just remotely probably drunk.

Colin was on his fourth glass of scotch. *Or was it fifth? Or did it even matter?* His right hand held the glass. His left hand fumbled in his pocket with his phone. His mind muddled over the day and the thoughts that were stirred up because of his rumination.

They had had their moment.

What more could he ask of Naomi?

What?

That she should forget about her life?

She should give up everything because he wanted her too?

Wasn't he just the asshole-of-the-hour!

To come in, like an angry hippo on meth and tell someone whom he loved that he deserved them more than someone else. That what he currently had for a life was just shit compared to the alcohol fueled fantasy he was now trying to convince himself could be real. The scotch was supposed to have prevented such an action. Stupid scotch not doing its job. His mental world was supposed to be a wasteland of smoking ash, but somehow a sunflower was still able to sprout.

Colin looked at the half-filled lost count glass. He looked at the table where the small slider sandwiches, cheese and crackers, and other miscellaneous food items were located. He looked back at his glass. Earlier he had managed to eat several of the small sandwiches. He knew he had eaten them, because he could still feel the aggravating weight of them in his rebellious stomach. Colin just wanted the night to be over.

He attempted to move from the wall he was currently holding up, to a bench that needed to be weighed down. Instead found himself slowly trying to get the phone out of his pocket. The left hand wasn't doing a such a good job of it. The right hand wanted to help but was currently occupied trying to get the glass up to the mouth.

Why didn't the brain just shut down when he needed it too? Why couldn't life just be simple?

Why couldn't the fantasy just end and not bleed into his reality?

Colin mentally slurred to himself that life was supposed to be simple. He understood that now, even thru the cloudy haze of the liquid amber Colin understood. He was ready for simple.

It was supposed to be simple.

Sleep was supposed to be simple.

Naomi, even after three drinks lay in bed with her eyes burning holes into the ceiling.

Climbing the stairs was supposed to be simple.

Colin, however, found himself death-gripping the handrail and pulling himself forward as much as he was holding himself up.

Naomi quietly slipped out of bed. Brad locked in sleep snored several times and remained oblivious to her actions.

Colin woke with a disconcerting and distinctly uncomfortable feeling in his body.

Outside in the cool night air, the light night breeze drifted with the lingering aroma from morning's rain.

Noisily stumbling from the bed and lurched to the bathroom.

Alone, sitting on the front step of the house she watched the clouds lazily float across the stars and moon and listened to the soft sounds of leaves and grass brushing together.

His stomach decided it didn't want to keep its current contents and would be returning them to the mouth.

With only the simplicity of nature to bear witness, Naomi opened her armor and cried.

Colin violently puked for several minutes.

Finally, the tears ended,

Finally, there was nothing left to return,

Naomi crept back in,

Colin shakily walked,

Naomi lifted the blankets,

Colin fell onto the bed,

Sleep came but provided little comfort.

Chapter 27

Monday morning and Naomi survived the weekend. The worst was over. The consuming fireball of emotion that had ripped through her body had passed. The smoking ruins had been mostly cleaned up. Now the reconstruction process could begin. Naomi looked at her coffee cup and smiled at the memory. It would be okay. She would make it okay. She knew how strong she could be, of that she was certain.

The weekend had been tough. There were moments when she fought tooth and nail to keep herself from completely losing control. Just giving up and staying in bed.

However, that same strength and resolve that lived deep down inside her and gave her the strength to leave her first husband, to go to school, to become a success at whatever task she set before herself, that conviction set in stone before her by the finger of her own hand, Naomi knew she would survive this part of her life as he had survived all the other parts of her life.

Despite all her personal resolve and inner strength, the next walk in the park was the hardest moment. Needing some alone time, she left Brad to work in the garage doing whatever it was he did or did not do there. Late in the afternoon the cool May evening started. She wanted to be there for the fog to come in off the pond. She wanted to stand there and try to become lost in it.

The cold air began to blanket the warm water and Naomi watched the white tendrils begin to lift up. However, the fog developed into only a thin mist and not the dense fog Naomi wanted. It didn't come up to her. It didn't hide her from the world. But Naomi did find solace there in her park, silence from the modern world lost in the sounds of the woods. And in the silence of the woods, she heard the plopping sound of drops of collected moisture as they hit the ground, having become too heavy to hang from her chin.

Now it was Monday and Naomi could sit at her desk and concentrate on the details of the cases on her desk. A sad smile found a way to her face. It wasn't much but it was enough. On the drive in that morning, she had already worked on her alibi, her reason for not appearing to be her usual self, especially after a long weekend. Her reasoning was airtight and would not be questioned, not even by the nosier of the office workers who never accepted any answer, either yes or no, without demanding an explanation. *Fuckers!* Naomi found a small genuine smile as she mentally cursed several of her coworkers.

It was around ten when her phone binged with a text. Out of reflex, not because she needed to, Naomi glanced at the screen. She already knew it was from Colin. That was his text tone. The one she set to let her know it was him. Naomi looked at the legal brief on her monitor while her mind thought about the text from Colin.

It was ten o'clock in the morning her time, eight in morning in California, in Colin's time. Colin would be in his studio. He probably had his Monday morning music playing. What it was depended on what he was preparing to do. If he were painting, it was Haydn. If setting up or cleaning, it was The Kills. The music on, the morning sun coming through the large window that looked out at his oak tree. She knew what his view was, he had sent her several pictures of how his mornings had started. He would have a cup of coffee.

For a moment, she hated herself for knowing how his Monday's started. For knowing so much about his life and how it worked.

She looked at her own cup of coffee. For some reason the Janis Joplin song *Maybe* came to mind. Maybe it was okay to look at the text. Maybe it was okay to read the words. Maybe it would be okay to feel the feelings that came with the words. Maybe it would be okay between them. Maybe all she had to do was try. Maybe. Maybe. Maybe.

Naomi donned her armor, girded her loins, even added some new reinforcements and a few extra hard edges to her armor and reached for her phone.

"Hey."

That was all it said. Naomi read it again wondering if somehow, she had missed something.

"Hey."

Naomi didn't know how it was supposed to go. She had gotten ready. Brought up the extra defenses and prepared to kick some ass. All she got was "Hey." She wanted to be angry. She wanted to be sad. She wanted to feel something she had prepared herself to feel. That fucker Colin still knew how to get to her. The son-of-a-bitch, motherfucker! Naomi felt better after her mental rant at Colin. She was right though. He knew exactly what to say. Naomi knew him well enough to know right now, being the hopeless romantic goof that he was, Colin was hurting just as much, if not more, than she.

The simple "Hey" said so much. That simple "Hey" must have cost him so much. Those three simple letters were Colin's way of letting her know he was there. He would honor their pledge to try and be as they had been, to be special friends. That simple "Hey." was what Colin would have sent on any given day. It was exactly what it was supposed to be, it was a friend saying hello. Naomi felt everything. Every feeling was coming at her again. It was time to retreat, to regroup and prepare again. It was time for a bathroom break.

In the morning sun, Colin sat alone on the grass. His back leaning against the outside eastern wall of his studio. His coffee cup in his hands. His phone resting on his legs. His feet pushing at the acorns lying about. He had just sent Naomi a text. Now all he could do was wait.

He spent several miles of his morning run trying to think of the perfect line, the perfect thing to say. Then he realized there was no perfect thing to say. There was only saying something and go from there. They had made an agreement. That agreement was just as valid as the other established deal of delete everything. If Colin was to remain true to the deal that was what he had to do, no matter what it cost. Delete everything.

He sat on the grass as the morning sun was rising strong in the sky, just coming over the top of the neighbor's house and privacy hedge, just starting to break through. Colin thought it would a perfect moment, hackneyed and cliché, but still a perfect moment for Naomi to respond to his text.

He glanced at his phone as overwrought soap opera ideas played out in his head. He wanted to chide himself for being so over-imaginative, but he could not. He had to be over-imaginative because he did not know what he would do if Naomi did not respond.

It was around nine his time when the chime assigned to Naomi on his phone chimed. Colin had moved from his earlier stage mark outside on the grass to the new one inside his studio. Now on his third cup of coffee, The Kills coming from the speakers, he had decided to dedicate his morning to the tedious task of signing limited edition giclée prints. Colin hated signing them. Signing his name, a hundred times along with numbering the prints, one of one hundred, two of one hundred and so one until finally his hand hurt and he wanted to burn down his studio.

The best and most coveted were the errors. His hand working on its own, his brain not really thinking about what it was supposed to be doing. Apparently, Colin had several times in the past signed something else, screwed it up somehow and like an upside-down airplane stamp, those prints became desired collector items. Colin was on twenty-seven of one hundred when Naomi's chime broke the moment.

Colin tried to show some control. To display some personal dignity. To not immediately drop everything and run over to the window where he had left his phone.

Although it wasn't a run, the studio was too small for that, instead he took several hurried steps, almost tripping over an easel. He wanted to know everything was still okay between them. That Naomi was okay. Colin needed to know they were still friends. He opened her text and almost dropped the phone from laughing.

"Hey."

Several days after the initial text Naomi and Colin were moving back to where they had been before their rainy day. Naomi tried not to think about it too much, the memory was still fresh, the wound was too deep, but it was healing. It was odd, but then again, maybe not she thought. Afterall, they were friends. They always had been. So, they had a moment together, something special. It didn't mean their lives were any different. Naomi had slept with guys before, some of them she stayed in contact with, they were still friends, in a sort of, roundabout, maybe casual sort of way.

As Naomi thought about it, yes, it was weird, but if she had the ability, the option to take it all back she would not. In that day she let herself be herself and free of everything. Not afraid of letting someone get to close. Not afraid of being manipulated and used because of her looks. Not afraid of her emotions. Colin gave her that, and in exchange, she returned the favor. For that one day there was only the two of them fully exposed and trusting each other. For that one-day Naomi had fearlessly abandoned herself to love.

Chapter 28

Naomi found she and Colin moving forward again. There were tough spots and Naomi told herself, "*When the waves come, you face 'em.*" That was never truer than the next time it rained. Naomi felt the waves of emotions swell, rise, and crash down against the armor of her breaker wall. Naomi felt herself start to cry. She stood alone in her yard and let the cool spring rain soak her, let her tears join with the world around her. She faced her waves and knew it would get easier. It just took time for wounds to heal. And when the next time it rained Naomi didn't cry, almost. She had a little laugh at almost not crying, it was good. Eventually only the rain came down.

It helped that in their texts, without having to say or hint at anything, they never mentioned their moment together. It had been deleted from everything except their memories. Besides, thought Naomi, what good would it do to talk about it? It wasn't like they were likely to meet again. What happened was just their moment, not some tawdry affair. They were better than that.

The texts were slow at first, with banal chit-chat topics about weather, work, weekends. The general bullshit minutia of which life was composed. As May became June their texts were almost back to normal. Naomi started to wonder about Colin, if he was okay. His texts were guarded, he wasn't as open as he had been. Naomi thought about it, about some of her texts and realized she had become the same way. It would seem their moment of intimacy did have a price, although a small one, the debt still had to be paid.

Colin may have been withholding emotionally, in other aspects of his life he was still open and sharing. Naomi laughed out loud when Colin, for the first time since that day, called her because he just had to tell her something.

He told her about how he let one of his former art teachers bring a small group of students to his studio. It was their chance to talk with an artist who had actually become successful. An actual artist who had navigated the art world and was able to make a living at it while still alive.

During the visit, and before Colin could think to do or say anything to prevent it, one of the students hurriedly asked to use the bathroom as they were already walking to it. Through the laughter coming from his voice, it apparently didn't go as bad as it could have. The young woman didn't mention anything specific about his bathroom artwork, except to say, she liked the Banksy quote. The situation then became more complicated and uncomfortable when the other students wanted to see what the girl was talking about. Colin for several embarrassing minutes then had to talk about graffiti art and how it fit into society. As he spoke, his puta challenged him and everyone in the class.

Naomi after, her fit of laughter subsided and her stomach stopped hurting, was finally able to talk and managed to finally cajole Colin into sending her several pictures of his bathroom. Including and especially of his so-called puta.

Naomi wanted to be shocked when she first saw it but wasn't. Colin had made mention of some graffiti stuff he had painted in his bathroom, but he had never sent actual pictures so she could only imagine. She had already seen some of the graphic tattoos he would draw on the guys back in school. Plus, there were all the nudes he painted and continued to paint. So a naked woman was neither shocking nor surprising to her.

What did surprise her was the graffiti itself. It was alive with energy and wild abandon. His paintings were always of a calm contemplative life. An image or scene where a person found themselves pulled into it, wanting to be there. But his graffiti had a vibrant and edgy quality. The colors garish, the edges big and rounded with deep contrasting colors. In his graffiti she saw the part of Colin she knew in high school. The shy guy turned rebellious teenage Joey Ramone-looking punk.

That Colin, the Colin who had started to find his strength and understanding of who he was and what wanted to be was still there. Her heart felt warm knowing that version of Colin was still around. Naomi also smiled at the thought of the students and how they might have reacted to the puta. The two of them were getting back into their groove. It was slow, but worth it. Colin could still make her smile. She still had her friend.

Colin loved and hated summer in the Sonoma. He loved it because of the long summer days. He loved to be able to open the widows to his studio and let the warm air move out the stale winter paint smell.

He loved his oak tree now full of large dark green leaves, tangles of long filament moss, and acorns of various sizes. The tree had dropped almost all of last season's acorns, almost. Those errant acorns continued to fall from the branches with tips and taps and plips and plops and cover the yard around the tree.

Several squirrels did their best to eat and bury them, but even they couldn't keep up with all the acorns. Even though they left a mess that Colin would later spend some lazy afternoon raking into a pile, he loved the acorns as much as he loved the tree.

He also loved the vineyards. All the grape vines heavy with deep aubergine or pale almost transparent white wine grapes. The mountains whose grass mixed in shades of deep living greens and dormant summer golds.

Those good and calm aspects of summer were juxtaposed with the tourist season. Colin wanted to hate weekenders from out of town, from San Francisco and further away or from out of state. The roads choked with traffic. All the shops and restaurants constantly busy with people.

Colin leaned his mesh backed patio chair against his oak tree and watched the afternoon sun slowly going down. Sipping at his bottle of cold beer he watched the Saturday traffic go by. He lived several blocks down off the main road. But that didn't mean people wouldn't try to shortcut around the traffic lights and stop signs, which of course didn't work.

Colin knew all too well that all roads led to the stop signs and the long jam of afternoon traffic. Colin had long ago determined he didn't actually hate the summer tourists. He just really disliked them. Although, sometimes he wanted to hate them. Mostly, he disliked them because they disturbed his peace, his sense of quiet solitude. Being there under his tree is where he would recharge his soul. No matter how much, or how hard people fed on him, striping him of his energy. Just spending an hour sitting with his magnificent and ancient friend could restore his wellbeing.

The current problem with all the summer tourists was, Colin thought as he took another sip of beer, and as a delinquent previous fall acorn deciding it was time to drop with a plip, tap, plop to the ground next to him; the problem with even disliking those people was because they paid for his life. Several times a week he would receive calls from local galleries asking him for new work or old prints because some out-of-towner had heard of local resident artist Colin Meyer, loved his paintings and wanted one.

However, there were also some people who didn't respect privacy. They didn't respect his attempt at being invisible and tried to find out where he lived. But because Colin did try to live an invisible, private life, no one usually found out where he lived—invasive jerks. But right now it was just him and his tree. For better or worse, or maybe just fate, his life once again had a simple singular quiet to it.

Colin took another satisfying pull from his beer and relaxed into the sunset. Tip, tip, tap, plip, plop, thud. Off in the distance he could see the Mayacamas mountain range.

It was the line of mountains separating Sonoma Valley from Napa Valley. Although it was one long generally unbroken range, the grape growers had designated smaller sections of the range into appellations because of how the grapes grew.

Colin understood the generalities of the process, he had lived in wine country long enough. However, the intricate details of wine making were beyond his level of caring. Just as the winemakers were beyond caring about Colin's level of obsession with brushes and pantones. However, in the end they both appreciated each other's efforts.

Colin looked at the Mayacamas range and finished his beer. Plip, plip, tip, tap—twack!—tink, thud. Colin winced and rubbed at the spot where an acorn hit him on his head, then bounced of his chair before it hit the ground. Colin looked once more at the mountain then to his empty beer bottle. He tipped his chair forward, back onto all four legs, told the oak tree he would be back later, and walked into this studio.

Chapter 29

It was late August when Naomi's phone rang. Wednesday morning, sitting at work drinking coffee and waiting for Colin to send her his good morning text, letting her know he was up and in his studio. Then her phone rang with a number from an unknown caller. Naomi muted the phone and out of habit let the call go to voicemail. When the voice mail icon appeared, Naomi was surprised. Robo calls never left voice mail. She called her voice mail to find out what was going on, who had left her a message.

Saturday at ten in the morning, as scheduled, a black Mercedes sedan and a large panel van turned into her driveway. It wasn't the car but the delivery van that surprised Naomi. It bigger than she had expected and that had caught her attention and started to again make her anxious and start to worry. Naomi had been expecting, hoping, something smaller, something friendly looking something that wasn't a large panel van.

On the previous Wednesday, after listening to her voice mail Naomi text Colin. She didn't care if he was awake or not. She didn't care if he was alone or not. Naomi knew Margo was aware of Colin's friend from school with whom he texted and sometimes talked. If he had to, Colin could just tell Margo it was an emergency, Naomi needed a friend to talk to, they had done it before. She sent him the text to call her.

"NOW!"

It was an infuriating hour and two cups of coffee and several bathroom trips later when Colin sent her a text. "Talk?"

This was one of the few times Naomi missed the ability to jab buttons or turn the dial of a phone. There was a simple cathartic pleasure in that physical act, especially when strong emotions were involved. All she could do now was touch her finger to Colin's picture on her phone. It was a selfie. One of him in a paint covered shirt, in his studio holding a gin and tonic. Her stupid smart phone took the pleasure of jabbing at buttons away from her.

"Hi. What's up? Everything—"

"What do you mean I'm getting a delivery!"

"Oh. I guess the gallery there called you. Yeah. Sorry. I thought you would have liked the surprise. Happy Birthday or Merry Christmas or something?"

Naomi could hear the humor as well as some apology in Colin's voice. He genuinely wanted to do something nice, and maybe a little fun. He had wanted to surprise her with something, which that something she learned was a painting that had to be delivered. But that wasn't why she was angry.

"And how am I supposed to explain this to Brad you ass clown."

"Did you just call me an ass clown?"

Naomi suddenly forgot about being angry. It was too funny. She didn't mean to say it. She wasn't even sure how or where the name came from, but yes, she had just called Colin an ass clown. They both laughed. It had been several months since either one of them had honestly let loose, put down their emotional guard and returned to the point where they shared honest genuine feelings with each other. The laughter was good, cleansing, and all it took was for Naomi to call Colin an ass clown.

It was several minutes before they were able to talk again. Meg Richardsen who shared the cube next to Naomi even started to laugh, not knowing why she should, giving Naomi a questioning look of "What's so funny?" Naomi waved her off, she would try and explain later. Finally, after realizing the rest of the office was probably listening as she called someone an ass clown, Naomi got up and walked down the hall to someplace a bit more private.

"Yeah, I thought that might be a problem. But just tell him the truth."

"Now I know you're an ass clown. Tell him the truth!"

Naomi heard Colin once again laugh as she once again called him an ass clown. She mentally admitted it was a funny metaphor. She liked it and apparently so did he.

"Now you're the ass clown. He knows you and I are old friends. He knows we text and sometimes talk. He knows I'm a painter. Just tell him it's a gift. And that is exactly what this is, it's just a gift. For those days when you can't get to a museum or a gallery or out to your park. It's just something to help you recharge your batteries when the rest of the world has fed on you and drained you emotionally empty. Naomi, it's just a gift."

Naomi thought about it. Colin was right. Everything he said was right. It was just a gift. If she tried to make too much of it, then Colin would know something was up. That she might still be feeling something from their time together. Furthermore, Brad did know about Colin, there was no way for him not to know. Colin was part of life and he had entered into general conversations between her and Brad. Although it was never anything more than just idle comments made in passing.

"Alright. But I didn't get you anything."

"Yes you did."

"What?"

"You called me an ass clown."

They started laughing again.

Chapter 30

Now it was Saturday.

After hanging up with Colin she called the gallery and made the proper arrangements for the delivery. Naomi didn't think anything about the situation, thinking it was a normal part of the process when the gallery manager said he would be there to help with the installation. Also, that Naomi would need to find ample open wall space for the picture. When she asked more detail, she was a little surprised and intrigued.

The black Mercedes sedan rolled up the driveway and stopped in front of the detached garage. The van stopped next to the sidewalk that led to the front of the house, to the porch where Naomi was currently and anxiously standing.

Nerves drove Naomi from sleep and bed before the sun came up. Pacing around the moonlit kitchen she wondered how the day was going to go. Naomi could not understand her anxiousness, and yet, at the same time she understood it all too well. Finally, after a few calming breaths, instead of trying to get around the problem, Naomi once again turned to face the waves coming at her. With nothing left to do but wait, she filled a cup with coffee and still in her pajamas walked barefoot in the dewy morning grass and watched the sun rise into the ever-brightening blue sky.

Naomi never understood why people insisted on wearing shoes. She always enjoyed being barefoot. It made her feel connected to the earth and today it helped to calm her. But now Naomi was dressed in blue jeans, a loose knit shirt, and unfortunately shoes. She could have really used the connection with the earth just then as she stood nervously waiting for the pending the delivery.

As soon as she saw the car and van turn into the driveway she walked out onto the porch. A man in a casual dark sport coat and pants exited from the Mercedes. He walked over to the van and spoke to the driver as he exited from the cab. Another man got out of the van on the passenger's side and the two workmen went to the back of it as the man in the suit strolled with enthusiasm up the sidewalk towards Naomi.

The man in the sport coat was short, a little overweight with a hook nose and course black hair. His polished black leather shoes making rapid scuffing shuffle sounds against the cement as he walked, his hand already coming forward in greeting. His open and gregarious nature was feeding Naomi's anxiety. She instead tried to not concentrate on the two workmen in the clean white coveralls opening the back of the van.

"Good morning. You must be Naomi. I'm Steven Krenshaw from the gallery. We talked on the phone."

"Yes. Good morning. Hi. Wow, that's a big van for just a painting."

Naomi thought her quip was at least a little funny, but Steven just stood there giving her a puzzled look. From behind her Naomi heard the screen door squeak open and with a metallic bang, snap shut. Brad had joined them.

"Hey. I'm Brad."

"Hello Brad. Steven Krenshaw."

"So how big is this thing. I was hoping I would still be able to get a sixty-inch flat screen for the bedroom wall."

Brad gave his token sarcastic laugh as he said it. His sarcastic laugh he would use when poking fun at Naomi, when teasing her because that's what people do when they love each other. That was something Naomi didn't enjoy, no matter how many times of saying so, thus she never returned that love. Naomi knew what Brad was actually saying, but Naomi couldn't help but notice the look on Steven's face. There was no way he would have known and she became even more puzzled. There were some details Colin had failed to mention and something wasn't what she thought it was.

"I'm guessing from both of you asking similar questions Colin didn't give you the precise detail or size of the paintings?"

Naomi started feel some panic set in. Paintings—there was more than one? What had Colin done! How was she going to explain this? She looked at the van where the two workmen had unloaded three large wooden crates. Naomi knew the paintings weren't that big. The boxes were oversized for protection. But even so, she estimated the crates to be four feet high, three feet wide and about eight inches in depth. Brad's dream of a sixty-inch flat screen television in the bedroom was never going to happen now. Naomi looked from the boxes back to Steven.

"No. Colin didn't give me a lot of details. He just said he had a gift for me and to find some wall space."

Naomi watched Steven make a small humorous smile while shaking his head, a small snort of breath to go with the light laughter. Apparently, Colin's surprise was still a surprise. Naomi hated him for this awkward moment. She also felt something else but refused to acknowledge that emotion. Fortunately, and Naomi was momentarily relieved by it, Brad took control of the situation.

"Hey, Steve can we get you a cup of coffee or anything?"

"Thank you, but no. I'm good. However, could you show me where you would like the paintings to be hung?"

Brad still in charge. Brad who many years ago was a setup, a blind date for Naomi by some of her friends. Brad who was a solid, decent, hard-working, whom even with all the years behind them, Naomi could still find him attractive. Brad who provided for them as much as Naomi did, even though it seemed to Naomi she still got stuck with the house cleaning chores while he worked in the garage but never seemed to accomplish anything. Naomi tried not to think like that, she tried not to be negative. He was a good man. She had her hard edges. That was how life worked.

"I guess the wife here said it's supposed to go in the bedroom. I leave that decorating stuff to her to figure out. I guess you should show him where you want them hung, Naomi."

Naomi put a smile on her face. She looked at both of them. She took a quiet cleansing breath and did her best to lower her quills. For some reason Brad was baiting her. No, not for some reason thought Naomi, there was one big reason that came in three pieces. She wanted to hate Colin for putting her in this uncomfortable relationship and emotional situation. She wanted to hate him. In fact, she might actually decide to hate him. There are some things that can never be forgiven. Right now, Colin's fate was contained in three boxes.

"This way. I'll show you."

It was about thirty minutes later when the Brad came back into the bedroom. Naomi hadn't left the room since the paintings were, with painstakingly tedious detail, correctly hung on the bedroom wall. It took everything inside Naomi to not react when she saw the paintings for the first time.

Chapter 31

The workmen that came with Steven were not only there to deliver the paintings but to also hang them. The men were as courteous as they were professional. They brought in protective padded drop-cloths for the floor. Each crate was brought in one at a time, opened, the painting still in a protective cloth, was removed and carefully leaned against another protective padded drop cloth. The process repeated two more times. Each painting, unframed, measured at forty-two-inches high, thirty-inches wide. Several times Steven confirmed the location for the still covered unknown paintings to be hung.

Naomi nervously watched him as he surveyed her bedroom. He walked to the windows and looked at the wall. Walked to the wall and looked at the window. He paced around the room several times always looking at the lines and the space of the room. Naomi knew he was looking at the light, the flow of the room. And even though she knew it was purely professional, she still didn't enjoy someone walking around her bedroom.

After the brief minutes that felt like hours, Steven made several small suggestions about how the pictures should be hung and placed and were Naomi and Brad okay with his suggestions. Brad remained silent and nudged Naomi's shoulder, letting her know he wasn't going to answer. This was in no way his decision and it was up to her to deal with the situation.

Naomi felt another little emotional cut in her soul. Naomi smiled down the sudden welling of emotion, blinked several times and told Steven sure, the little changes would be fine. Steven motioned to the workmen who came in with a toolbox and more drop-clothes. Opening the toolbox, they brought out stud detectors and heavy-duty fastener and hangers and levels. Steven politely let Naomi and Brad know they didn't need to stay unless they wanted. He would make sure everything would be handled and he would let them know when the pictures were up.

Naomi didn't want to leave.

She wanted to see the paintings.

The last thing she needed was a to have had Colin paint a series of nude images of her, because at the moment that was all she could imagine. Her naked body in three different and intimate poses for Steven Krenshaw, the two workmen, and Brad to all gawk at as she tried to explain. Naomi wanted to be there so when that first glimpse of pink nipple or blushed ass cheek appeared, she could stop everything before it was too late. She didn't get the chance.

Steven was both professionally and politely stern and even though it was her bedroom and her home, Steven was gesturing for them to exit. Suddenly, Brad was in his authoritative man-of-the-house mode, and Naomi found herself anxiously sitting at the kitchen table holding a coffee cup in her hands but not able to drink. Her fingers feeling for a brown cardboard jacket to pick apart.

It was about an hour later when the workmen came out of the bedroom carrying their tools, the protective padded drop-cloths, the empty crates, and the final protective wrappings that had been around the paintings and walked out the door. Steven follow them to the kitchen where he stopped and with perfervid expression and asked them both to come back and inspect the paintings and their bedroom to make sure everything was in order. Naomi walked in with her eyes downcast, not wanting to face her doom and shame.

It took every ounce of self-control, every curse word, including several new variations she had never before thought of; every inch and seam of her armor locked into place. It took everything she had to just keep herself steady long enough for Steven and Brad to leave the room before she started to cry.

When Steven asked if *"everything, the room was as it was?"*, that the paintings were *"hung in a manner to their satisfaction?"*, the only response Naomi was capable of was to absently nod her head in an up and down, yes, motion. She knew that if she had tried to talk, even a simple guttural sound and her armor would have shattered into millions of splinters and left her emotional and defenseless. She felt her finger nails dig into the palms of her hands. Naomi repeatedly told herself, *she could do this.*

"Huh. They're nice, but I don't get it."

Naomi almost wished for Brad to explode he as stood there. The only thing that kept Naomi from making that wish was she didn't want his blood and gore splattered across the paintings.

"I have some final paperwork for you to sign. Verifying the paintings were delivered undamaged, hung properly according to artist instructions, and some appraisal forms for your insurance."

Naomi didn't hear a word of what was being said. She absently raised her hand and pushed on Brad's arm. He wanted to play the role of authoritative and in-charge husband, then he could go take care of the paperwork for a change. She wasn't going to. She was going to stay right there.

Chapter 32

It was about thirty minutes later when Brad came back into the bedroom. Naomi was still sitting on the end of the bed looking at the clouds. Colin had painted her the clouds. He had painted the scene in three parts, from the perspective of standing there on the mountain, just as he had described it to her that day they shared together.

She was there.

She was in the painting.

Naomi was in the clouds.

The first panel and Naomi found herself standing on the mountain and looking slightly upward. The evening sun was brilliant on the horizon. Colors of yellow, red, purple and every shade in between lit the sky. The trees and grass on the other mountains around her were shades of deep fall greens and the dormant summer golds. Below her, there were vineyards, but now too far away to see clearly. Naomi didn't care about them anyway. Why would she? Because above her the clouds were gathering. Some of the higher mountain peaks already gone, lost. Naomi could smell the ocean on the cold air pushing in from the Bay area. The warm dry Sonoma air being pulled upward brought dust and grass and the ground under her bloomed with petrichor. As those cold and hot air masses came together the clouds started to form and Naomi was sure that if she were to raise up her hand, she would have been able to touch a cloud being born.

The second panel and Naomi found herself enveloped in a world of shades and layers and shifting flowing movements of white and gray and mist and moisture and she was now lost in the clouds. She was wrapped in a blanket of puffy living air. Naomi remembered as a child lying on the grass and looking up at the clouds, finding shapes and figures and faces; now all she had to do was look around her. Naomi had become one of those shapes, the ever morphing, turning changing shapes that for one moment were one thing and with a light brush of her hand, or breath of exhaled air created something completely new. Naomi had become a cloud.

The third panel and the clouds had left her, making her mortal again. They had become too heavy and were drifting, slowly sinking down around the mountain leaving a heavy layer of dew covering everything they passed over. The spotlight sun now set; the curtain of clouds descended. Now Night dressed in a black dress with flashing sequins made her entrance. She sparkled with millions upon millions of stars as she moved across the sky. Tonight, Naomi was Nights chosen dance partner. And Naomi knew, just as Colin had told her, all she had to do was believe she could, to believe so hard in the impossible that she could make it possible, and she would have been able to start dancing with Night across the clouds.

As long as in her heart and soul she believed.

As long as she had the clouds to stand on.

Naomi could go anywhere.

The world was hers.

Colin might not have been able to bring her to the clouds, but he had been able to bring the clouds to her.

Chapter 33

Brad came in as the worst of the tears had passed. Her face was a teary snotty mess. She didn't care. Brad was going to ask about all the crying. Again, she didn't care. Naomi only cared about the clouds. Her body hadn't moved from the end of the bed. Her soul, however, was high on the mountain and dancing with Night across clouds.

"Wow. You must really like those things. Or you really hate them. I guess it doesn't matter, although if it was the latter—"

Naomi heard the tone. Even up there dancing on the clouds with Night.

Another cut.

"Do you know what they're worth?"

It was the tone of his voice, not what he was saying, the words were meaningless. Just the wind coming up from the valley floor. However, it was the incredulous accusatory aggrandizing inflection and tone of his voice that caused Naomi to lose time and step, to stumble on the dance floor of clouds.

"What?"

"The forms that Steve guy from the gallery needed signed. The ones I signed for you."

Another cut.

The dance came to an end.

Her new partner had left.

And now the old one was there, tapping on her shoulder, moving in to take the space vacated by Night. Naomi so negligently knocked down from the clouds didn't have time to prepare herself. She didn't have time to put her armor back on. She had to take it off when she was on the mountain. It was too heavy to wear when she was in the clouds. It had been in the way. Suddenly that all changed.

She wasn't in the clouds.

She wasn't on the mountain.

She wasn't dancing with Night.

She was sitting on the end of her bed in her home trying to get her armor back on. The softness of the clouds being replaced by the hard edges of reality.

"The insurance on those things is going to be crazy. We're supposed to update our homeowner's policy and we're supposed to claim them on our taxes as an investment. Those fucking paintings are worth almost a hundred grand!"

It wasn't just the tone. It was the attitude. It was the selfishness. It was again, failing to see something beyond the end of his own nose. Naomi felt her quills stand up, points hard, sharp, and ready.

"Why would your friend Colin give you something like this? This expensive? Is the guy nuts or something?"

Naomi didn't care if his blood and gore were splattered all over the paintings. It would have been worth it. Once again, it took every drop of self-control she had to keep her emotions in check. She kept her response civil, but the tone carried mental death rays that would have obliterated Brad. There would have been nothing left of him.

"I had told Colin how I like to watch the clouds and the fog in the park. How I liked hiking the mountains up north. He told me if he had time, he would paint something special for me, to make up for all the missed birthdays and Christmases. I guess when he painted them, he didn't do it thinking of money. He was just doing something nice for a friend."

"Easy honey badger. I was just making a comment. Don't get all ferocious on me."

Another cut!

"But, ya know something to think about. If this Colin never knew; I mean like we could take a picture of you standing next to them, you could send to him. We could sell these things, pay-off all the bills and still be able to get a new television and surround sound system for in here."

Naomi heard the sarcasm in Brad's voice. It was his *I'm just joking* tone. However, there was another octave under that tone. That was where he tried to mask all his insults and his true feelings with his I'm just teasing you because I love you bullshit. In that octave he was actually serious. And in that disguised seriousness, his sarcastic I'm just joking voice, were built the layers upon layers of all his little insults and jabs that his I'm just joking voice tried to hide.

The voice that because the insult was veiled as a just having some teasing fun with you, what he said wasn't meant to be taken seriously. And because it wasn't supposed to be taken seriously, Naomi was just supposed to tolerate it as usual. Because he loved her and that was his way of showing it.

But this time the tone of the sarcasm was too thin. The insult was too strong to be completely veiled. Because she had been so brusquely knocked from her clouds and mountain, she was defenseless, her heart and soul exposed. Naomi felt the cut and it hurt her. It was sharp and it was deep and it this time Naomi wasn't sure if she could stop the bleeding.

Naomi found she didn't want to cry, what good would it do? *I've shed enough tears to know they don't change anything.* She found she didn't feel angry or the even the desire to be mad. *How had all her previous shouting at him changed anything?* This new feeling Naomi found was curious to her. Seconds before she wanted to use some imaginary telepathic powers to make Brad explode. Naomi understood, just like all the tears and shouting, her anger was just as meaningless. It did nothing but let him know he had been able to make her react. Naomi found herself, body and heart and soul, going numb. Usually, the numbness made her feel like a deep ocean shark. Spending its life living in the dark cold depths. Its black almost lifeless looking eyes seeing nothing but the darkness around it. Barely moving, just enough to bring water over its gills. Doing just enough to stay alive.

This time the numbness moved on and evolved into something else. In her numbness Naomi understood so much of her life had been wasted on little petty worthless things that in the end were meaningless. Even the paintings Colin had given her, these so-called valuable works of art were now meaningless. The numbness grew into an understanding that you don't own life, you just borrow it for an undisclosed and non-negotiated length of time.

This time Naomi found everything around her disappeared because it no longer mattered. It was all replaced with an understanding. It was pure and simple. It was absolute and it was uncomplicated. This understanding started in the marrow of her soul and radiated outward filling her with such surety that Naomi did not doubt her ability to do it. She stood on the mountain and walked out onto and across the clouds.

Chapter 34

It was late in the afternoon, the sun heavy on the horizon filled the sky with streaks of orange, red and purple. Naomi stood there on the peak and she could feel the cool evening air pushing in from the Bay carrying the tangy brine of the ocean. At the same time the warm grass and dust scented air was flowing upward from the sunbaked valley floor. The two air masses swirling around her she both shivered from the cold and sweat from the heat.

Naomi's body could feel the air pressure changing around her as much as she was changing. She was there. This was the spot that Colin told her about. Everything was exactly as he described it to her. From where to park, to how to find the trail, to where to stand where she would meet Night and dance across the clouds. It was exactly how he had painted it. Once again, as with all his others, she was in one of his paintings.

The movement of the air quickened and a mist took hold, gathering around her. Naomi looked up and watched as the clouds started to form over her head. In a matter of minutes, she was able to reach up and touch them and they her. As the dew began to gather on her body, as the clouds came down around her hiding her from the world, she didn't feel alone. She felt stronger, freer than she had ever felt in her life. As the clouds descended, she let her quills fall away. She softened all her hard corners. She took off all her armor. It was all too heavy and would only hold her down. In the clouds, on Night's dancefloor she didn't need any of them. Besides, her defenses were useless anyway.

Night is my partner
Spotlight stars shine, dance floor clouds
Where   sky   touches   earth

About the Author:

Not much I want to say about myself. Sorry about that. Besides, I'm not interesting especially when compared to Tic Tok videos.

Thank you for reading my book.

www.ingramcontent.com/pod-product-compliance
Lightning Source LLC
Chambersburg PA
CBHW050121030726
47505CB00007B/1982